every star that shines

every star that shines

TALENA WINTERS

MY SECRET WISH
PUBLISHING

Published by My Secret Wish Publishing
www.mysecretwishpublishing.com

Every Star that Shines (Peace Country Romance Book 1)
Copyright © 2022 by Talena Winters. All rights reserved.
Contact the author at www.talenawinters.com.

Summary: When an aspiring actress gets cancelled, she returns home to piece her life together and reconnects with the high school sweetheart who broke her heart. With all the obstacles between them, will wishing on stars make their dreams come true?

ISBN (eBook): 978-1-989800-10-2
ISBN (paperback): 978-1-989800-11-9
ISBN (hardcover): 978-1-989800-12-6

Cover design by Talena Winters
Developmental editing by Jennifer Lindsay, thewriterswellspring.com
Author Photo © Amanda Monette. Used with permission.
Printed in the United States of America, or the country of purchase.

To the Peace River arts community,
with all my love and gratitude.

THIS BOOK IS written using Canadian English, spelling, and idiomatic or regional language.

It also includes brief mentions of domestic violence.

So be prepared, eh?

T.W.

Chapter 1

DELANIE FLETCHER HAD to be the happiest woman in Vancouver. Her cheeks ached from smiling so much.

It's finally happening. Took a little longer than I hoped it would. Okay, a lot longer. But that's in the past now. And tonight, I'm going to enjoy my success.

She stretched her champagne flute across the steakhouse booth toward her friends' raised glasses.

"To dreams coming true," said Desmond Sun. The Korean-Canadian film editor grinned at Delanie from across the table, the bling on his bright pink rhinestone cowboy outfit glittering with every movement.

"Word," said Delanie's other best friend, Marie Daramola, from her seat near the wall next to Desmond, her large gold hoop earrings swinging against her curved jaw beneath her afro. As per usual, Marie exuded polished glam, her upslanted amber eyes accented with perfectly done golden eyeshadow and dramatic glittering teal eyeliner, and the body-conscious striped scoop-neck tee and jeans she wore drawing the eye of every guy in the room—and a few girls. Marie took the glances of both genders with an equal nonchalance that Delanie envied. Delanie's own glittering black tank and skinny jeans may be drawing eyes, too, but that only made her self-conscious.

"Thanks, you two," she said, tucking a long lock of golden

hair behind her ear. Her face warm, she touched her glass to the other two, the satisfying *clinks* audible even above the din of the busy restaurant. After taking a sip, she said, "It still feels more like a dream than reality, though. I don't know if it will truly sink in until I'm on set."

The effervescent liquid bubbling in her belly buoyed her almost as much as that afternoon's news—the show she had landed a main role in, a cowboy romance called *Trueheart*, had been approved for production, and she'd been offered a three-season contract as the female lead's best friend. It was the kind of job security every actor dreamed of. The kind that could launch her career.

"About bloody time you got your break, I say." Marie snagged a piece of garlic toast from the complimentary basket in the middle of the table and tore off a piece. "I can't believe it took a decade for the idiots in this town to see what they were missing out on. At least your loser producer boyfriend has that much going for him." She placed the bread chunk in her mouth.

Delanie's smile faltered. Marie made no bones of her dislike for Josh, but when it came to Delanie's career, she'd been a true believer since they met at film school. With Marie, what you saw was what you got. It was one of the things Delanie loved about her. Most of the time.

"Thanks, Marie." She chose to ignore the barb—a well-established habit by now. As a costume designer, Marie didn't have to worry about the things she said to others quite the same way Delanie did. Her frankness was part of her charm.

Marie swallowed. "My turn." She raised her glass again. "To Delanie Fletcher, Canada's rising star."

"Hear, hear." Desmond clinked his flute with theirs, then downed the remaining liquid in a single swig before slamming the glass down next to his half-finished Caesar. He blinked away the carbonation, the far-too-curled brim of his white straw cowboy hat shivering back and forth as he shook his head.

"Easy, there, cowboy." Delanie laughed and put out a cautioning hand. "You don't want it to come out your nose and ruin that shirt."

She wrinkled her nose at Desmond's outfit doubtfully, questioning whether that might not be better. To honour Delanie's new role in a western, Marie had chosen the steakhouse as the celebration venue—and Desmond had worn a fringed western shirt and matching pants with enough oversized rhinestone studs to *blind* a cow into submission. If anything, the clothes made the editor look less cowboy-like than usual, which was saying something, given his normally fashion-forward aesthetic. Good thing there weren't a lot of cows in Vancouver.

"Says you," he said. "That's my best party trick. Totally works on the ladies." He wiped away the moisture at the corner of his eyes, then gave a small belch and hit his chest with his fist.

Marie smirked and placed her elbow on the table, supporting her head on her bent wrist. "Not in my experience. Is that something guys find appealing?"

Desmond looked thoughtful. "Maybe if *you* did it. Why don't you give it a shot? Here, let me top you up."

He snatched the champagne bottle and moved it toward her glass to follow through on his threat, but Marie gave him a playful shove in the arm. Resisting her shenanigans, he managed to refill her glass halfway before she yanked it out of reach and a stream of golden bubbles splashed on the table.

"Hey, that's my victory champagne you're wasting." Delanie scrambled for some napkins to toss on the mess.

Marie rolled her eyes. With an exasperated sigh, she set her glass down—out of Desmond's reach—and helped Delanie clean up. Desmond grinned and emptied the remaining champagne into his and Delanie's flutes, then took another generous swallow. Turning around, he beckoned at the server, who had paused across the room to survey her section. Picking up his Caesar, he pointed at his cocktail and made a circular motion toward Delanie and Marie to indicate a request for another round, and the woman gave a nod before picking up a tray and bustling over to the bar.

Marie tossed the sodden napkins onto the outside edge of the table for the server to collect when she came, then turned to Delanie. "So, girl, now that you're going to be rich and famous, are we still going to be able to do monthly games nights? Does Desmond need to quit his job to be your bodyguard? He's got that yellow belt in Taekwondo . . ."

Desmond, who'd been taking a sip of his cocktail, snorted and choked. When he recovered, he said, "It was only a yellow *stripe* belt, remember?"

Delanie polished off her margarita and placed the empty glass at the end of the table. "What's the difference?"

"About three months of training and a lot more gluttony for punishment." Desmond smirked at Marie. "Can you really see me as a bodyguard?"

"Absolutely. You'd be like a less broody Korean Kevin Costner." She gave his outfit a wry look. "But you might have to wear more black, less bubblegum pink."

He frowned down at his shirt. "What's wrong with this?"

"Nothing." Marie laughed. "If you're a rodeo clown."

"Marie," Delanie chided.

Marie rolled her eyes, and Delanie chuckled despite herself. She turned to Desmond.

"Fun as it would be to have you on set, I think your skills are put to better use in the editing room. And you can wear whatever you want there." She gave a sideways look at her friend.

"Actually," said Desmond, putting his hand to his chin in mock pensiveness, "being your bodyguard might be more fun than being an editor. I'd get to be around people all day. We could play UNO in your trailer while we wait for the lighting techs to set the stage for your next shot. I would get to eat the food, right?"

He patted his belly, obviously thinking of the generous spreads that were usually available twenty-four-seven for the cast and crew to graze from. "And would we get to talk to the extras during breaks?"

Marie shook her head. "You'd be on high alert, I see."

"I would." Desmond grinned at her. "For crab cakes and pretty girls."

"Let's not get ahead of ourselves." Delanie's face grew warm. "I mean, this role as Maryanne is a start, but I won't be at body-guard-level fame anytime soon. I'd be happy if I just started making rent regularly."

"I'd be happy about that too." Marie arched a brow at Delanie, but her grin belied the sarcasm.

Delanie smiled back. She and Marie had been roommates since their second year of film school, and over the past nine years, Marie had often pitched in for more than her fair share of the expenses. Not for some time, though—not since Delanie's YouTube channel had started paying a few of her bills and a bit more. For the last year, her supporters had helped carry her through when callbacks had been few and far between and tips from her waitressing job had been sparse. Sometimes, knowing she had a community of fans that believed in her enough to give her even a part-time income—on top of what she paid Marie and Desmond to help her produce her videos—still blew her away.

Of course, now she'd be able to pay for a lot more than a couple of bills. Maybe she'd even get to go home to Peace Crossing to visit Nan soon. Her grandmother's eightieth birthday was coming up, and it would be nice to surprise her. Not for the first time, Delanie regretted how far Vancouver's film industry was from her northern Alberta hometown, and not just because of Nan.

Caleb Toews's face flashed unbidden to her thoughts, and she pushed it away. He didn't deserve her regret after what he did to her.

The server brought their refills with the promise that their dinner would be out in a few minutes. The alcohol had started going to Delanie's head, and she left her new margarita untouched. Guilt that she hadn't already called Nan with the good news about her role pinched her. Of all people, her grandmother deserved to be among the first to know.

Marie held up her phone, its glittery purple case sparkling in the dim lighting. "C'mon, Delanie, come sit on this side so we can do a selfie. This is definitely going on social media. Hashtag *move over, Meryl.*"

Delanie chuckled, resisting the urge to roll her eyes at her friend's confidence. Maybe she could borrow some of it. "Okay. We should do one with mine too."

She slipped her phone out of her purse, then swung around to sit on the bench next to Desmond, leaning into him despite the rhinestone pressing into her bare shoulder. He draped his arm around her shoulders, and they grinned at the phone Marie held at arm's reach until they heard the click.

"Okay, now mine." Delanie shifted position, as did her two friends, so she could get all three of them in the frame from her end of the bench. She took two quick shots, and then her phone chimed with an incoming text message. The preview flashed the name Josh Rosenburg.

"Ooo, what does Josh want?" Desmond was already halfway through his second Caesar, and it showed.

Marie rolled her eyes. "What are you, twelve? It's probably about work. Josh is the least-clingy boyfriend I've ever seen, which is saying something after that guy I dated in second year. Josh is so unclingy, it's like he's not even here." She gave a meaningful look at the empty bench across from them.

"It's just because he's so busy with the show." Delanie knew she sounded defensive and moderated her tone. "He's got a lot of responsibilities as producer." She stood and moved to her own side of the table. "Maybe he's finally able to join us."

"I don't care if he *is* the show's producer, he should have been here celebrating with us," Marie said fiercely. "This is your big break."

"Which he gave me," Delanie said pointedly.

"True. But you still deserve better."

Delanie sighed and tapped on Josh's text to pull it up, while Desmond retorted to Marie with a sassy quip, then laughed at his own joke while she rolled her eyes. Sometimes she wished Desmond would just get up the nerve to ask Marie out and get it over with. The endless flirting was getting on her nerves. She glanced at her phone.

Twitter is blowing up. Have you seen this?

That didn't sound good. She clicked the link Josh had included, which took her to a thread she'd been tagged in. A quick glance was all it took to set her heart racing. Words like *cancel* and *outrageous* and *#byeDelanie* jumped out at her.

"What's wrong?" Desmond said, no longer laughing.

Delanie glanced at her friends' worried faces, her heart thundering in her ears. "I . . . I don't know. Something about my latest video."

Marie started thumbing around on her phone. Her eyes widened, and she looked at Delanie in alarm. "I didn't notice anything bad in that video." She looked at Desmond. "Did you?"

He shook his head in bewilderment. The video they had posted yesterday had been right on-brand for Delanie—a one-person musical skit offering scathing commentary about superstar actor Nathan Tait. The former Sexiest Man Alive had been accused of abusing his wife, though he said it was the other way around—as if that was likely. Delanie had made a video of the musical theatre classic "Modern Major General", dubbing her version "Modern Major Terrible". The righteous indignation that had fuelled her writing while she'd created the skit now fizzled in astonishment at her fans' reaction to it.

Desmond pulled out his own phone and scanned Delanie's Twitter feed. "Oh, no. No, no, no."

"What?" Marie demanded.

"It's not about yesterday's video. It's about that one you made about Nathan three years ago."

Delanie swallowed, her mind scrambling. "Three years ago?"

"Yeah, the zombie one."

"What?" Delanie frowned. She had used a zombie blockbuster Nathan had starred in to make a statement about multi-national conglomerates preying on mom and pop stores. "But why are they mad about that?" Delanie scrolled further down, looking for answers. She found a tweet with the answer just as Marie started reading a similar one aloud.

"'Nathan Tait is the scum of the Earth. I can't believe Delanie Fletcher would defend him on any level. She needs a wake-up call. Hashtag cancel Delanie.' Well, they certainly blew that out of proportion. No one even knew Nathan Tait was a wife-beater back then."

Desmond scowled. "No one's even sure of it now."

Marie drew back. "You saying you believe him that he's the victim here?"

Desmond held up his hands defensively. "I'm only saying we don't know, and it's up to the courts to figure out which of them is telling the truth."

"I don't think the Internet is going to let a court decide my fate." Delanie's voice sounded hollow in her ears. How could the outpouring of hatred and bile on her Twitter feed be directed at her? She wanted to crawl under the table and hide her burning face. "I have to explain what happened." She started to type a response.

Marie's hand closed around hers. "No. You don't respond to this, not right now. Maybe not ever. You'll only fuel the flames."

"But if I don't, they'll think I don't care," Delanie objected, tugging her hand out of Marie's.

The server brought their food, but as the T-Bone steak she'd been looking forward to was placed in front of her, she knew she wouldn't be able to eat a bite. Not now.

Her phone chimed with another text from Josh. *Call me ASAP*. Her throat closed, and she cleared it.

"I'm sorry, guys, but I think I better go home and deal with this. I need to call Josh, and I don't want to talk about this here."

Marie gave her an understanding look, then told the server they would take their meals to go. The server nodded and, with a sympathetic glance at Delanie, went to get containers. Delanie wondered how bad she looked.

"What can I do?" Desmond asked. He looked kind of helpless and pathetic. "I have a yellow stripe belt in Taekwondo. I could beat someone up. As long as it only involves simple blocks and breaking free from a very specific hold, I could beat someone up."

Delanie gave a half-hearted chuckle, but shook her head. "Thanks, but no. And Marie, you don't have to leave yet. You stay and enjoy the meal. I'll call an Uber."

Marie looked about to object, but Delanie shook her head. "Please." She didn't know what Josh would have to say to her, but she knew she didn't want any witnesses for it.

Marie gave her a long look, then nodded. "You don't start tweeting before I get home. I'll know." She tapped her phone with a pointed gel nail painted in pumpkin orange and silver swirls.

Delanie gave a reluctant nod. As she made her way to the foyer to wait for her car, she barely noticed the cheerful goodbye from the hostess or the crowd of people waiting to get in. She was too busy doomscrolling through her social media feeds, fear tightening her chest more with every post she read. The furor had already escalated to death threats.

For an innocent mistake?

The notification that her ride was there popped up. With shaky hands, she dropped her phone in her purse and went out to the car.

Chapter 2

THE NEXT MORNING, Delanie stumbled out of her room, still in her pyjamas—shorts and a pink tank top with a cartoon cat on it. She blinked at the light streaming in through the living room window of the small but airy apartment she shared with Marie.

How can the sun be so cheerful and enthusiastic when my life is falling apart? And when I only got four hours of sleep?

Marie sat at the small dining room table in front of the balcony doors, sipping coffee and sketching in a spiral notebook, looking as put-together as usual even in no makeup, lounge pants, and a headscarf. She glanced up when Delanie walked in.

"Good morning, sunshine. Things look any better by the light of day?"

Delanie rubbed her bleary eyes and went over to the coffee pot on the counter. She grabbed a mug from the cupboard above, relieved when steam rose from the black nectar as she poured. "I don't know yet. Is that daylight, or a spotlight on my career going up in flames?"

"Aw, girl, it ain't that bad." Marie pushed the notebook aside and leaned back in her chair, her hands encircling her coffee mug. "You just got to ride this thing out. If you wait long enough, the mob will forget about you and move on to their next helpless victim."

Delanie took a sip of black coffee. "So you think I'm a helpless victim?"

"No, but they do." Marie indicated her phone, which sat next to her notebook. "Don't act like one, and they'll get bored and move on."

"Hmph."

Delanie wasn't awake enough to come up with a better response than that. She took another sip of coffee, hoping Marie wouldn't mention the tweets she'd made the night before. Marie had been right about not replying to the Twitter mob, of course. The responses Delanie had received had gone from bad to worse, until she'd thrown her phone across the room and sobbed herself to sleep. Her puffy eyes and crusty face told her she probably looked like death warmed over. She smoothed her tangled hair with her fingers—*as though that will make everything better.* She snorted at herself.

"What did Josh have to say?" Marie asked.

Delanie cringed. Josh had had a *lot* to say, but most of it wasn't something she wanted to tell Marie. It would only justify her friend's dislike of him more. "He said he would try to smooth things over with the executive team and get back to me. He was optimistic this wouldn't change anything."

Marie snorted. "By *smooth things over,* he means *do whatever Crystal McLean tells him to,* of course."

"He's not like that," Delanie said, too tired and too annoyed to let it go this time. "You don't give him enough credit."

"Don't I? Do you remember when he told you he knew the director of *Skyscraper,* and he'd get you onto the set so you could meet Dwayne Johnson? Then he said that they had already finished filming and Dwayne had gone home before he could work something out?"

Delanie narrowed her eyes, not sure if she could handle more negativity right now. "Yeah . . ."

"Well, I have it on good authority he lied. He doesn't even know Rawson Thurber. He was just saying that to impress you."

Delanie froze, stunned, then shook her head—whether in disagreement or in denial, she didn't know. "Well, it worked. And until this moment, the thought that he'd tried made me feel better."

She glared at Marie over the rim of her mug, and her friend shrugged unapologetically.

Marie cocked her head. "Is that your phone ringing?"

"There's No Business Like Show Business" pumped through Delanie's open bedroom door. She had turned up the ringer volume while they were at the restaurant last night, and the phone now blasted loud enough that the neighbours could probably hear it. She dashed into the room and scrambled to retrieve it from behind her dresser, answering just before the call went to voicemail.

"Hi, Josh," she said.

"You're out of breath. Are you out running?"

"No, I'm . . ." No way she was going to tell him what had actually happened. Best to change the subject. "Do you have any updates?"

"Yeah, about that . . ."

In the silence, Delanie's gut tightened into a hard ball.

Josh sighed. "Look, there's no easy way to say this, so I'll just come right out with it. You're off the show. The executives don't want to risk the kind of negative publicity this situation could bring them. Fans of sweet cowboy romances look down on this kind of controversy."

Shock choked her for several seconds, then dissolved into anger as his words sank in. She was being fired, just like that?

"Well, then," she spluttered, "maybe the *executives* should have thought of that before they hired me." She drew a breath. "They knew I run a YouTube channel satirizing current events all along. Didn't they realize that's bound to bring some occasional controversy?"

"Hey, babe, this wasn't my idea. If it was up to me, you wouldn't be going anywhere. But you know how Crystal is. When she makes a decision, there's no changing her mind."

"Did you even try?" Delanie seethed. She'd never seen Josh stand up to Crystal about anything. "Wait, don't answer that. You know what? I think Marie was right about you." Much as she hated to admit it.

"Now wait a second, Delanie—"

"No, *you* wait a second, Josh. You think because you're a producer and you gave me a break that I owe you something. Well, I don't, not if you're not going to fight for me the instant things get tough. We're through."

"But—"

"And you don't even know Rawson Thurber!"

She mashed her finger on the screen to end the call, hanging up on his protests, and threw the phone down on the bed. When it rang again immediately, she picked it up, rejected the call, and put her phone on vibrate. Turning, she found Marie leaning against her door frame with a sympathetic expression.

"That couldn't have been easy. I'm sorry, hon."

Delanie bit her thumbnail and nodded. "Probably for the best. My life just turned into a dumpster fire. If he's not going to support me, then he's adding fuel to the flames."

Marie nodded approvingly. "Well said. Glad you finally see it."

Delanie drew a breath, not sure how she wanted to respond to that. The apartment buzzer sounded, and Marie glanced over her shoulder. Delanie's heart sank. She couldn't handle company right now, maybe not even Desmond.

"You expecting someone?" she asked, wincing internally.

"Just the Cinnabon delivery guy. Thought we might drown our woes in carbs and a *Grey's Anatomy* marathon today."

Delanie's heart lifted slightly, then she frowned. "I thought you had plans."

Marie shrugged. "Cancelled 'em. I can go to the mall with Cheyenne anytime."

Warmth pushed aside some of the constant dread that had filled Delanie since she'd received Josh's text last night. "Thanks, Marie. You're the best."

"I know." She smirked and went to answer the buzzer.

Delanie's phone vibrated in her hand—a ring, not a text. Annoyed, she glanced down to reject the call and saw that it wasn't Josh. It was her mom.

She hesitated, trying to decide if she wanted to try and explain everything to her mom right then. Cheryl Fletcher hadn't been the most supportive of her daughter's choice of career, and the last thing Delanie needed was to hear her mother say *I told you so*. Not only that, her mom could be a little out of touch with modern culture. Sometimes Delanie thought Cheryl didn't quite understand what social media was, even though she'd set her up on Instagram a couple years ago. Cheryl definitely wouldn't understand what *being cancelled* meant, nor why it was such a big deal to Delanie.

But an intense longing to pour out her troubles to a listening ear made her answer the phone at the last second.

"Hi, Mom. How's it going?"

"Hi, Delanie."

Something in her mother's tone stopped Delanie from jumping into her story—Cheryl's tone, and the fact that she hadn't responded with her typical cheery *Better than a bushel of barley*.

"Is something wrong, Mom?"

She heard a stifled sob on the other end, and her heart stammered. Not more bad news.

"Are you sitting down?" Cheryl asked.

Delanie sank to the bed. "Mom, you're scaring me. What happened? Is Dad okay?"

"Dad's fine." After a slight pause, Cheryl said, "Nan died.

Last night. I called her this morning like I always do, and when she didn't answer after a few tries, I came over to her house to check on her. Looks like she went while she was sleeping. I'm just waiting for the ambulance now."

Delanie's chest constricted, and her gaze snapped to the photo of the sweet-faced white-haired woman on her dresser. How could Nan be dead? She was supposed to live forever.

"I'm so sorry, honey," Cheryl said. "I know she meant a lot to you, and—"

"When's the funeral?"

"Well, I have to talk to the funeral home yet to work things out, but we'll try for this Saturday."

"So soon?" That was only four days away.

"Will you be able to make it? I never know what your work schedule is like."

"I can make it." Delanie swallowed a lump the size of an apple. No job, no boyfriend, a deep desire to escape from the disaster that was her life . . . she could definitely make it. "Maybe I'll even stay a while. It's been a minute since I was home."

"Would you?" The hopeful surprise in her mom's voice needled at her. "That would be wonderful." Cheryl paused. "How long would you be staying?"

Delanie tensed. Her mother was notorious for turning Delanie's trips home into meetings with one eligible bachelor after another masquerading as get-togethers with old friends or family. Not that Peace Crossing had much to offer in the *eligible bachelor* department, but there was a reason Delanie usually only flew home for the weekend. After Caleb, Delanie had no interest in dating a small-town guy ever again. They were too rooted down to be able to handle her and her ambition—they wanted small-town girls, girls who would stay and support their small-town dreams. And one betrayal like that was enough. "Why do you ask?"

"Well, it's just . . . I could use some help going through Nan's things. She's got this farmhouse to sort through, and she was such a hoarder."

Delanie thought of the tidy home with the full but well-organized closets she had known as a child—a far cry from the jam-packed houses she'd seen on reality TV. She shook her head. Her mother had a very different definition of *hoarder* than she did.

"Isn't there anyone else to help? Uncle Roger? Aunt Lily?" Her mother's other siblings lived too far away, but Roger and Lily both lived in the area. Delanie knew her younger sister, Savannah, wouldn't be an option—Savannah would have just started her classes, and medical school students couldn't afford to take time off.

"I'm sure they'll lend a hand here and there. So if you don't want to help, I won't be left in the lurch. I just thought, if you'd be home for a bit, it would be nice to have your company. You're so good at organizing things, and you probably won't be as emotionally attached to everything as I will be."

Delanie tugged on a strand of blond hair, wrapping it around her finger. She didn't know about that. But it didn't sound like Cheryl wanted to organize a meet-n-greet. And the thought of doing something tangible and helping to organize the earthly possessions of the woman Delanie loved and admired most in the world held a lot of appeal.

"I'd love to help with that, Mom."

"You would? Wonderful. Thank you."

Cheryl started muttering. Delanie heard Savannah's name, and the names of Cheryl's siblings, plus the local funeral home, and realized her mother was going through the mental list of people to tell about Nan's passing. She bit her nail, her eyes filling with tears. *How can Nan be dead?*

Marie poked her head in the door. Holding her hand up to her ear like a phone, she mouthed *Who is it?*

My mom, Delanie mouthed back.

What's wrong? Marie mouthed.

Delanie moved the speaker away from her mouth. "I'll tell you in a minute," she whispered.

Marie nodded and held up the brown paper delivery bag, then indicated that she'd be in the living room. Delanie nodded back.

Then her mother said something about Violet and the play.

"What about the play?" Delanie asked before she could stop herself. Nan had been the director of the fall community kids musical in Peace Crossing for as long as Delanie could remember. It was where her own love of acting had begun—that, and listening to Nan's tales of her glory days on the stage as a young woman, before she gave up her career to marry Delanie's grandfather and move to Peace Crossing. Since this was the first week of September, the play would have just finished casting. Rehearsals should be starting this weekend.

"Oh, nothing you need to worry about, honey," Cheryl said. "I just need to remember to let Violet Butler know about Nan. Violet has been the musical director of the play for years now. I don't know who they'll find to take over directing the play on such short notice though. It's a pretty heavy commitment, and not many people have that kind of free time, let alone the expertise or the desire to—"

"I'll do it," Delanie said without thinking, then slammed her mouth shut. What was she saying?

"You will?" Cheryl said, her voice filled with delight. "You'll be here that long? Don't you have to work?"

Delanie paused. She could probably get her job back at the café if she asked. And just because she'd been fired from *Trueheart* didn't mean she couldn't get other acting work. She was still waiting to hear back from a few auditions.

Who was she kidding? If the studio that had already offered her a series contract didn't want to be associated with her controversy, why would anyone else? And the last thing she wanted was to go back to the Vintage Café with her tail between her legs and ask for her waitressing job back. The day she'd handed in her apron had felt almost as good as learning she had landed the part of Maryanne.

If she was going to *ride this thing out*, as Marie advised, what better way to do that than by disappearing for a couple of months? She didn't have much saved, but she had her Patreon supporter income—assuming she still had any supporters left. Besides, directing the play would be the perfect distraction from her current problems. And maybe getting away from Vancouver would give her the perspective to figure out what to do next.

"No, I can stay for a couple of months. I'll need a day or two to wrap things up here, but I should be there by Friday. I'll drive, so you don't have to worry about picking me up from the airport." The trip would take two days, or one if she pushed it, but a drive through the Rocky Mountains would be the perfect way to start her mental reset.

"Oh, Delanie, that's wonderful. I'm sorry the circumstances are so trying, but it will be lovely to have you home. And I'm sure Nan will rest easier knowing you're the one taking over the play."

She won't know. She's dead. But Delanie didn't say that. Though she didn't share her mother's spiritual beliefs, she couldn't claim to know what happened to the dead. Let her mother have her comforts—especially as she was obviously reeling a bit from Nan's death. Besides, Delanie could think of no better way to honour Nan's memory than by keeping her legacy alive.

"Just one request," Delanie added.

"What's that, honey?"

"Don't tell Caleb's mother I'm coming home."

Chapter 3

CALEB TOEWS PULLED up to the worn curb in front of his ex's yellow split-level bungalow and shifted his Ford pickup into park. His nine-year-old daughter peeked at him through the picture window, holding one gauzy curtain aside, her dark hair tumbling over her shoulders. When Emma saw him, her warm brown eyes lit up and she disappeared. Probably to collect her things.

He shuffled some work orders and a time sheet he still had to submit to the office at Martens Electric from the passenger seat to the clean back bench of the extended cab. Taking a deep breath, he got out of the truck and walked to the front door.

It was a beautiful fall day, with only a hint of crispness in the air. The mountain ash in the front yard had turned bright red, and the aspens lining the bank of the Peace River at the end of the street and climbing the hill behind the subdivision on the other end were a glorious shade of yellow. Autumns in Peace Crossing were often come-and-go events—as in, they had often gone as soon as they had come. But this one had been mild and surprisingly warm, with barely a hint of leaf drop yet, despite the frost a week ago. He hoped that meant they'd see the Indian summer called for by the Farmer's Almanac—his job was more pleasant when the weather was good.

He rang the bell, and, seconds later, Monica opened it. She

looked as beautiful as ever, her dark brown hair framing her perfectly made-up face. He'd once let her pretty blue eyes and pouty rosebud lips get under his skin—much to his everlasting sorrow. But as Emma ran down the stairs to the front landing yelling his name and threw her arms around his waist, he retracted that sentiment. He could never regret having the little girl who was the jewel of his life.

"Hi, Chickadee," he said, squeezing her shoulders. "Did you have a good week?"

"Yep!" Emma let go of him, and Monica stepped aside so their rambunctious daughter could grab her shoes.

"Hi, Caleb." Monica gave him a warm smile, then glanced affectionately at the little girl.

"Hey. You look good," Caleb said. There was something different about her, but he couldn't figure out what. A gleam in her eye that wasn't usually present.

Monica beamed. "Thanks."

Before Caleb could comment further, Emma started chattering up at him while trying to pull on a turquoise canvas lace-up shoe with unicorn decals on the sides.

"Daddy, you'll never guess what happened at school today." She missed her foot because she wasn't paying attention and tried again, but kept talking. "Addison gave me a friendship bracelet that she made herself. See?" She held up her wrist to display a pink-and-purple striped bracelet made from knotted embroidery thread. "Mom said she's going to teach me how to make them so I can give her one back."

Caleb grinned. "That's awesome. I'm sure Addison will love it."

"Do you think Hannah would want one?"

Caleb shook his head. Hannah was his sister Rachel's youngest of four children. Of all Emma's cousins, Hannah was the only other girl, and Emma could hardly wait for her to get old enough to play pretend with. "Hannah's only two, which is a little young for friendship bracelets. Maybe when she's a little older."

"And maybe I can teach *her* how to make them by then, too." Emma picked up her second sneaker and tried to force it on her foot.

"Maybe," Caleb agreed.

Monica chuckled, then crouched to help Emma get the shoe over her heel and tied the laces, double-knotting the bow. "Sweetie, remember I said I wanted to talk to Daddy for a minute? How about you go wait in the truck?"

"Sure, Mom." Emma leapt to her feet and threw her arms around her mother's neck. "See you next week."

"Actually, it might be sooner." Caleb eyed his ex-wife. "Unless you won't be able to make it to the parents' meeting on Sunday?"

"For the play? Is that still running now that . . . you know?" Monica stood and gave Emma a wary glance.

Caleb held back a frown. He wanted to protect Emma's innocence as much as possible, too, but death was a part of life. And it's not like Molly Davis was Emma's grandmother. At the thought, he wondered how Delanie was taking the news, then pushed the question aside. None of his business.

"My mom said Cheryl Fletcher told her they found a replacement director already, but she didn't say who it was. So I guess the play is still on." Caleb gave a sardonic snort. "Better be—I'm working on the sets with Noel Butler tonight."

"That's good news. Emma's been practicing her song, haven't you, sweetie?" Monica played with Emma's silky brown hair, pulling it out of the neckline of her pink fall jacket.

Emma nodded enthusiastically. "I already know all the words by heart."

"Wow," Caleb said, impressed but unsurprised. Emma had only been cast as Lucy the Talking Cricket in the *Pinocchio* play a week ago. Monica had been a bit worried when Emma had landed a main cast ensemble part in her first year in the play, but he knew she would be up to the challenge. He could see he had been right.

"Okay, Emma," Monica said with one last stroke of Emma's hair, "I guess I'll see you Sunday. Maybe we can start on your friendship bracelet while we're at rehearsal."

"Yeah? Cool! Can we do green and red? Wait. That's for Christmas. How about blue and yellow?"

"I think I have some floss in those colours." Monica's mouth twitched in an amused smile.

"Awesome! I'll see you soon then, Mom!"

Before Monica could respond, Emma pushed past Caleb and dashed to the white truck near the curb.

Caleb shoved his hands in his jean pockets. "So, what did you want to talk about?"

Monica glanced down and twisted her fingers, looking un-usually shy. "I, um, have some exciting news."

Caleb's gut tightened. Had she and Dave finally decided to tie the knot? It would be about time—they'd been living to-gether for two years already. And, call Caleb old-fashioned, but he would rather Emma's mom be married to the guy she was living with, even if it wasn't him. Not that he wanted it to be him . . . not even close. It was more of an example thing.

But a cursory glance showed Monica's ring finger to be bare.

"Are you going to tell me, or should we start playing Twenty Questions?" he joked.

"I'm pregnant," she blurted.

The tension in Caleb's gut vibrated like a plucked guitar string. "Er . . . Congratulations."

"We just found out. Emma already knows, and she's super excited to be a big sister."

Caleb smiled. "She would be. And she'll make a great one."

"I know." Monica hesitated. "Also, Dave asked me to marry him. And I said yes. We're going to Grande Prairie tomorrow to pick out rings."

Caleb drew in a deep breath. "Congratulations again. I'm happy for you."

Her face softened. "Really?"

He nodded. "Really. You deserve to be happy, Mon. And Dave's a great guy. Just answer me one thing, if you would."

When she saw his face, her brow furrowed. "Of course."

He stepped closer and lowered his voice. Dave was probably still at work, but Emma had rolled down the truck window, and he wanted to be sure she didn't overhear.

"Tell me you're not marrying him because of the baby. That didn't work out so well the last time."

She laid a hand on his arm. "I'm not. I learned my lesson, I promise." When he didn't relax, she said, "Trust me, Caleb. This is what I want."

He searched her brilliant blue eyes, then stepped back. "Okay. Good. Have you set a date?"

"Not yet. I'll let you know when we do."

Caleb nodded, then glanced toward the truck. Emma's head was down. She was probably drawing.

"How about you?" Monica asked. "Any prospects on the horizon? How did things work out with Kate?"

"They didn't." He and Kate had only gone on a couple dates before Caleb knew it wasn't fair to her to keep seeing her. Just like he'd known with the two or three other women he had tried dating in the six years since he and Monica had split. It was always for the same reason Monica had ultimately left him—his heart wasn't truly available. None of them were Delanie.

"You're going to have to get over her someday, you know," Monica said quietly. She wasn't talking about Kate anymore.

He looked toward the river and nodded. "Someday I will. See you Sunday."

He strode toward the truck, not looking back at the house until he clicked his seatbelt into place.

By then, Monica's door was closed. Like his heart.

Emma glanced up at him, a pink coloured pencil in her hand. "Look at the picture I drew for Hannah. It's Lucy!"

He glanced at the partially coloured, fairly realistic drawing of a cricket wearing a pink polka-dot dress and smiled. "Great job, Chickadee. Hannah's going to love it."

Emma grinned. "I thought it might remind her to always follow her conscience." She returned to her colouring, already re-absorbed in her work.

He watched Emma a moment longer, then put the truck in gear.

As proud as he was of his daughter's moral compass, he wished he could find the words to tell her that following one's conscience didn't always work out.

Sometimes, it left you heartbroken and filled with regret.

He sighed and pulled away from the curb.

Chapter 4

------◆ ◆------

DELANIE SLOWLY TILTED her head from side to side to stretch her tight neck and shoulders, keeping one hand on the wheel and her eyes on the road. After driving for the better part of two days, her muscles had started to cramp up. In front of her, the straight highway stretched between partially harvested golden fields of grain like a dark ribbon through yellow hair. On her left, the sun brushed the treed horizon, causing her car to cast a long shadow on her other side that jumped erratically with the shifting terrain of the ditch and field. At least this was the final leg of her journey. Her neck wasn't the only body part that would be glad to be out of the car.

She had told her mother she would be home by supper that night, but when she had passed through Whitecourt at five o'clock with three hours to go, she realized that wasn't going to happen. Ignoring her guilt at how late she had dragged herself out of her hotel room that morning—postponing her inevitable return home, if she were honest—she had called her mother to let her know. Then she had swung through the Starbucks drive-through for a chai latte and banana bread to tide her over until she got to her parents' place.

Delanie took the final cold sip from her paper cup and tucked it into the cup holder in the console with a twinge of sadness. That was the last Starbucks she would get until she left Peace

Crossing and passed through Whitecourt again. Though she had to admit that the lattes at Cool Beans, the local coffee shop in town, were almost as good, and their food was much better.

Good thing—ever since the events of Tuesday night, she had been constantly exhausted and had barely slept. Strong coffee was the only thing that had kept her going. She would probably be stopping at Cool Beans every day.

At the thought of all she had endured that week, the familiar pressure built behind her eyes. Frowning, she pushed the thoughts aside and cranked her music, tapping her thumbs on the steering wheel to OneRepublic. She had already cried enough today to leave her cheeks raw. She didn't want to start again.

Driving northeast across British Columbia from the coast had been like driving from the middle of summer to late fall, though she knew the weather would have only started turning a few weeks ago. She was amazed that the trees in northern Alberta were still in full leaf—there had been more than one autumn in her childhood when the second week of September saw every leaf on the ground and the threat of snow in the air. But when she crested the hill that allowed her to see the Peace River Valley bathed in the last auburn glow of the setting sun—which now shone directly into her eyes until she lowered her visor—she caught her breath.

The thickly forested valley was a bonfire of gold, fiery orange, and deep red leaves slashed by uneven trails of dark, thick evergreens. As she started her descent, she came around a turn in the highway and caught sight of the Peace River snaking its way between the hills and the graceful turquoise arches of the bridge that spanned it—the lone connection between the two sides of the sprawling, scattered town. Some of the tension eased from her shoulders. Peace Crossing might be a million miles from civilization, but it made up for its remote location with its breathtaking beauty.

Her phone vibrated somewhere beneath the travel detritus of
to-go bags, napkins, and snack wrappers that had accumulated
on the passenger seat, and she tensed. At Marie's insistence, she
had deleted her social media apps from her phone, even if she
couldn't bring herself to delete her Twitter account completely as Marie had advised. However, Josh had called and texted
multiple times in the last few days, to the point that every time
her phone gave her a notification, she worried it would be him.
She should just block his number, but there was always the pos-
sibility he might be calling with news that Crystal had changed
her mind. Well, he could definitely wait. She wasn't pulling
over now, not on the winding, steep highway into town with
its almost non-existent shoulders—it wasn't safe.

She came around another curve in the road and gasped. The
sun had sunk behind the horizon, leaving a dusky sky painted
with streaks of red and pink and purple. The streetlights on
the bridge flickered on, and the other lights in town soon followed, turning the scene into something from a postcard. She
had been so eager to get out of here as a teenager, to make her
mark on the world. Now, she felt a twinge of regret that in two
short months, she would once more have to leave behind the
little treasure of a town to return to the asphalt jungle and fight
to regain the dream she'd worked so hard to build.

She ground her teeth. She had made *so* many sacrifices, taking acting jobs she didn't even want so she would get noticed
by the right people to help her career. She had thought it had
paid off, that she was about to get her mythical *breakout role*.
But none of that mattered now, did it?

Tears threatened again, and she shook her head to push them
away. When she showed up at her parents', she didn't want her
mother's first comment to be how frightful she looked.

Hmph. As though I'll be able to avoid that after a day on the
road.

She glanced in the rearview mirror and smoothed her hair,

trying to detangle it with her fingers while keeping the other hand on the wheel. Maybe she should stop somewhere to freshen up before heading out to her parents' acreage. The gas station at the far edge of town should still be open. She would pop in on the way by.

Delanie glanced toward the dusky west—the general direction of her parents' place—and gasped. The first star had just winked into sight in the darkening sky.

Stars. Except for the occasional ski trip out of town, or that time an ex-boyfriend had taken her on an overnight sailing trip, she had rarely seen the stars since moving to Vancouver. The glorious night skies of the Peace Country, with the splash of the Milky Way and dancing aurora borealis and constellations so bright you could touch them, were one of the things she had missed most . . . besides Nan, of course.

At the thought, tears sprang to Delanie's eyes anyway, the salt stinging her cheeks. She plucked one of the tissues from the box she had put on the passenger seat for easy access and dabbed at the moisture, sniffling to stifle further sobs.

A tidal wave of longing washed through her—longing to reconnect with the roots of the dream that now lay in shambles around her, and with the woman who had inspired it. *The play should help.* Her mom had brought home the director's script she had found at Nan's house, along with Nan's binder full of notes. Delanie looked forward to reading them in nervous anticipation, trying to ignore the needling suspicion that she was in over her head. If Nan's notes were as organized and extensive as her craft cupboard, Delanie would be fine.

As she rounded the final hill, Peace Crossing's quaint downtown area came into view. Delanie glanced greedily over the familiar buildings, but the aching hunger in her chest remained. She could barely see the theatre from here—it was farther away and lower down, near the river and behind the Anglican church tower.

When she approached the exit that would take her downtown instead of across the river, she found herself slowing down and signalling. The theatre was probably locked up at this time on a Friday night, but she could at least drive by. On her way to the gas station on Main Street, of course, which would also be open—she hoped. Besides, she could use every extra minute she could get to collect herself before she had to deal with Cheryl Fletcher in person.

She parked across the street from the ancient hall. Both the Mackenzie Playhouse and the church next door shared a similar design aesthetic—a white stucco exterior accented by dark brown painted wooden beams. Some scaffolding next to the church suggested renovations in progress—maybe the congregation was doing some restoration work on the old structure.

The front light of the church was on, illuminating its concrete stoop and the several steps up to the front door, and so was the light next to the theatre's main entrance. Two trucks—one black, one white—sat in the small parking lot the hall shared with the church. Pickup trucks were another thing she didn't see much of in Vancouver. Here, they were the most common form of transportation—and for good reason, given the kind of work and weather that dominated the area. Both trucks had locked metal tool boxes filling their beds.

Delanie frowned at the two vehicles. While the church's front light was probably left on every night as a safety measure, the unlit windows suggested the building was empty. Were the owners of these trucks in the hall, which had hardly any windows to let tell-tale light escape into the night? If so, why? Even if the theatre was also being renovated, it would be fairly odd for anyone to be there now. Carpenters in Peace Crossing didn't make a habit of working late on Friday nights, the last she knew.

She shrugged and turned off her older-model Honda Civic coupe. If the hall was open, she could freshen up there. Before getting out, she fished her phone out from under the tissue box to check on the notification. The text had been from Marie, asking for an update.

Just got to town, Delanie quickly typed back. *Thanks for checking.*

The response of a heart and a thumbs-up emoji was almost instantaneous. Delanie smiled and climbed out of the car.

The right side of the brown metal double doors leading into the theatre was unlocked. Cautiously, Delanie opened it, and the hinges let out a loud complaint. She stepped onto an empty landing no bigger than her apartment bathroom. A short flight of stairs on the left led down to the basement reception hall and dance studio, and the one on the right ascended to a somewhat larger foyer that led toward the bathrooms on one side and into the auditorium on the other. The musty odours of old carpet and wood assailed her nose—the smells of the best parts of her childhood. Filled with reverent awe, she made her way up the steps.

One of the brown-painted wooden double doors into the auditorium was propped open with a doorstop. She glanced through it longingly, then turned aside into the small carpeted lobby across from it. After pausing to glance at the old play posters crowding the walls, she made her way to the cramped two-stall ladies' room. The room had recently received a thorough coat of nondescript cream paint, adding to the decades-thick layers already there and covering up any professions of undying love that may have been left on the stall wall.

She relieved herself and washed her hands, then used the mirror above the sink to help her tidy her smudged makeup and comb her hair. She assessed her reflection. Her eyes weren't all that red, but her makeup had worn off, revealing the dark circles beneath them and the fading red splotches on her cheeks and forehead.

"Who am I kidding? Mom is gonna know I was crying all day in a hot second."

Sighing, she left the bathroom.

When she got back to the landing that would lead her either down the stairs or into the auditorium, she hesitated, staring at the open door into the theatre. Filled with a strange trepidation, she crept through it onto the small landing. The narrow landing's far side was bounded by a partial wall which was still taller than she was, topped with a rail, beyond which sat the last row of seats of the auditorium's centre section. Steps ascended off of either side of the landing to the auditorium's two aisles. Taking the left set of steps, she held her breath as the dimly lit hall came into view.

The hall was both smaller and more impressive than she remembered. Now that she'd seen more of the world, she sometimes found it hard to believe that little Peace Crossing had such a great community theatre. The room's dark decor gave it a sombre atmosphere, even with the lights on. Delanie fixed her gaze on the stage. The heavy black velvet curtains had been pulled wide open, and the lights shining down on the painted black stage floor revealed scuffs all over it—repainting the stage would be one of the last things done before the performance weekend. She could almost see Nan standing before the stage, organizing kids and volunteers in her firm but kind way, turning their raw energy into a top-calibre production that would be packed out for every performance.

It wasn't until Delanie was halfway down the aisle that she noticed the little dark-haired girl sitting on the left side only a few steps away. The child's head was bent over a sketchbook, and with another step, Delanie spotted a decent drawing of a unicorn's purple head with a spiral horn coloured like a rainbow.

"That's pretty good," she said.

The girl's head snapped up. When she saw Delanie, she grinned. "Thanks! My dad says if I keep practising my art, I could be an animator someday, and make movies and everything."

"Wow, your dad must be pretty special."

Her own dad hadn't been nearly so supportive of her larger-than-life dreams. More supportive than her mom, whose response when Delanie had announced her intention to enter film school had been to leave pamphlets for Grande Prairie Regional College on her bed with the education and drama programs circled, subtly reinforcing Cheryl's *you need a career to fall back on* mantra. But when Delanie came home to visit, even Bill still looked at her with quiet worry in his eyes—even if he had also driven her and all her stuff to Vancouver when she'd moved.

Delanie squatted next to the girl. "That's a pretty bracelet. Did you make that too?"

The girl looked at the pink-and-purple friendship bracelet on her wrist and shook her head. "My friend Addison gave that to me today, but my mom's going to show me how to make them. Then I can make one for my cousin Hannah and one for my little sister."

"I remember making those when I was your age. What's your sister's name?"

"I don't know yet. My mom just found out she's pregnant." The girl got a thoughtful look. "I suppose it could be a boy. He probably wouldn't want a friendship bracelet." A dejected look came over her face.

"You never know. I have a friend named Desmond who would probably wear one. Especially if his sister gave it to him."

"Really?" The girl's joy returned, shining from big brown eyes with full lashes set in a dimpled face. She was about the most adorable thing ever. "That's awesome."

"I'm Delanie. What's your name?"

"Emma."

"And why are you here all alone, Emma?"

"Oh, I'm not alone. My dad is backstage working on the sets. But guess what? I get to be Lucy in the play!"

Delanie frowned. "Lucy?" She knew the play was an adaptation of *The Adventures of Pinocchio*, but she hadn't read the script yet and had no idea who the characters were.

"Yeah. You know, the Talking Cricket? Her full name is Lucetta, but she hates it when people call her that."

Delanie chuckled. Emma's energy and enthusiasm were contagious. And the trucks outside suddenly made sense. They probably belonged to the Butler brothers. Violet had mentioned her son Noel was building sets for the play, and he had probably conscripted his brother and business partner Derrick into helping. Thinking of the two brown-skinned boys she had gone to school with, Delanie wondered which one of them this little cutie belonged to. Emma didn't much resemble either of them. Her mom must be as fair-skinned as Violet.

"You are going to be a *great* Lucy." Delanie grinned at the little girl.

"Thanks!" Emma looked curious. "Were you ever in the play?"

"As a matter of fact, I was. I started when I was about your age. But I didn't get any speaking roles until I was much older."

"Yeah, Daddy says most kids don't. But they needed someone little for Lucy, I guess, and I'm great at memorizing things. I already have my song memorized, even."

Delanie chuckled. "I bet you do." Tired of squatting, Delanie stood and stretched to work out some of the travel kinks. "That's an important skill in theatre . . ."

She froze.

Caleb Toews stood at the bottom of the aisle, staring back at her with his mouth slightly agape. He hardly looked different than the last time she'd seen him—the large-check plaid shirt with the sleeves rolled up was blue instead of red, and his dark-wash blue jeans still hugged a slim, athletic frame. He now wore his dark brown hair short, she noticed, so she couldn't see the waves, and his chin was covered with dark stubble. The good looks he'd had when they had dated in high school had matured into a rustic, casual magnetism he still seemed completely unaware of, but which made Delanie's mouth go dry.

Her stomach did a weird flip. She tried to think of something cool and intelligent to say, but what came out was a choked, "Hi."

The word seemed to break his trance. He walked up the aisle toward her, turning his attention to the little girl.

"Emma, are you ready to go?"

This is Caleb's kid?

Emma closed her sketchbook. "Yes, Daddy." She started closing the zipper on her pencil case. "This is Delanie. She has a boy friend named Desmond who likes wearing friendship bracelets. Isn't that funny?" She giggled.

"He's, um, not my boyfriend," Delanie stammered, wondering why she was explaining herself. "He's just a friend."

"No," Emma said, "I didn't mean *boyfriend,* I meant boy, friend. They're not the same thing." She gave an exaggerated roll of her eyes and tucked her sketchbook and pencil case into her mint green backpack.

"I see." Caleb's voice sounded a little thin, and he looked at Delanie as though he'd seen a ghost. "What are you doing here? Oh, wait. Molly's funeral." His brow furrowed. "I'm sorry for your loss."

"Thanks." Where had all her good words gone? "And congratulations on your new baby."

He blinked, looking confused. "What? Oh. No, I'm not . . . Monica's pregnant, but we haven't been together for years." He raised an eyebrow at his daughter. "Are you sure Mom wants you telling people about the baby already?"

Emma looked sheepish. "Oh, yeah. She said I was only supposed to talk about it with you. Sorry, Daddy."

"It's alright, Chickadee. I know it's hard to keep exciting things to yourself. Just try to do better." He turned his attention to

Delanie. "They just found out, so if you could not tell anyone, that would probably be best."

Delanie nodded dumbly. Caleb and Monica had split up? Her knees shook.

She and Caleb had dated all through high school, dreaming of the day they would go to film school together—she for acting, he for screen writing. In grade twelve, Monica Fehr had become obsessed with Caleb, doing everything she could to draw him away from Delanie. He had laughed off her attempted manipulations, claiming he found it annoying.

Then his dad got sick with cancer, and he had chosen to stay home after graduation to help with the family farm. Delanie couldn't see how they could keep dating from so far away, so she had broken up with him and gone to Vancouver alone, all the while hoping it wouldn't be long before he would join her and they could pick up where they had left off.

But, six months later, she had heard he was married to Monica with a baby on the way. The way her mother told it, he had been seeing Monica for months, which meant he'd been lying about why he had stayed behind—not about his dad's cancer, which her mother had kept her apprised of. But if Caleb had truly loved her as he'd said he did, how could he have gotten together with Monica so soon after the two of them split up? Or, as was more likely, even before?

Ever since, every time she thought of Caleb, the bitter taste of betrayal filled her mouth. For some reason, knowing that Caleb and Monica had broken up years ago and she had never known—that he had never once reached out to her—made it worse. Why hadn't her mom said something, at least?

He drew in a breath and tucked his hands in his pockets. "Well, uh, we best get going. This little jumping bean needs to get to bed." He tilted his head at Emma. "I guess I'll see you at the funeral tomorrow."

Delanie nodded. "Emma said you're building the sets. I

thought that was Noel Butler's job." She indicated the stage.

"Yeah. He roped me into helping him."

Delanie tried to sound casual. "I'll be seeing a lot more of you then. I'm directing the play."

He nodded slowly. "That explains why Cheryl didn't say who it was," he muttered. He gave her a tight-lipped smile, but his tone was sincere when he added, "I can't think of anyone better for the job."

Emma stood before him with her backpack on over her light jacket, and he urged her up the aisle with a hand on her back.

"See you around, Delanie. Noel's still here, so don't worry about locking up."

"Bye, Delanie!" Emma waved over her shoulder, then tore up the aisle.

Delanie cringed at the inadvertent reference to her recent humiliation, but neither Emma nor Caleb seemed to notice.

"No running," Caleb called, striding after his daughter. "And that's *Miss Fletcher* to you," he said as they reached the stairs.

"Okay, Daddy." Emma adjusted her pace, then gave Delanie another wave before pounding down the stairs at an only somewhat restrained pace.

"Bye," Delanie said with a half-wave of her own.

With a last glance at Delanie, Caleb followed his daughter down the stairs and out of sight.

Delanie watched them go, her chest filled with cold dread and her stomach with an unwelcome nervous flutter. After being so hurt and angry with Caleb for nearly a decade, how could she still feel *anything* for him? Oh, why had she said she would direct the play? Not only had she never directed anything but her own YouTube videos before, it also meant she would likely see Caleb on a regular basis.

She sighed. It was too late to change her mind now. Violet had been so thrilled to have her on board that Delanie suspected her mother's assessment had been right—finding someone else to step into the director's role at this point would be unlikely, jeopardizing the entire production.

Well, as long as Caleb was only helping with sets, she could manage to be civil when they crossed paths—as long as her heart didn't start pounding like this every time she saw his face. Ugh. Maybe she could get the producer, Anne Erickson, to deal with set stuff.

She waited a full five minutes before she left the theatre to give Caleb a chance to leave. When she made her way back to her car, the white truck was gone, and her heart stuttered in relief . . . and a touch of disappointment.

Yep. This was going to be interesting.

Chapter 5

TWO DAYS LATER, Caleb held the truck door open for Emma while she climbed in—carefully, to avoid damaging the fluffy dress she'd worn to church that morning—and then he handed her the brown paper bags from the local sandwich shop. After she tucked her dress under her legs, he shut the door and made his way around to the driver's side. He would have preferred sandwiches from Cool Beans, but they weren't open on Sundays. And, with so little time between church and play rehearsal, he and Emma didn't have time to go home, prepare lunch, and get back to Mackenzie Playhouse. If he had been thinking ahead that morning, he would have made sandwiches to bring with them. At least he'd had Emma grab a change of clothes at the last minute. She could change out of her dress at the hall.

He wasn't normally this disorganized, but ever since he had seen Delanie on Friday night—and again yesterday at Molly's funeral—he hadn't been able to get her out of his mind. Oh, he had tried, but she hadn't made it easy on him. Not with the way she kept glancing at him from across the church reception hall yesterday, nor with how sensational she had looked in that slim black dress. Every time he had caught her looking at him, she had quickly looked away. And when he had gone to give her his respects, she had said only enough to be polite. *Can you blame her, Caleb? It was her grandmother's funeral, not a high school reunion.*

Still, he had hoped to pull her aside and ask how she was doing, maybe make up for how awkward he'd been the night before. She'd caught him by surprise, appearing in the hall like that, talking to Emma, and looking even better than the last time he'd seen her—though, understandably, a little shaken up. He had probably sounded like an idiot. He'd certainly felt like one—his leaden tongue had been as helpful as a green-broke horse.

Maybe it was for the best that he hadn't had the chance to talk to her. She didn't owe him anything, not really. And he would be seeing her often enough over the next two months—there would be other chances.

But should I take them?

He frowned at the voice of wisdom in his head. Knowing he should leave well enough alone and doing it were two entirely different things.

As he jumped in the driver's seat and closed the door, the jangle of an old rotary phone pierced the air. It was loud and shrill enough to catch his attention even on the job site, but he would have to remember to put his phone on vibrate when they got to the hall. Lucky he hadn't received a call during church. This time.

The moment he saw his older sister's name on the screen, his gut tightened with guilt. He already knew why she was calling.

"Hi, Rach. You're probably wondering why I'm not at Mom and Dad's right now."

Toews Sunday Dinner was a family institution, when all of his local siblings and their families would descend on Marcus and Adelaide's sprawling farmhouse to feast and reconnect after a busy week. He had been so distracted by Delanie and the funeral that he had completely forgotten to tell his mom or Rachel about the regular Sunday afternoon all-hands-on-deck play rehearsals that meant he and Emma wouldn't be at dinner for the next two months.

"Actually, I was hoping you would still be in town," Rachel said. Caleb could hear car noise in the background. Oliver must be driving. "Can you stop at the store and buy some coffee cream on the way out? Mom asked me to do it, but it slipped my mind. Ivan was up all night—he's still teething that nasty molar, I think—and neither of us got a lot of sleep."

Caleb sighed. With four kids under eight, it seemed Rachel was always up at night with someone. He didn't know how she managed it. "Sorry, I wish I could, but actually, I won't even be there today. Emma has play rehearsal every Sunday afternoon for the next two months, and I'm helping with sets. Maybe Dinah can bring it. Mom should have asked her in the first place."

Twins Dinah and Isaac, the youngest of the Toews siblings, were both still single and childless. Isaac lived in Calgary, so he usually only made it to the farm for holidays and special occasions these days. But Dinah lived in town, where she worked as a hairdresser at a local salon. As the only single sister in the family, Caleb thought Mom should call on her a little more often to step up for things like this. At the same time, he knew why she didn't.

"Is that Aunty Rachel?" Emma asked through a mouthful of sandwich, and Caleb nodded distractedly. "Say hi to Hannah for me!"

He shifted the phone down to answer his daughter. "Okay, Chickadee. I'll tell her." Into the receiver, he said, "Emma says hi to Hannah."

"Okay, I'll tell her," Rachel echoed him. "Um, maybe I'll call Abby," she continued. "Dinah is probably out there already, anyway."

"Sure." And even if she wasn't, she would probably forget the request the second she got off the phone. Caleb could never decide if Dinah were too self-absorbed to take note of others' needs, or if she was just an airhead. Probably a bit of both. And Abby and her husband, Jake, had been perpetually late since their second son had been born a few months ago, so chances were good they were still near a grocery store. "Sorry I couldn't help."

"No problem. Who did they get to direct the play?"

Caleb hesitated before replying, "Delanie Fletcher."

Silence hung. "Are you alright?"

"Why wouldn't I be? Things were over between Delanie and me a long time ago."

Emma glanced up from her grilled cheese with bacon and eyed him.

"There's over, and then there's *over*," Rachel said slowly.

Caleb glanced at Emma, who had gotten distracted by something out the window, and lowered his voice. "What's that supposed to mean?"

"I'm just worried about you. Can't a big sister care?"

Caleb sighed and started the truck. "I'm fine, Rach. Thanks, though. And please give my love to everyone. We get Thanksgiving Sunday off, so I'll see everyone in a month. Emma's with me this year, I think." He frowned, not sure about that.

"Feel free to stop by before then if you need to talk."

"I said I'm *fine*." He sounded grumpier than he meant to and drew a breath to calm himself.

"Okay." Rachel sounded unconvinced, but, thankfully, she let it drop. "Tell Emma hi from Aunty Rachel, and I hope you both have fun."

"Thanks. Bye, Rach."

"Bye." He could hardly blame Rachel for not believing his assertions that seeing Delanie several times a week for the next couple of months wouldn't be a problem for him. Not when he hadn't yet been able to convince himself.

"Did you and Miss Fletcher used to date?" Emma asked, startling Caleb.

Caleb set the phone in the console before turning his attention to the rearview mirror to watch for a gap in the after-church Main Street traffic. "A long time ago, before your mom and I got together."

"Huh. She's nice. I can see why you liked her. Do you think you would date her again?"

Caleb swallowed before answering. "Somehow, I don't think she'd be interested. We haven't been on the best terms since then."

"Too bad." Emma shrugged, then tore an oversized bite from her sandwich, her mouth too full to say more.

Seeing his opportunity in the mirror, Caleb reversed into the street and slammed the truck into drive. He glanced at his daughter, her words pinging around inside his tight chest. Ever since Delanie had appeared at the theatre the other night, he had wondered the same thing. But there were some hurts that *shouldn't* be forgiven—and he didn't mean the fact that she had left. Delanie had hurt him when she had broken up with him, yes. But she had left the door open, telling him that when things settled down with his dad and he came to Vancouver, they could get back together . . . but that if the worst happened and he had to stay behind, they were both free to focus their energy on the tasks that lay ahead of them. He hadn't liked her reasoning, but at least he had understood it.

But how could he ever make her understand his hasty marriage to Monica? He could never regret having Emma, but he still punished himself for the one moment of weakness that had changed his life forever. And if he couldn't forgive himself, why would Delanie?

Chapter 6

"QUIET, PLEASE," DELANIE called over the crowded auditorium, but she could barely hear her own voice over the din of excited children's voices.

She stood onstage at Mackenzie Playhouse next to the petite Violet Butler, trying not to be overwhelmed by the number of kids filling the theatre—seventy-eight of them, if everyone who had come to auditions had shown up today. The middle section was about two-thirds full, with kids arranged by grade from the front. Parents dotted the outer sections—some visiting quietly near the back, others staring at their phones, and some watching the proceedings with interest. Or disinterest, as the case may be.

Caleb and Monica sat near each other about halfway up one side. Delanie's heart skipped. The last thing she needed was to embarrass herself in front of those two. She had done plenty of that already at the funeral yesterday. Every time she had thought about going to talk to Caleb, her feet had stubbornly refused to move. He must have gotten tired of catching her looking in his direction, because he had eventually come to talk to her, like polite people do—and she had said something so utterly inane, she could no longer remember what it was. It was like her brain had frozen in the past, and all she could think about was what she *wished* she could say to him. But calling your high school sweetheart a lying cheater at your grandmother's funeral wasn't exactly in good taste.

"Attention, everyone! Quiet down!" she tried again, with similar results.

"Hi, Miss Fletcher," came the voice of one little girl.

Delanie spotted Emma gazing up at her from the front row. When Emma saw Delanie look at her, she waved excitedly. Delanie waved shyly back, then glanced at Caleb and Monica to see their reaction. She needn't have bothered. They probably hadn't even noticed. She wondered if the man in a puffy quilted vest on Monica's other side was her netw man.

"Hi-ho, Silver!" called Violet Butler in a voice that could probably be heard in the next county.

"*Away!*" came the unified response of most of the kids, and they quieted, their attention now fixed on Violet and Delanie for the most part. The littlest ones sitting near the front giggled and reacted in loud excitement, but after the older kids and the surrounding parents gave a few hisses of warning, they got the idea and settled down.

Delanie gaped at the smiling music director. She'd known Violet Butler for most of her life, but she was always amazed when such a big voice came out of such a slender woman. Violet's indigo eyes sparkled behind the youthful-looking woman's thin-framed glasses, which were perched on a patrician nose. Violet had started keeping her thick, straight hair cropped short in the back since Delanie left, and what had once been black was mostly silver now—though she had dyed a chunk of the bangs framing one side of her face dark purple, almost the same colour as her eyes and her drapey dark blue sweater.

"We did *The Lone Ranger* a few years ago, and we've used that catchphrase as a signal to the kids that it's time to quiet down ever since," Violet whispered.

"I'll have to remember that," Delanie whispered back. "Have you seen Anne or Liam yet?" Delanie had only met the woman

who had been volunteering as the show's producer for the last
several years for the first time yesterday, at Nan's funeral, and
had never met Anne's son Liam, who had been cast as Luigi the
Fox in the play. Anne had said she would arrive early, despite
having to drive a half-hour from Berwyn, but she hadn't been
at Delanie's rushed pre-rehearsal meeting with Violet.

Violet glanced over the hall and shook her head, her brow
wrinkling and smoothing so quickly it might not have happened. "I'm sure she'll be here any minute. She probably got
stuck behind a baler on the bridge or something."

"Sure." Delanie turned back to the audience. Seventy-eight
pairs of eyes, plus at least half that many more belonging to
the parents, stared back at her expectantly. Her knees started
shaking. *Breathe, Delanie. You're an actress. So act like you know
what you're doing.*

"Hi, everyone!" Good. Her voice didn't even wobble.

A few curious *hey*s and *hello*s came from the kids.

She put on her most polished smile. "My name is Delanie
Fletcher. Molly Davis is . . . *was* my grandmother." Her breath
hitched, and she paused to collect herself. "And I'm going to be
directing the play this year."

At that, some of the parents who'd been visiting or looking at
their phones started paying attention.

"I ask that you bear with me as I get my feet wet. I've had
a chance to read the script and go through some of Molly's
notes, but it's been a few years since I was sitting in your chair."
She pointed at Emma, who giggled. "Or even yours," she said,
gesturing a little farther back at the older kids, who smirked.
"However, I'm sure that if we all work together, this is going to
be a great year."

A woman with short auburn hair and a determined set to her
chin stood up in one of the side section rows near the front.

"Question?" Delanie said.

"Yes, hi. I'm Amber Leclerc. I was just wondering if you'll be reviewing any of the casting choices. My Celeste is in Grade Eleven and deserves a main cast role like the Blue Fairy, not Judy the Puppet."

Delanie glanced at the rows of senior high students, and noticed a pretty girl covering a face as red as her long tresses of hair with two hands while her companions giggled. Her heart pinched for the girl. She glanced back at Celeste's mother.

"I'm sorry, Ms. Leclerc, but I trust the judgement of Violet, Anne, and Molly, and stand in support of their decisions." She turned to take in the whole room. "And I want to remind everyone that *every* role is important, even the chorus. We couldn't put on a play without every one of these roles being filled."

"And one might almost think that kind of question could have been asked privately," Violet said to Amber in a voice full of both steel and velvet.

Amber's face flamed almost as bright as her daughter's, but she didn't sit down. "I'm just wondering, Miss Fletcher, after all that's happened to you recently, if *your* judgement might also be in question." She arched a brow. "We do have the Internet, even in Peace Crossing, you know."

Delanie's throat closed, and she couldn't think of a thing to say. She stood there frozen, staring into Amber's condemning eyes. What was happening? She never froze! But in the face of Amber's accusations, the weight of her collapsing career nearly crushed her, and she could only gawp like a fish yanked from the water.

Violet frowned at the woman. "Please have a seat, Amber. You may come talk to us later about your concerns. Now," she said, turning to the room at large.

The kids had started to get restless and noisy again, and Violet once more did her call of *Hi-ho, Silver!* This time, now that the little kids knew what to do, the response of *Away!* just about deafened Delanie. Amber huffed, but did as she'd been told.

Violet took over, getting the kids and parents oriented as to what to expect from the production, the schedule, and how they would proceed.

Delanie glanced at Caleb, wondering if he had heard about her recent cancellation, then scolded herself that she even cared. But it wasn't only Caleb she had to worry about. She was sure the judgement of every person in that room was bearing down on her, especially the parents and the older kids, who probably *all* knew about Delanie's humiliation. How stupid had she been to think she could retreat to Peace Crossing for a couple months and lick her wounds in a place where no one would know what had happened to her?

Her heart thundered in her ears as she glanced around the hall, but thankfully, most people were listening to Violet. Anne still wasn't there. Happy for the excuse to avoid eye contact, she pulled out her phone and sent Anne a text, but didn't get a response back. If Anne was driving, that made sense. Delanie would have to call her once the kids dispersed.

Violet assigned different chorus groups to different locations around the building to start learning their songs, and then reminded the parents that there would be a parents' meeting in fifteen minutes in the basement. Bless her—Delanie had forgotten to even mention it.

Violet dismissed the kids to their groups, and volunteer parents took charge to herd the younger ones to their practise areas, where those who had volunteered to help with music would start teaching them their songs. Delanie sighed in relief, her knees still weak. First hurdle down.

"I'm going to call Anne," Violet said to Delanie, moving toward the side door that led backstage. "This isn't like her. You can get to know the cast while you wait," she said, indicating the kids, most of them older teenagers, who were making their way to the front rows. Emma sat cheerfully where she'd been, her legs short enough to swing from the folding theatre seat.

"Thank you," Delanie said, chewing her thumbnail. If even

Violet's optimism had faded, her own brewing concern might have merit.

Just then, a woman with a dark brown ponytail hurried down the aisle, working her way against the flow of retreating kids, her phone clutched in her hand.

Violet spotted her and paused. "That's Anne's sister, Erin," she said under her breath to Delanie.

The look on Erin's face made Delanie's gut clench. Something was obviously very wrong.

"Anne was in an accident on the bridge," Erin said without preamble as soon as she reached them. "Liam was with her. He's fine, but she's in surgery. I don't know how serious it is. Frank—that's her husband," she said to Delanie, "didn't know much. I have to go to the hospital. If my wife can't make it here to pick up the kids before rehearsal ends, Monica Toews will take them."

"Oh, my," breathed Violet. "That's terrible. Poor Anne. I'll be praying she's okay. Please keep us posted when you have time."

"Thanks," said Erin, then spun on her heel and hurried along the now much-cleared aisle.

Delanie swallowed. First Nan, now Anne? What was happening around here?

And how was she, a newbie, supposed to direct a play without an experienced producer to help her out? Violet knew a lot, but she had enough on her hands with just the music. Delanie wasn't the praying type, but she couldn't help breathe a little petition to the Universe that Anne would be perfectly fine, even if she was embarrassed that her reasons were mostly selfish. She sent up a final word to make it clear she wanted Anne to be okay for her own sake, too, not just Delanie's. She didn't know if the Universe cared about the motivation behind the prayer or not, but better safe than sorry.

Pushing her trepidation aside, she turned to face the kids she'd be leading for the next seven weeks. Whether she knew what she was doing or not.

CALEB SHAMBLED DOWN the stairs toward the lower hall behind Dave and Monica along with the other parents. Watching Delanie at the front of the room earlier—uncomfortable, though he doubted many but him could tell, yet fiercely pushing ahead with her task—reminded him of why he'd fallen in love with her so long ago. Delanie had always been fearless.

No, that wasn't true. She had fears, just like anyone else. She just didn't let them stop her. It was a trait he admired . . . and, if he were honest with himself, even envied. If he'd been a little more fearless, maybe he would have gone to Vancouver with her a decade ago. How different would his life have been then?

"Can you believe that woman?" came Amber Leclerc's voice from somewhere behind him. "Just because she's Molly's grand-daughter doesn't mean she'll make a good director. What does she know about theatre, anyway? They should have asked me to do it."

Whomever she was speaking to made a non-committal sound in her throat.

Caleb clenched his jaw. When he stepped off the last step, he turned around enough to meet the woman's eyes.

"I can answer that for you, Amber. Delanie has been a work-ing actor for the past ten years, and she grew up on that stage up there. She might be new to directing, but she's one of the most brilliant actors this town has ever known, aside from Molly herself. If you're smart, you'll stay out of her way and let your daughter benefit from Delanie's experience."

Amber's face puckered. "If she's so brilliant, why has she only ever done a few commercials and a part in some student film I've never heard of?"

Caleb flicked his glance to the phone in Amber's hand. "Is

that what your little Internet search told you? That that's all she's done? Huh."

He turned around and walked through the double doors into the reception hall, letting Amber stew on that for a while. He hadn't kept close tabs on Delanie's career for the sake of his own mental health, but his mom had shared tidbits she had heard from Cheryl Fletcher over the years. And Molly had told anyone who would listen about Delanie's stage career, including her most recent run as a supporting cast member in a production of *Legally Blonde: The Musical.* No, it wasn't exactly going to make her a household name, but it wasn't nothing. And if Amber had only searched Delanie's film credits on IMDB, like most people would, that wouldn't have come up.

The parents had assembled in a loose circle near the outer edges of the large open room, leaving space clear at the front where a door and pass-through window led into the dark kitchen beyond. Another doorway beside the kitchen window opened to a wide corridor that led to the basement walk-out entrance.

Delanie came in through the double doors at the back of the room with two binders in her arms and made her way to the front, a troubled look on her face. Violet followed a step behind.

Delanie set the thicker of the two binders on the rectangular grey plastic table that had been set up in front of the pass-through window. Opening the other binder and bracing it against her abdomen, she pulled a pen from the front pocket and started moving it down the page as if checking items on a list. Finally, she looked up at the assembled parents and cleared her throat, and the quiet murmur of visiting friends stilled as everyone gave her their attention. From the corner of his eye, Caleb caught Amber glaring at him before glancing back down at her phone and swiping upward as though reading a long piece of content. He focused on Delanie, but couldn't keep from smiling a little. *She must have found it.*

"Hi, everyone," Delanie said. Though her voice carried through the large room, she had lost the exuberance she'd had upstairs.

Caleb tensed. What had happened between then and now?

"Thank you so much for coming today," Delanie continued. "As you know, we couldn't run a production like this without our volunteers. Unfortunately, I just received some disheartening news, and it has left a big gap on our production team. Anne Erickson has been in an accident on the bridge, and she is currently in surgery."

Gasps and soft whispers of shock and sympathy filled the room. Caleb swallowed. He didn't know Anne personally, but any tragedy in a community this small would have ripple effects. And he was pretty sure he knew where Delanie was going next.

"Do you know how bad it is?" asked one of the moms.

Delanie shook her head. "Unfortunately, we don't know much yet, including how long Anne will be unavailable. I think it's safe to say, if she's requiring surgery, that she won't be jumping back into the production immediately. Which means the first volunteer position we need to fill is producer. For Anne's sake, we'll call the position Assistant Producer for now, in case she is able to return to her role."

Uncomfortable shuffles and throat clearings drifted around the room.

"What would be involved?" asked Rachel's brother-in-law, Dan Wood. His older two kids were in the play.

Delanie found Dan in the crowd and met his gaze. "You'd be involved in a lot of the hands-on work with the play, such as creating and posting schedules, communicating with parents and department heads, keeping volunteers organized, getting the souvenir T-shirts made, *et cetera*. Basically, anything involved in running the play that doesn't have to be done by me would be done by the producer."

"And you would be part of our planning meetings," added Violet.

Caleb's chest tightened as he fought the urge to volunteer. Being producer would mean spending more time with Emma over the next seven weeks and making sure her first year in the play was a positive experience. But it would also mean spending a *lot* more time with Delanie. And he didn't think that would be good for either of them. So he waited, hoping someone else would speak up.

Amber stepped forward, her eyes gleaming. "I'd be happy to do it. I've been involved in the play for years now, and I've filled almost every parent volunteer role. I know exactly what to do."

Delanie hid her consternation well, but Caleb recognized her aversion to the idea in the way she curled a lock of long blond hair around her finger and tugged.

"Okay, um, thanks, Amber. Can I call you Amber?" Delanie smiled brightly, but it was a little stiff.

Amber nodded shortly, a victorious smile on her face. Caleb could only imagine the living hell it would be for Delanie to work with the smug busybody for seven weeks. After everything she'd gone through recently with losing Molly, she didn't need that too. Before he could rationally think it through again, he heard himself say, "I'd be willing to do it too."

Relief flashed across Delanie's face as she looked for the person who had spoken. When she saw him step forward, her hopeful expression disappeared in wide-eyed surprise.

"Caleb. Yes, you'd certainly be a good choice, as well. Um . . ."

Violet touched her arm, and when Delanie glanced at her, Violet turned her body away from the parents, urging Delanie to step away to chat. They murmured back and forth for a few minutes. A low buzz of voices filled the room, making it impossible to hear anything Delanie and Violet were saying, even if Caleb had tried. He could feel Monica's gaze boring into his back, and Amber's animosity drilled into him from across the room. But despite his misgivings, he stood his ground. Once he had committed to something, he wasn't the kind to back down. He had thrown his hat in the ring. Now he would have to deal with the consequences.

And if Delanie chose Amber over him, he would know exactly where they stood.

Finally, Delanie and Violet finished their quiet consultation. Delanie stepped forward with a bright smile on her face, but her clenched hands on the top of the open binder forced the bottom edge into her midriff.

"Thank you both for volunteering," she said, taking in Amber and Caleb in turn. "Your willingness is deeply appreciated. It was a tough choice, as these things always are, but I think I'll ask Mr. Toews to take the position."

Something in Caleb's chest released, even as Amber's face darkened.

"I should have known," she muttered, glaring once more at her phone.

Delanie glanced uncertainly at Amber, her brow furrowing. "However, Amber," she added, and when Amber glanced up at her, she continued, "since this role is a big responsibility that could easily be divided, I was wondering if you would be willing to assist. Your varied experience with the play would be a helpful asset to our team."

Amber straightened, raising her head as though she were considering the offer. Finally, she nodded stiffly. "Very well. I don't want Celeste's experience ruined by an inexperienced production team. What would my title be?"

Caleb resisted the urge to roll his eyes and quip that she would be the Assistant Assistant Producer, obviously, just to see the look on her face—but he successfully bit his tongue.

Instead, Delanie said, "Assistant Director. I would value your expertise and help with the decisions I'll be making during the production."

Amber gave a surprised smile, then nodded, obviously mollified.

Well done, Delanie. Caleb smiled. Delanie had always been good at handling prickly people. Amber would likely see Assistant Director as at least equal to Assistant Producer, if not better. It was the perfect solution. As for Caleb, he could care less about titles. He would help Delanie out in whatever way she needed. He ignored the quiet voice in the back of his head that asked if he would have done the same for anyone else in the role, focusing on what Delanie was saying to him and Amber.

"If you two would stay after the meeting, we can make arrangements for our first planning session."

"Sure." Caleb stepped back to his place near the wall.

Amber nodded earnestly. Her earlier outrage seemed to have evaporated.

Delanie and Violet went through the rest of the orientation, laying out the volunteer needs and pointing parents in either Caleb's or Amber's direction several times to connect about certain jobs. When Caleb saw Amber start taking notes on her phone, he did the same, begrudgingly admitting to himself that it was a good idea. He wished he had a notepad and pen— he hated swiping around on his screen. He would be more prepared in the future.

After the meeting dispersed, Caleb met up with Delanie, Violet, and Amber at the front of the room. Violet gave him a knowing smile, and he wondered what she was thinking.

"Thanks, again, you two," Delanie said, glancing quickly past him to Amber. "I know it's a lot all at once. Would you be available to meet at Cool Beans to discuss everything before Wednesday night rehearsal? I think Violet and I can handle the principal and supporting cast rehearsal tomorrow night by ourselves, but if you could make that too, that would be helpful."

"I'll already be here for rehearsal because of Celeste," said

Amber. She swiped around on her phone. "Would Tuesday afternoon at two-thirty work for the meeting?"

"Works for me." Delanie looked at Violet and Caleb for confirmation.

"I'd have to leave at three so I could teach music lessons," said Violet, "but you and I could meet earlier to go through our part and you could pass it on to the others."

"Sure. Unless everyone could meet earlier. Caleb? Do you have to work?"

She finally met his gaze, her big brown eyes soft and unguarded for once.

He cleared his throat to banish the sudden tightness and looked at his phone as if that held the answer she sought. He definitely wasn't looking at it because he was afraid of what she would see looking back at her.

"Yes, but I'll take a few hours off. I have extra time accrued, so it shouldn't be a problem. And I'll already be here tomorrow night, too—I was planning to work on sets with Noel. I'll come out to observe for a few minutes if I can."

"No need to do that," Delanie said. "Thanks for making accommodations for everyone. How does two sound instead?"

After a round of agreement, Delanie beamed. "Great. Guess it's a date for Tuesday. I'll see you all then . . . and tomorrow night. Now, the kids should be finishing up, so we better go wrap things up upstairs. If you could go ahead, I'll be just a minute."

Amber and Violet headed toward the door as Delanie turned to gather her binders, but Caleb hung back. Delanie saw him standing there and busied herself with arranging her binders on top of each other on the table. He wondered if she were avoiding his gaze. Maybe he should just go.

But no. He wanted to know where they stood. Despite his misgivings, he stepped toward her.

"Hey, Delanie, are you sure this is alright with you? It won't be too weird, will it?"

She straightened, flashing him a sunny smile. "Weird? Why would it be weird?"

"Well, you know . . . Things seemed a little awkward between us the last couple days. I don't want to make you uncomfortable."

Delanie's expression hardened, and she stepped toward him, staring into his face. "Nothing you could ever do would make me uncomfortable, Caleb Joseph Toews. I stopped giving you that privilege a long time ago. We're professionals. So let's act professional and do what we have to do to make this a great production for the kids. Agreed?"

He should have stuck to his instincts and kept quiet. "Agreed."

With that, she whirled and stomped away across the tile floor. *Using my full name and stomping angrily away—very professional.*

He snorted. Despite what she had said, his suspicions were confirmed—she must still hold a grudge because of what had happened a decade ago. He sighed. It was nothing less than he deserved, he supposed. Still, didn't he have a right to be hurt, too? She had broken up with him, not the other way around.

Whatever the case, he would make the best of it. And maybe he could finally find a way to put his feelings for Delanie in the past.

But when he followed her, he could still feel the brush of her breath across his face.

Chapter 7

DELANIE STOOD IMPATIENTLY on the wooden porch of Nan's farmhouse with several nested empty cardboard boxes in her arms, waiting for her mother to unlock the door. The breeze had a bite to it, and she wished she had worn a warmer sweater.

When she followed Cheryl inside to the small entrance leading directly into the living room, the scents and sights plunged her into nostalgic memories. There was the same couch covered with a floral slipcover where she'd often whiled away an afternoon reading. There was the living room gallery wall, covered with framed school photos of Delanie and her sister, her cousins, uncles, and aunts, all surrounding a large photo of Nan and Pops taken on their fiftieth wedding anniversary. Pops had died a year later from a heart attack. Beneath the staleness of the air caused by the house being shut up for a week and a half, Delanie detected hints of lavender from the potpourri Molly kept on the coffee table and the pungent smell of dried roses from a shrivelled, dusty bouquet hanging upside-down near the photos.

She put down the boxes on the living room floor and set her purse—which she'd brought in to hold her phone and keys— on the bench near the door, then took off her calf-high leather boots. The floor was probably cold, but there was no reason to make it dirty and make more work for them later.

"The first thing we should do is go through her food," Cheryl said, hanging her coat in the closet and bustling toward the kitchen. She had given up her typical slacks and blouse to wear a more appropriate ensemble of jeans and a T-shirt, but still managed to look as elegant as ever. Her blown-out short blond hair and full-face makeup helped. "I took the perishables home with me last week, but she has quite a few things in the root cellar already. And we'll have to come back and dig up the rest of her carrots and potatoes soon before it freezes."

"Sounds good." Delanie touched a photo of her and Nan that had been taken after Delanie's first opening night in the kids' play. Delanie had been nine, the same age as Emma now, and still in her mouse costume. They had been doing *Cinderella* that year. Both faces in the photo were split in wide grins.

Oh, Nan, what advice would you have for me now? Now that she had messed up the only dream she'd ever had.

A row of photo albums on the bottom row of a nearby tall bookshelf caught her eye. *Nan's scrapbooks.* Delanie chose one that looked particularly vintage and opened it, cradling it on her arm as she turned the pages with her other hand. Inside were photos of Nan in various roles next to programs with stiff pages that had yellowed with age—relics of her life before she had met Pops and given up acting to move to Peace Crossing. Delanie stared at a black-and-white photo of a young, vivacious Molly Wright in costume for the role of Anna Leonowens in *The King and I* on a Toronto stage, her voluminous ball gown accentuating her tiny figure.

"What's that?" said Cheryl.

Delanie looked up to see her mother leaning against the archway leading to the kitchen. "One of Nan's old scrapbooks from her acting days. Did you know she played Anna Leanowens once?"

"I think she mentioned it, yes." Cheryl came and peered over Delanie's shoulder at the photo. "She didn't talk too much about her early days on the stage. She was always more focused on the present than the past." She smiled. "Beautiful. You know, you look like her when she was that age."

"I do, don't I?" Delanie touched the plastic page protector, tracing the lines of Molly's face. "Would it be okay if I kept this?"

"I don't see why not. I'll ask your uncles and Aunt Lily, but I doubt any of them will want it. Lily never took much interest in Mom's acting career, and the boys . . . Well, Walter's the most sentimental, but he's not the type to keep photo albums around. I'll probably end up putting most of these in storage in our basement." Cheryl stooped and pulled several more albums off the shelf, piling them in her arms. She opened the top one. "Looks like this starts after Roger was born. You know, I think I'll ask him if he wants it after all. But you can keep that one, for sure."

"Thank you. I haven't looked through this one since I was little." Delanie closed the album and set it on the bench next to her purse. She could hardly wait to look through it later.

Cheryl grabbed one of the boxes and set it on the floor near the bookshelf, then put the pile of albums inside, propping them so the spines faced up. She pulled a few more off the shelf, glancing inside the front cover of each as she did, her face pensive.

"On second thought, I probably shouldn't assume that everyone wouldn't want these albums. They are our childhood, after all. I'd like to find the one from when I was born." She looked at Delanie. "Would you mind going through these at home later and helping me decide who should get what? I'd rather not worry about that right now when there is so much other packing to do. We might even need to split the photos up if everyone just wants their own memories."

"Sure, Mom. Here. I'll do this. You go start in the kitchen." Delanie took the stack of albums from her mother's arms and placed them in the box with the others, then tucked the one she was keeping into the box at one end where it would be easy to find again. As tedious as divvying up family photos sounded, a part of her tingled with excitement to see what she might learn about her family, and her grandmother especially, in those pages.

"Thanks, honey." Cheryl released a deep sigh, looking around the room with a flash of overwhelm on her face. She dabbed some moisture out of the corner of her eye with her finger before collecting the remaining cardboard boxes and bustling back into the kitchen. "Why don't you take that box out to your car when you're done, and check the shed on your way back in," she called over her shoulder. "We're going to need a lot more cardboard boxes."

"Sure," Delanie said again, glancing around the overstuffed room. She still couldn't call Nan a hoarder, but her grandmother had certainly made use of every inch of available space. The books alone would require boxes and boxes to pack. "Do you think we should ask everyone if they want any of Nan's other things?"

"Lily already came and took what she wanted," Cheryl called from the kitchen. It sounded like she was already opening cupboard doors and pulling things out. "So did I. Beth said she and Roger didn't need anything except Nan's salad spinner because hers recently broke, so I put that aside already."

That explained why there was a salad spinner sitting in her mother's laundry room. Delanie had wondered.

"But what about the books? Uncle Frank likes to read."

"He said Mom already let him take his pick years ago. And I brought Savannah over yesterday while you were at rehearsal. She took a few things, most of which are in my basement now."

Given how small Savannah's apartment in Edmonton was, that didn't surprise Delanie. She had barely had time to catch up with her sister after the funeral before Savannah had headed back to the city yesterday, which was unfortunate. Maybe while Delanie was in Alberta, she would drive down to Edmonton to see Savannah again—and hope her sister had some time to spend with her while she was there.

Cheryl appeared at the kitchen door again holding an unopened jar of pickles, which she used to gesture around the living room. "I'm afraid most of this will just need to go in the yard sale. And whatever we can't sell will be donated to charity. You're welcome to take anything you like, of course."

"Thanks. Not sure if there's much we need either. Our apartment's pretty small too. But I'll take a look through the kitchen things." Delanie put the last of the albums in the box, then stood and looked around at the possessions Nan and Pops had accumulated over a lifetime. They had held so much meaning and value to Nan, and now they had become castoffs to be sold as cheaply as possible. It made Delanie a little sad.

She stooped to put on her boots. "I'll be back in to help in a few minutes."

"Thanks, honey," Cheryl said, turning away. Then she paused and gave Delanie a warm look. "I'm so glad you're here. Thank you for agreeing to do this."

Delanie flashed a smile at her as she zipped up her second boot. "No problem, Mom. I'm happy to help." Surprisingly, she meant it.

As she carried the box of albums out to her car, she realized that for the past fifteen minutes, she hadn't thought about her career troubles once. And it had been wonderful.

Yep, maybe this was exactly what she needed.

SEVERAL HOURS LATER, Delanie and her mother had packed up the kitchen, putting items to donate in a pile in the shed and stacking the boxes of things to put in the yard sale in the living room. After a break to eat lunch, which consisted of some reheated homemade chunky soup from Nan's freezer, they had tackled Nan and Pops's bedroom. Cheryl was sorting the closet, and Delanie sat on Nan's dressing table stool, deciding what to do with the collection of vintage perfume bottles and the other brass and glass items Nan had kept on the table. *Nan did like her sparkle.*

"So, how are things going with that young man you're seeing?" Cheryl asked, taking an old blue button-down men's shirt off a hanger and inspecting it.

Delanie studied the vintage glass perfume atomizer she had just picked up from Nan's dresser, avoiding her mother's gaze. "They're not."

In the dressing table mirror, Delanie saw Cheryl turn to her in surprise. "What happened? It sounded like he was a real gem, getting you that big role you wanted and everything."

Delanie sighed. She put the atomizer in the box of things to sell on the floor beside her, then sat erect and tucked her hands together between her thighs. "Yeah, about that . . . he did get me that role, and then he took it away from me. We broke up."

That wasn't exactly accurate, but Josh may as well have taken her job away, even if the decision hadn't been his. He hadn't fought for her at all, and he had been the one to give her the bad news. Marie had been right about him all along. Chalk one more mark under *Delanie only dates losers who stab her in the back.*

"Oh, honey. I'm so sorry." Cheryl's arms encircled Delanie's shoulders in an awkward hunched-over side-hug before Delanie even realized her mother had come around the queen bed. Then Cheryl straightened. "Well, I guess it wasn't meant to be. There'll be someone else, you'll see. I met a nice young man when I went to the clinic the other week for my check-up, a new doctor. He said he's planning to stay in town for a while. *And* he's single."

There it was. Delanie rolled her eyes and picked up another bottle. Trust Cheryl Fletcher to start plotting Delanie's next failed relationship in the breath after she had heard about the last one. Delanie wasn't even shocked that her mother had asked about the new doctor's relationship status—not after ten years of Cheryl trying to set her up.

"Mom, I appreciate that you're trying to lift my spirits, but I'm not here to date anyone. I'm only here for two months, and then I'll be going back to Vancouver. Besides, my love life isn't exactly my biggest concern right now."

"Oh?"

Surprisingly, Cheryl didn't press, just kept pulling clothes from the closet and folding them in mid-air before arranging them in neat piles on the floral quilt. Delanie let the question hang while she sorted several other items between the *give* and *sell* boxes, then turned to her mother. She was going to have to explain the situation sooner or later. Might as well get it over with. She just wished her stomach would loosen its death grip on her spleen while she did it.

"So, do you remember my YouTube channel?"

"Yes, the one where you do little skits and songs and such? What about it?"

"I got cancelled last week."

Cheryl frowned. "Cancelled? How can you get cancelled from a publicly available website? Did they close your account?"

Delanie had been afraid of this. "Not cancelled by the platform. Cancelled by my fans."

Cheryl's brow furrowed deeper in confusion.

Delanie sighed. "Some people got upset about a video I made a few years ago, and there was a huge deal about it on Twitter. That's why I lost the job. The studio didn't want to be associated with the controversy." She picked up a tiny lead crystal bud vase, relishing the bumpy texture in her hand. "So I'm back to square one in my acting career. Worse, actually. I'm like a leper in the acting community now. No one wants to work with me."

Cheryl came and sat on the edge of the bed next to Delanie. "So you got *cancelled*"—she made air quotes around the word—"because of something you did years ago? And that lost you your job?"

And my boyfriend. And at least half my Patreon supporters . . . so far. There was no need to say that out loud though. Delanie nodded, her throat tight.

Cheryl shook her head. "There's just no grace nowadays. What was the video even about?"

"Something that had nothing to do with why they're mad."

Delanie explained the situation as briefly as she could, and what Marie had advised her to do. Saying it out loud again, she had to agree with her mother. That she should be cancelled for *that* made no sense to her.

Sure, she had painted Nathan Tait as a hero in the original video, because, at the time, he was the spokesman for a U.S. *Shop Local, Shop American-Made* campaign. It was the reason she had chosen Tait's latest blockbuster as the source material for her skit in the first place. No one was shouting that you shouldn't shop local now because Nathan Tait turned out to be a dirtbag. No, they had chosen to ruin *her* career, not his—not that his career was in any great shape either. He had already lost several big movie franchise contracts for roles he'd been filling for years. Still, he had earned his consequences, and she hadn't.

Like her mother said, where was the grace? What happened to the years of putting out excellent content that her fans loved? Did those videos—and all the raving and approving comments that had gone with them—now mean nothing?

Had the trolls finally won?

"Well, that sounds ridiculous to me," Cheryl declared. "I think your friend Marie is right. If you let this thing blow over, everything will go back to normal. People's memories are short, you'll see. And just like with the guy, this job must not have been meant to be. That means something better is waiting in the wings."

Delanie gave a small smile. "Did you just use a theatre metaphor?"

Cheryl chuckled. "Honey, I grew up at that theatre every bit as much as you did. Mom didn't just direct the kids' play, you know—she was involved in many other productions too. And that doesn't even count the guest roles she sometimes took in other communities. It would be more surprising if it *hadn't* rubbed off."

Delanie laughed. "I guess you're right."

She hadn't ever thought about how Nan's love of the theatre had affected her own children. Cheryl had always put Delanie and Savannah in the play, of course—at least until Savannah reached high school and declared she no longer wanted to participate—but she hadn't exactly encouraged Delanie's acting dreams otherwise. Nor had she ever stood in the way—Delanie had to give her that. It was like Cheryl couldn't care less either way. Maybe that's what bothered Delanie the most.

"Anyway," Delanie said, looking away, "I wish I shared your optimism, but people's memories have gotten a whole lot longer since the Internet came around. Case in point—that video is already three years old, and they're getting angry about it now. Even though my latest video actually supports their views."

Cheryl waved her hand dismissively and went back to her task. "Three years is a drop in the bucket. Your life is still ahead of you. You've got lots of time. Three years from now, you'll probably be in an even better position than you were two weeks ago before this hubbub started. You just never know."

"Three years is a long time from where I'm sitting," Delanie muttered. "Three years ago, I was playing a bit part in a production almost no one came to see that only ran for three weeks. This was my first big break."

She'd had other roles, of course, but, for one reason or another, they never lasted long. Plays closed early. Pilots weren't accepted. Doing a few commercials had kept her afloat, between that and her waitressing job, but just barely. That's why *Trueheart* had been such a breakthrough. Until last week, she had hoped that three years from now, her agent would be renegotiating her contract to get her an even higher salary on what had become a hit show.

She sighed. At least Sandra had done her job. The agent had gone to bat for her with Crystal McLean, stepping in where Josh had been too cowardly to do so, but nothing had changed. And even Sandra had agreed that laying low for a while in Peace Crossing would be a good idea. *Everyone's pretty worked up right now, but I'll talk to a few people and see what I can find out. In the meantime, maybe you should avoid posting any more videos.*

That wouldn't be a problem. In the aftermath of last week's Twitter-storm, all of Delanie's creativity had disappeared. And she couldn't even bring herself to create an apology video—not when she didn't believe she had done anything wrong. She wouldn't grovel.

But she couldn't completely ignore the desperation that clawed at her heart, trying to convince her that her acting career was over for good. And without acting, who was she?

Delanie picked up an antique hand mirror by its long brass handle, staring at herself in the reflection. The silver backing had started to flake away from the mirror, leaving the edges of her face obscured by dark spidery-looking lines. It felt like a fitting metaphor for her fracturing identity.

"Why didn't you tell me Caleb and Monica had broken up?" she asked before she had even thought about it. Why was that still bothering her?

"I didn't think you needed to know." Cheryl's tone was light, but she looked sideways at Delanie while she continued to fold. "Was I wrong?"

Delanie drew a breath. "No. Yes. I don't know. What he does doesn't matter to me anymore, I guess. It just would have been nice not to be caught off-guard."

"You saw him?"

"Yeah, his daughter's in the play." She paused. "And he's my new producer. Anne won't be coming back this year."

Erin had called that morning to tell her that Anne would be in the hospital for several weeks. She had broken several ribs and her leg, which was in traction. Erin had mentioned that the doctor said Anne was lucky to be alive, then she had muttered that the new bridge couldn't be finished fast enough. Delanie agreed. The lone two-lane bridge that connected the two sides of town along the main highway route was one of the primary sources of traffic congestion and collisions in the small town and was long overdue for an upgrade. Unfortunately, while construction on a second bridge had finally begun the previous fall, it wasn't scheduled to be finished for almost two more years.

Cheryl cast Delanie another sideways look. "You chose Caleb as your producer? Interesting."

Something in her mother's tone raised Delanie's hackles. "Options were limited."

Of the two people who had stepped forward, Violet had pushed Delanie toward choosing Caleb, mostly because of his more easy-going personality. Despite Delanie's reasons to say no, she had agreed that his stable presence would be a good asset to the team, even if she had disagreed with Violet that Caleb always followed through on what he said he would do. He did for most things, she supposed—just not the one time it had mattered to her the most.

"I'm sure they were," Cheryl said knowingly.

Delanie stood and rounded on her mother. "You can stop whatever train your thoughts just boarded before it pulls out of the station. Things are over between me and Caleb, and that's not going to change. That's why it doesn't matter that you didn't tell me he got divorced. I. Don't. Care. His choices have nothing to do with me."

"The lady doth protest too much, methinks." Cheryl's amused expression faded, and she met Delanie's gaze. "All teasing aside, I'm actually glad to hear you say that. After what Caleb did to you, and then leaving Monica in the lurch, I don't think he's the kind of man who is worth getting involved with. That's the reason I never brought up their divorce. I was afraid *you* would get ideas."

Delanie frowned. "He left Monica in the lurch? What, is he not paying child support?"

Cheryl shrugged airily, adding another blouse to the pile of women's clothes. "Oh, I'm sure he does what he can. He has always taken his financial responsibilities very seriously—just look what he did for his father, taking over the farming until Marcus was recovered enough to do it on his own again. But who divorces a woman with a three-year-old? And after cheating on you to get her pregnant in the first place!"

"He technically didn't have to cheat on me to do that," Delanie offered. Though, thanks to her own feelings on the subject, her voice lacked conviction.

"He must have though." Cheryl paused her folding, her knuckles white around the shoulders of a floral-print dress. "Otherwise, how could he have dated you for two years, and then the moment you leave town, that Fehr girl is just 'suddenly' knocked up?" She shook her head and resumed folding the garment. "I don't care what Adelaide says. Caleb made his bed with that woman, and he should have lain in it."

The note of finality in Cheryl's voice indicated she had no more to say on the subject, and Delanie was glad to move on. Except her thoughts weren't so congenial to the idea. From what she had seen of Caleb and Emma, he took his responsibilities as a dad pretty seriously too. And no one had mentioned a new woman in *his* life, so maybe he simply wasn't good at romantic relationships. He had certainly made a mess of theirs. If she had stayed behind with him, maybe *they* would be divorced with a kid by now. There was no way to know.

Relationships ended for all kinds of reasons. People fell out of love. People weren't who you thought they were. People couldn't get along anymore. Or they moved away and moved on to bigger things.

But what happened when those people came home and that old wound wasn't quite as scarred over as they thought it was?

The question occupied Delanie's circling thoughts for the rest of the day.

Chapter 8

"DELANIE FLETCHER, is that you?"

Delanie glanced up from the debit machine at the till of Cool Beans and peered at the slim young woman moving toward her on the other side of the counter, trying to place her. The chin-length wavy rich brown bob was a new style, but the pretty face with high cheek bones and flawless warm ivory skin was familiar. Unfortunately, the woman wasn't wearing a name tag. Smiling to cover her lapse of memory, Delanie handed the debit machine back to the cashier to buy herself some time, her other hand clenched around Nan's binder. Then she remembered. Her high school friend Stephanie's younger sister.

"Autumn? Autumn Neufeld?"

The woman smiled. "It's Autumn Lambert now. Wow, I haven't seen you since you and Stephanie graduated. You look fabulous! Are you in town for a visit?"

Delanie moved aside to allow the next person in line access to the cashier, facing Autumn from across a glass display case full of scrumptious-looking home-baked goods. "In a manner of speaking. My grandmother just died. I came to town for her funeral, and I'm taking over her role as director of the kids' play, so I'll be in town for a couple months."

Autumn's big dark brown eyes widened. "Oh, I'm so sorry. I hadn't heard."

Delanie shook her head dismissively. "It's fine. She lived a long, full life." She pushed aside the pinch in her heart. Ever since her mom had given her the news last week, she couldn't help but feel that she had squandered so many opportunities to spend time with Nan. She should have come home more, or called more often. Now she couldn't. "So, how long have you been working here?" she said, anxious to change the subject.

"Oh, forever." Autumn swept the counter area and its small hive of worker bees with a glance and a heavy sigh that was at once anxious and weary. "My parents own this place, and I've been managing it for years now. I do most of the baking, too, so I'm usually stuck in the kitchen."

Delanie blinked. "That's amazing."

Autumn smiled wistfully. "The mornings are pretty early, but it means I get afternoons with my son. Stephanie helps out sometimes on her days off too."

Her son? The dark circles under Autumn's eyes made sense now.

"Stephanie's still in town too?"

Autumn nodded. "She's a nurse up at the hospital."

"I see."

Delanie wondered if Stephanie was married with kids too. Sometimes Delanie felt like she was the only one in her graduating class who had opted to leave Peace Crossing to pursue her career instead of settling down to have a family. She wasn't sure if that made her feel isolated or relieved that she had found a way out of this little town with its small dreams.

She forced a smile. "Good for you. I'm looking forward to sampling your carrot cake in a minute."

"And I better get started on your latte," Autumn said. "Excuse me. Jeff will bring your order out when it's ready."

"Thanks. Tell Stephanie I said hi."

Autumn flashed her a brief grin. "I will. She'll be thrilled to hear you're in town."

Autumn moved away down the counter and began working the espresso machine. Delanie looked around the small coffee shop to find a table, and noticed that Violet had slipped in and sat down since Delanie had walked in. The music director already had a steaming white mug and a binder on the table in front of her. *She must have been in the washroom.*

Delanie picked her way through the labyrinth of square and rectangular tables, taking in the changes since the last time she had been in here. The room was full and cluttered in the coziest way possible. Tables were tucked between short barriers of double-sided open shelves made of stacked squares. Some of the cubby-holes held worn copies of well-thumbed bestsellers in a variety of genres, while others contained unusual antique items that looked mostly coffee-related, like old grinders and stainless steel and ceramic pots. Potted succulents and trailing plants that Delanie was pretty sure were real sat on top of the shelves, offering some privacy between the tables. Oil paintings and large framed photographs covered walls painted a misty grey, with the exception of an intense green between the large rectangular windows along one side. In the far corner stood another tall bookshelf full of board games, which sat next to a small sitting area—a love seat and two overstuffed chairs around a coffee table near a gas fireplace insert. The overall effect was like being welcomed into a sunny, inviting living space.

Finally, Delanie reached the table for four that Violet had chosen near a window not far from the sitting area. The blinds were open partway, but the sun had already moved around to the west side of the building, giving them a great view of the gorgeous September day outside without any glare.

Delanie set Nan's binder on the table and pulled out the chair across from Violet, who glanced up from her notes. When the older woman saw her, she gave a warm grin.

"There you are."

"Here I am." Delanie slung her purse over the back of the chair and unbuttoned her long cabled knit cardigan coat before she sat down. "Caleb and Amber aren't here?"

"They just walked through the door," Violet said, gesturing beyond Delanie.

Delanie turned around to see that such was the case, returning Caleb's smile and Amber's nod of acknowledgement with a little wave, then faced Violet.

"I saw you catching up with Autumn," Violet said, gesturing toward the counter. "Isn't it a marvel what she's done with the place? All of these paintings are by local artists, you know, and they're for sale. There's so much talent in the Peace Country."

Delanie looked around at the canvases of quirky portraits, paintings of the Peace River Valley, and macro photographs of local flora and fauna. There was one large framed photograph of the northern lights that took her breath away. It had been a long time since she'd seen the aurora. "Indeed. Sounds like a lot of work, but she's obviously doing a great job."

"I'm glad her parents have been able to help her out like this. It's so hard to lose a spouse, and so young. And her little guy kept her on her toes even before she was working full time. I don't know how she manages now."

Delanie swallowed. "What do you mean?"

Violet cocked her head. "You don't know? Autumn's husband died in a quadding accident nearly two years ago. Now she's raising Julien alone, and he's quite the little handful."

"Oh."

Autumn had been two years behind Delanie and Stephanie in school, which meant that she must be around twenty-six years old. At twenty-six, Autumn was a mother, managed a thriving coffee shop, and had already been married and widowed. That felt like a lot of living in the only eight or so years since she had graduated. Despite the loss Autumn had suffered, Delanie couldn't help wonder what her own life had to show in comparison. Had her string of short-term acting gigs and collection of failed romantic relationships been worth the time she had spent away from home?

"But has she ever watched a Shakespeare play under the summer stars in Stanley Park while eating fresh caramel corn?" Delanie muttered.

"Pardon?" Violet said.

Oops, that had been Delanie's outside voice. "Never mind." Her face flamed, and she busied herself flipping through the binder to find the notes she took the previous night. Who else would hear about someone losing her husband and make it all about themselves?

Fortunately, Caleb and Amber arrived just then. As everyone exchanged civilities, Caleb pulled out the chair next to Violet—but before he could sit down, Amber smiled at him and sat in it.

"Thanks, Caleb."

"Uh, you're welcome." With a bemused grin, he pushed in her chair, then took the seat next to Delanie, placing a spiral notebook and ballpoint pen on the table in front of him.

Delanie would have smirked at Amber's presumption if she weren't so uncomfortably aware of how near Caleb was sitting. And the fact that it hadn't been *his* first choice either.

"So," she began briskly to cover her discomfiture, "now that everyone's here, I have some notes from the rehearsal last night. I think we will need to work with Joe to help him loosen up more. Geppetto is supposed to be a bit uptight, but not *that* uptight. There's this great exercise we used to do in college that might help."

Caleb nodded. "I agree. A few of the other kids could probably relax more too. Some of that will just come in time as they get more comfortable with their roles and with being on the stage."

"Emma didn't seem to have any trouble relaxing." Violet's

eyes twinkled behind her gold frames.

Caleb chuckled and shook his head. "Well, that's Emma. I hope she wasn't too rambunctious. She seemed okay while I was in the room."

Violet patted his hand. "She was just fine. Don't you worry about a thing. You and Monica are doing great with her."

"We do our best," Caleb said with a small smile.

For some inexplicable reason, the reminder that Caleb and Monica still shared parenting duties made Delanie even more uncomfortable. She flipped around in her binder until Violet turned to her, then glanced up as if she'd truly been distracted from her search.

"I could extend the warm-up exercises with the kids at the beginning of every rehearsal," Violet said, picking up her mug. "Joe isn't the only one who could loosen up a little." She raised her cup to her lips and blew across the top.

Amber fished a tablet and digital pen out of her voluminous purse and put it on the table. "Not that Celeste needs it, but the other kids would probably benefit." She swiped around on the screen until she brought up a note-taking app.

Delanie fought the urge to roll her eyes. She drew a breath. "Thanks, Violet."

Violet finished taking a sip from her mug, then set it down. "Molly always used to say that a third of the play's success was giving the kids the tools to succeed. The second third was making sure they believed they could."

"What about the last third?" Caleb said.

"A healthy helping of prayer." Violet's eyes twinkled.

Delanie laughed along with the music director. That last comment was just the sort of joke that Nan would make, though she had no doubt her grandmother had, indeed, prayed before every rehearsal, just as she had seen Violet quietly do the other day. Molly had never been flamboyant with her faith—but Delanie had never known her to waver from it. "Nan was a smart cookie and a good teacher. In fact, I think I saw something about the acting exercises she used to do with the kids in her notes from the play last year."

Caleb blinked in surprise. "You found her notes from last year?"

"Yes. From all the years. Nan was astoundingly thorough and organized."

When Delanie had come across the shelf of binders in Nan's storage room, it had been like hitting the jackpot. She'd only taken a couple home to glance through, but her grandmother's neat cursive had filled page upon page in each. It would take her several days to read through even the binders she had taken back to her parents'.

"That, she was," agreed Violet. "She was an incredible woman and an astounding director."

Delanie nodded, loss tickling the back of her eyes and Impostor Syndrome crushing her ribs. When Violet's hand covered hers, she looked up.

"You'll get there too, my dear. You're already an incredible woman. As far as directing, that only takes practise, just like anything else."

Delanie absorbed the belief shining from the indigo eyes of the woman who had taught her how to sing and play piano, and who'd been a steady, encouraging presence all through her formative years. She smiled shyly, her face growing warm.

"Thanks, er, Violet." She still struggled with referring to her old teacher by her first name instead of as *Mrs. Butler*. Glancing sideways, she noticed Caleb watching her, an intense look in his eyes. The heat in her face intensified, and she looked toward the counter instead, relieved to see a tall, thin server in a green apron making his way toward them with a tray full of mugs and snacks.

After the server left, they settled down to business. For the most part, the discussion was productive, with everyone offering good ideas and observations. Caleb volunteered to head up finding backstage volunteers and to work with the theatre manager to figure out lighting, all while continuing to work on the sets.

"Which reminds me." Caleb flipped his notebook open to a pencil sketch of a backdrop design depicting an Italian village by the sea. Though it looked like the drawing had been done in a rush, it had obviously been made by a practised hand. He turned the page to reveal designs for other set pieces. Delanie moved the sketchbook to the centre of the table so the other women could see, too, then started flipping slowly through.

"I had Noel sketch these up last night so you could see what our plan is," Caleb continued. "He had discussed these concepts with Molly, but he never got the chance to show her the designs. He said we could still make changes if you want. We've got the materials, but we haven't started on the big piece yet."

He flipped the page and pointed at a drawing of an open-mouthed whale facade to be made from plywood and put on casters. Delanie glanced over the drawing, impressed. From the looks on Amber's and Violet's faces, she wasn't the only one.

"This looks great," Delanie said. "Can I keep this?"

"By all means," he said with a gesture. "Samantha Crawford—you know, the mom of the girl playing the Blue Fairy—will be doing the actual painting. Noel and I will just be doing the building."

"Thanks." Delanie closed the notebook and tucked it into the front pocket of her binder. "I'll let you know if I think of anything else. But are you sure doing the producer job isn't too much of a time commitment? Sets and lighting alone is a big job, on top of helping me run rehearsals."

"Nah," Caleb said with a dismissive wave. "I'm good."

Violet smiled at him. "I'm so glad you're part of the production this year, Caleb."

Caleb shifted uncomfortably. "Don't mention it." He looked like he would really rather she hadn't.

"My husband, Luc, can run sound again," Amber interjected.

"Uh, great," said Caleb, jotting Luc's name in his notebook. "Thanks."

Amber nodded, making a note on her tablet too.

Delanie studied Amber, wondering if she had jumped in so awkwardly because she'd been feeling left out. Thankfully, the other points of discussion went more smoothly. Amber took copious notes throughout the meeting and made some rather astute suggestions. Perhaps not to be outdone by Caleb, she agreed without hesitation to take on organizing the wrap-up party, arranging for the posters and cast tee-shirts to be made, and overseeing the parent volunteer schedule. When Delanie complimented and thanked her, she looked as though she were trying to hide how pleased she was. Delanie made a mental note—even though Amber could be abrasive, perhaps she was only trying to find validation through her contributions. Delanie could relate.

"Now, about the costumes," Delanie said. "I had my friend Marie send me some sketches." She pulled up the images on her phone. She had been astounded when Marie had sent the gallery of photos that morning—not only had the designer sketched ideas for all the principals, but she had even done designs for each of the choruses.

You're the best, Marie, Delanie had texted back.

Don't you forget it, Marie had returned with a silly-faced emoji.

Delanie passed her phone to Caleb to look through while she kept talking. "The costume mistress—what's her name again? Becca?"

Violet nodded. "Becca Johanson."

"Becca may not be able to replicate these exactly, but these should be simple enough to make on a budget with only a few volunteers, Marie tells me."

"Becca's a miracle with a sewing machine," Violet said. "I'm sure she'll be able to come pretty close."

Caleb peered at the phone screen, sliding through images with his thumb. "These look great. Your designer friend knows what she's doing."

Delanie beamed. "Yeah, she's amazing. I'm hoping she can come out to see the play when we perform."

Caleb raised his brows. "That would be fantastic. Emma would be thrilled to meet her. She loves designing clothes—she's always making little sketches of dresses and such. She would probably talk your friend's ear off." He handed Delanie's phone to Amber, who snatched it and began scrolling.

Delanie shook her head. "Is there anything your daughter can't do?"

"Not that we've found so far." Caleb grinned back.

"Well, this won't work," Amber said, frowning at the phone.

"What do you mean? Which one?" Delanie glanced toward the screen, which wasn't visible to her until Amber laid the phone on the table between them.

The phone display showed the coloured pencil sketch of the costume for Judy the Puppet—Celeste's role—with its long pleated red bell skirt and simple white blouse under a long bib apron. Marie had even drawn a mole onto the hooked prosthetic nose, which Delanie had thought was a nice touch. She had laughed just looking at that outfit.

"What's wrong with it?"

"Why is this costume so unappealing? Celeste deserves to look better than this. I won't have her going onstage looking like some old biddy."

Delanie drew a breath. Didn't Amber know how acting worked? "That's just the role. The old Punch and Judy puppets always looked that way, because they were supposed to be ordinary folk, and they were meant to be funny caricatures. And I think it's perfect. Celeste will look amazing in it."

Amber shook her head emphatically. "I don't care what they

were traditionally, this costume has to be redesigned, or Celeste will need to be recast."

"What?" Delanie frowned. "We're not recasting now. Celeste did really well at the rehearsal last night—I can see why she was cast as Judy. Her comedic timing is exceptional." *And Punch and Judy's song is one of the easiest to perform of all the principal female roles.* But Delanie kept that to herself. Celeste was a delightful girl and a promising young actress, but her singing needed work. Her vocal tone was nice, but she was so pitchy that it had taken effort not to cringe. Delanie shuddered to think of Celeste trying to tackle the soaring runs and octave leaps in Stella the Blue Fairy's songs. Nope, Nan and Anne Erickson had cast Celeste wisely.

"But I don't want Celeste in the comedy role. I tried telling Molly that, but she wouldn't listen. She was just as stubborn as you are. I'm telling you, casting Celeste as Judy is a mistake. You're wasting her talent."

Delanie opened her mouth, but no sound came out. What could she say to that? Amber was obviously trying to work out her own issues through her daughter, and after Delanie's recent loss and cancellation, her patience for other people's drama had worn thin. She had enough of her own to deal with. She bit her tongue on the urge to snap that perhaps the real solution was for Amber to see a therapist, but no other kinder words came out in their stead.

"Every role in this play is a comedy role," Caleb said at last, glancing at Delanie, then piercing Amber with his scrutiny. "So what is your real issue?"

"I . . . I just don't want her to be made to feel ridiculous, that's all. And this costume is ridiculous." Amber tapped the phone screen, which had gone to sleep.

Delanie took her phone back and laid it on the table in front of her. "Have you ever been in a play, Amber?"

Amber's face went red. "Yes, a long time ago, but the part was very small."

She glanced away, and Delanie suspected that Amber's resistance was rooted at least in part in that experience, which must not have been very pleasant.

"I can appreciate that you want to protect Celeste's feelings, but I can assure you that being onstage and producing a laugh from the audience that you intended to manufacture is nothing like being laughed at in the school lunch room," Delanie said. "You don't feel embarrassed and ridiculous—you feel powerful."

Amber met Delanie's gaze and arched a brow. "Oh? And what about when the audience starts throwing tomatoes and tweeting death threats? What then?"

Delanie froze, her whole body hot and her heart hammering in her chest. How dare this woman bring that up? Delanie tried to think of a response, even a retort, but her mind had gone completely blank. She was back in her apartment in Vancouver, crying herself to sleep in bed while her life fell apart around her.

Violet cleared her throat. "One of the lessons I try to teach my choir students is that everyone's voice is a vital part of the whole, and each one matters. We cover for each other's mistakes, and we lift each other up when we struggle. That's also the way Molly, Anne, and I have always run this play. Amber, if you can't adhere to that standard, whether for yourself or for Celeste, then perhaps you don't belong on this team. And if Celeste doesn't want the part of Judy, she should come talk to us, but there is no guarantee she would get a speaking role at all otherwise."

Amber glared at Violet. "You're not kicking Celeste out of the play altogether."

"No, but there are only so many roles she is suited for," Violet said. "I think she will make a particularly fine Judy. But if you don't want her there—"

"No, it's fine." Amber snapped her tablet closed with a glare.

Yanking her purse off the back of her chair, she jammed the tablet into it. "Thank you." She stood and looked at Delanie, her expression cold. "I'll text you about the posters once I talk to Alexander. We're lucky his daughter could make it work to be in the play this year. He's one of the best graphic designers in town."

"Great," Delanie said stiffly, her mouth dry. "Thanks."

Violet glanced at her wristwatch. "I also have to go so I can get ready for my first lesson." She began packing up her things as Amber pulled her jacket off the back of the chair and put it on.

"Violet," Caleb said, "Didn't you tell me after Emma's last lesson that one of your voice students is moving soon? Would that slot be available for Celeste if she wanted it?"

Violet glanced at him in consternation, but then turned a warm smile on Amber.

"That's true. I have a waiting list, but it's not long. It can be tough to fill a slot once the school year has begun because everyone already has their schedule full of activities, so it may be that none of the folks on the waiting list can even jump in. A year of voice lessons might really open up Celeste's options in the play next year."

Amber huffed and glared at Violet again, then Caleb. "She doesn't need voice lessons. She needs to be in a town that recognizes real talent when it sees it. I'll see you tomorrow night."

With that, she spun on her heel and walked out.

Delanie exchanged bewildered glances with Violet and Caleb.

"You weren't kidding about her drama," Delanie said to Violet, regretting her decision to ask Amber to be part of the team. "I've never had to fire anyone before, but I'm seriously considering it now."

Violet gave her an understanding look. "Unfortunately, I think she would cause more problems if you did that than if you kept her on board. We'll keep an eye on her, but for now, I think it's best to leave her alone and try not to let whatever bee is in her bonnet get to you."

Delanie blew air through her lips and put her shaking hands in her lap. That might be easier said than done.

After Violet said her goodbyes and hurried out the door, Delanie turned to Caleb—suddenly hyper-aware that she was sitting alone at a table next to him.

"Are you regretting your decision to volunteer to do this as much as I am right now?" she said to fill the awkward silence.

"Not at all," he said, gazing at her with that intense look again. "Difficult people are part of life. I'm glad I can help." He paused and fidgeted with his empty coffee mug. "I hope *I'm* not one of the reasons you're regretting your decision."

Her heart skipped. "No, of course not. In fact, I'm glad you're here." She swallowed, surprised she felt that way. "Thanks for rescuing me back there."

"Rescuing you?" He frowned.

"When Amber got all aggressive. You'd think I would be better at handling stuff like that by now."

"Don't mention it." This time, the words weren't awkward but inviting, like the subtle curve of his lips.

She stared back at him, mesmerized by the way the afternoon light glinted from his warm amber brown eyes. They reminded her of maple syrup on pancakes.

She realized she was staring, and her heart sped up as she searched for something to say. The best thing to do would be to leave. Yes, that was what she would do.

She shifted away from him. "I should probably—"

Her phone buzzed with an incoming call. She glanced at the screen. The name Josh Rosenburg flashed up. Annoyed, she dismissed it. When she saw Caleb looking at her questioningly, the urge to flee intensified, and she reached for her purse strap.

"If you don't mind me asking," Caleb said quickly, "what

is it that Amber keeps hinting at? Did something happen in Vancouver that I don't know about?"

Delanie swallowed, her throat closing, and turned back to face him. "You didn't hear?"

"Sorry, no. I, uh, don't keep up on entertainment gossip."

Thankfully, Caleb shifted around to sit in the seat Violet had just vacated across from Delanie as he spoke. Not only was it more comfortable to talk to him that way, but once the table was between them, Delanie's heart slowed to a more normal pace.

"Not that I expect you to," she said, "but our moms talk."

Caleb gave a half grin. "When it comes to you, my mom tends not to say much."

"Mine seems to have the same philosophy about you." Delanie chewed her thumbnail and studied him. Was Caleb going to make her tell the whole story again? It had been bad enough explaining it to her mom yesterday. She considered snapping a pithy answer and leaving, but the intense look in his eyes had never left. He really wanted to know.

And, she was surprised to discover, she really wanted to tell him.

CALEB LISTENED QUIETLY as Delanie poured out the story of her recent cancellation and losing the studio contract she had been counting on.

"And that's why I'm here," she concluded. "I mean, I came home for Nan's funeral. But since I don't have any reason to head back right away, I decided to stay and help with the play too."

Caleb nodded, considering. "What are your YouTube videos about?"

She shrugged and looked away, obviously embarrassed. That

delightful dimple in her cheek he had adored in high school was still there. He took a deep breath and took the last sip of his now-cold coffee, firmly telling his heart to stop getting crazy ideas. He was supposed to be getting over Delanie, not falling for her again. And it was high time he did. *She's not staying here. And she shouldn't. I need to let her go.*

"Oh, nothing too amazing," Delanie said. "I do parody songs and skits based on movies—mostly classics—but I try to make them relevant to modern issues. If I had known going in how hard satire was to do well, I might have thought about it a little more." She laughed dryly.

He smiled, his chest warming. "Didn't we talk about doing something like that together, back in the day?"

She nodded, giving him an embarrassed look. "Yeah. I hope you don't mind that I stole your idea."

"Mind?" He shook his head. "I think it's fantastic that you took it and ran with it. Way to go. I'll have to go look your channel up."

"You will?" Her eyes widened, and she looked mock-nervous. "If you do, be kind."

He chuckled. "I'm sure you have nothing to worry about. Not if you're doing as well as you said."

"Not are. *Were.*" She sighed and stared at her empty coffee mug, tapping it with a fingernail.

He studied her lowered face. In high school, she had been pretty, though the admiring glances of all the boys in class had been lost on her. Now she was a knockout. He wondered who Josh Rosenburg was, and why she wasn't taking his calls. A boyfriend? Ex-boyfriend? Or someone else? But the haunted look behind her eyes probably had more to do with the trauma of her recent cancellation than anything else. *Who sends death threats about a satire video?* The stupidity of people astounded him at times.

Especially the one in his mirror.

"That producer was an idiot to let you go." Caleb swallowed and glanced away. Seeing her here like this, he couldn't help but be reminded of all he'd lost when he had stayed behind. But she deserved for him to be present right now, not dwelling on his past mistakes. He turned back to her, and the look in her brown eyes made his heart squeeze with longing.

"I know it feels like everything sucks right now," he said gently, "but if I've learned anything, it's that difficult times don't last. You'll get through this. You'll become the star you were always meant to be, and then that producer will be eating crow. You wait and see."

She looked at him, her eyes soft. "You always did know what to say, Caleb Toews."

His heart stuttered, and he resisted the urge to run his thumb along her curving jaw. He grinned instead. "Good to know I haven't lost my touch."

She smiled. "Speaking of that, whatever happened to that script you were working on back in the day? *A Million Miles from Everywhere*, or something like that."

He leaned back in his chair. "I finished it. It's collecting dust on my hard drive. That, and two others I wrote since then."

"Oh?" She rested her chin on her hand and tilted her head in interest. "More space operas?"

He shrugged. "One's a thriller, the other's a comedy. I can't seem to stay in one lane."

"So what are you going to do with them? Did you enter any contests or anything?"

He waved his hand dismissively, ignoring the familiar ache in his chest he felt whenever his long-lost screenwriting dreams came up. "Nah. My real life had too many responsibilities. I couldn't afford to run off chasing dreams."

Her expression froze, and he realized his mistake.

"I'm sorry, Delanie. I didn't mean—"

"It's fine. I know what you meant," she said, but her tone

was stiff.

Way to go, Don Juan. He had told himself he would avoid the topic of their breakup like the plague, worried it would bring up the hard feelings he was afraid were still there. Judging from the way Delanie was putting her phone in her purse with jerky movements, he'd been right to suspect as much. He tried to think of something to say to ease the tension, but a loud clang like a Chinese gong being struck emanated from his jacket pocket. Delanie glanced up from putting on her cardigan.

"That's my reminder to go pick up Emma from school." Caleb pulled out his phone to dismiss the notification so the alarm wouldn't clang again. "Sorry it's so loud. I have to make sure I hear my notifications above the noise of a job site. I should have put my phone on vibrate."

"You pick Emma up every day?"

"No, she usually goes to my sister's on the bus and I pick her up after work. But we're going to my parents' place for supper because we missed Sunday dinner this week. Since I took the afternoon off anyway, I told Emma I would pick her up from school and we'd head out early. Say, would you like to come out to my parents' for supper, too?"

Delanie's eyes widened and she stared at him like he had just told her there was an ax murderer on the loose.

Why on Earth did I say that?

"Um, that's sweet of you, but I think I'll take a pass. I have a lot of prep to do before rehearsal tomorrow night, and—"

"It's okay, you don't need to explain. I—"

"No, I'm not explaining. I'm just . . ." Delanie swallowed and glanced down, her attention focused on tying the belt of her cardigan. When she finished, she swung her purse over her shoulder and picked up her binder, then met his eye. "Thanks, Caleb. I guess I'll see you tomorrow."

"See you tomorrow, Delanie." Why did he feel as though he were saying goodbye, not *see you later*?

With a polite smile, she walked out the glass door, the bell jangling as she left.

He sighed and got up to go, carrying his dirty dishes to the bus bin near the door on his way out.

Too bad it wasn't as easy to be rid of the remains of his past with Delanie.

Chapter 9

DELANIE SAT ON her bed and turned another page in Nan's binder, scanning the neat handwriting for ideas—anything to get rid of the rumbling unease in her belly. After supper with her parents, she had declined her dad's invitation to watch Jeopardy, instead retreating to her room to go over the plan for the next night's rehearsal.

In the last hour and a half, she had already listened to the demo soundtrack twice, and now knew most of the songs by heart. She had read the script three times in the last three days. She had made a schedule of acting exercises she could use with the kids for the next six weeks, and was certain she could recognize each member of the main cast by name—their own as well as their character's.

Still, she couldn't evade the overwhelming sense of foreboding that hung over her head. That no matter what she did or how prepared she was, this production was doomed to epic failure because she was the one running it.

Volunteering to direct this play was simply another foolish thing she had done before thinking it through. Like her decision to leave Peace Crossing to chase a carrot that turned out to be as insubstantial as air. Caleb's words from that afternoon about having too many responsibilities to chase after dreams dug into her. She had been angry at him for staying behind for so long that she had failed to recognize what she had given up by leaving. Time with Nan. Time with her parents. Stability. Romance?

The look he had given her when she'd thanked him for rescuing her flashed unbidden to her mind, and the warm feeling that had curled through her at the time along with it. He didn't still have feelings for her, did he? Not after all this time. If he had cared for her at all, how could he have done what he did with Monica? And why hadn't he reached out to her after the two of them had split up?

And where was the familiar righteous anger that would let her brush that warm feeling and all these annoying questions aside? She tried to summon it, but it shrivelled under the memory of him encouraging her to keep chasing her dream. Why did he have to be so supportive and amazing after all this time?

Whether she deserved it or not.

She wiped away a tear just as her phone chimed—the same sound of chimes the read-along audiobook versions of her favourite fairy tales had used when she was a child to let her know it was time to turn the page. It was a text from Amber.

Alexander will have mock-ups by end of week.

Great. Thank you, Delanie texted back at the same time as Amber's next text came in.

Luc says we have a problem. The soundboard is dead. Will need to get it replaced.

Delanie blinked at the phone and swiped the remaining moisture off her cheek. That was unfortunate, but hardly surprising. Murray Jones, the president of the Peace Valley Community Theatre Society, had mentioned the aging wiring and sound system at the theatre when she had spoken to him. He said they had been fundraising for it, but the project was going to be fairly expensive, and they didn't yet have the money to tackle it. Delanie sighed.

I'll talk to Murray about it. She hoped they could figure

something out before the performance. They could hardly put on a play if no one could hear the actors. She bit her nail, thinking, then added, *Thank you for all you're doing to help me.*

It's for Celeste, came the almost-immediate response.

Delanie blinked at the phone, wanting to type back a reply that was just as terse and blunt. Instead, she opened up her conversation with Marie.

What have I done? I think I'm in over my head.

A few seconds later, her phone chimed with her friend's response. *Wanna video chat?*

Sure. Give me two minutes.

Delanie got off the bed and hurriedly checked her appearance in the mirror of the white dresser. The typical red splotches that covered her face when she cried were barely present.

Before she turned away, a strip of photographs stuck into the edge of the frame caught her attention—her and Stephanie Neufeld at a photo booth in West Edmonton Mall, taken on a tenth-grade school field trip. Stephanie had been one of her best friends in high school, but after Delanie had left, they had drifted apart. Delanie ignored a twinge of guilt—Stephanie had tried to keep in touch. It was Delanie who had been too busy to respond to texts or emails and had never called to get together during her rushed trips to town. *I guess I have time now.* She made a mental note to contact Stephanie soon.

Looking at her reflection, she wiped the last of the moisture from her eyes, smoothed back her hair toward her ponytail, and then settled herself on the bed with her laptop on her thighs, the chaos of her planning still around her.

A few seconds later, Marie's gorgeous, perfectly made-up face popped onto her screen. Behind Marie, the dining room pendant light was reflected in the night-dark glass patio doors.

"Desmond just texted, so I sent him a link to join too," she said. "I hope that's okay."

Delanie nodded, warmth filling her. *Desmond texted Marie?*

"You bet it's okay. I miss you guys. Have you been talking to Des much while I'm gone?" Despite the crush she was pretty sure Desmond harboured for Marie, Delanie knew that without her there, the two of them had few reasons to connect in person. If Desmond had sent Marie a text, maybe he had finally made his move.

Or maybe they were simply discussing how to get Delanie to smarten up and fix her wreck of a life.

Marie shrugged. "Once in a while. We went out for burgers last night."

Delanie blinked again. "You did? Just the two of you?"

"Yeah . . . ?" Marie said with a tone and an expression that said, *What are you getting at?*

But before Delanie could press further, Desmond's loading avatar—a photo of him with actor Carlos Valdes from the TV show *The Flash*—appeared in a separate little rectangle. When his video activated and he saw Delanie, his face broke into a wide grin. "Hey, bumpkin! How's life in the middle of no-where?"

He looked like he was holding his phone while relaxing on a couch. His hair was still shiny and gelled back from work, and instead of a sparkly rhinestone outfit, he wore his more typical dark button-down shirt with the cuffs rolled up to show off the tattoo of a cartoon version of the guy in the Gangnam Style video on his inner forearm.

Despite herself, Delanie laughed at his quip, then sobered. "Truthfully, it could be better."

"Has something gone wrong?" Marie asked.

"No. I just need you to remind me why I keep putting myself out there to chase a dream that doesn't seem to want me instead of getting on with my life like normal people do."

"Oh, sweetie," Marie said. "What happened?" She grew stern. "Have you been on Twitter? I told you—"

"No, no Twitter." Though Delanie had been tempted, she

knew nothing good would come of it. She glanced at the crumpled-up poster in her trash bin—the one of Nathan Tait that had been pinned to the ceiling directly above her bed for the last decade until she had gotten home on Friday night—and sighed. "And nothing's happened, not really. I've just been running into old friends, and they seem to be doing so much better at adulting than I am. They have kids, and businesses, and established careers. And what do I have?"

"Us, for a start," Desmond said. "I mean, we're pretty awesome."

She laughed. "And modest."

He gave an exaggeratedly enthusiastic nod and a thumbs-up, and she laughed again.

"Okay, so I have the two best friends a girl could ask for. But the parents and kids in the play don't have any confidence I can do this."

Desmond gawked. "They told you that?"

"Not exactly," Delanie said miserably, hating how whiny she sounded. "Well, one did. Amber. She threw my cancellation in my face, right in front of everyone."

Marie crossed her arms on the table in front of her and leaned into the camera. "That's only one person. I bet most of them are happy to have you." She frowned. "I know you're shaken up right now, but you can't let a mob of strangers decide who you are. They're wrong. *I* know they're wrong, *Desmond* knows they're wrong, and so does anyone else who actually knows you. Which this Amber obviously does not. You're a great friend, a talented actress, and a very capable person, no matter what the story in your head is saying. And you don't owe this Amber, or a fickle Twitter mob, or anyone else who doesn't see how amazing you are, one square inch of your mental real estate."

"Go, Marie." Desmond nodded appreciatively. "What she said, Delanie," he added.

Marie smirked. "Nothing of your own to add, Mr. Sun?"

Desmond looked thoughtful, then said, "You both look fantastic tonight. "

Marie rolled her eyes, and Desmond gave her a delighted grin.

Delanie bit her nail. "You're right. Of course you're right. And, despite everything, Caleb still seems to think I did the right thing in becoming an actress, for some reason." *You'll become the star you were always meant to be.' Has he never stopped believing in my dream?*

Desmond perked up. "Caleb? Who's that?"

Delanie swallowed. Why had she said anything about him? "No one. An old friend." She glanced at Marie, to whom she had mentioned Caleb more than once. Would Marie remember?

Marie's eyes narrowed. "Your old *boyfriend*, you mean. The one who broke up with you just before you left for Vancouver and then married your arch-nemesis six months later."

I guess she does.

"I broke up with him, actually." Delanie's voice trembled, and she took a breath to calm herself. Why did she suddenly feel the need to defend him? "After he told me he had to stay behind to help with the family farm."

"At *prom*."

"Well, yes. But I was leaving the next week, and they had just found out how sick his dad was. It's not like he meant to ruin our prom."

"I suppose," Marie said begrudgingly.

"Wait," said Desmond. "He stayed behind to help with the family farm and then got married to someone else within a year? He was, what, eighteen or nineteen?" He shook his head. "That's crazy. I don't care how into this chick he was, why would he do that?"

Delanie's shoulders tensed as Emma's grinning face popped into her mind. She remembered all too well the reason why, but the years that had passed since didn't make it less humiliating to talk about. While it wasn't all that uncommon for people from her hometown to marry young, nineteen was younger than most. Unless they had a very compelling reason.

"Monica was pregnant," Delanie said, the twinge in her gut a mere shadow of the knife that had ripped it open the night her mother had called to tell her all those years ago. Delanie had been in the middle of making Caleb a sappy Valentine's Day card when Cheryl told her he and Monica had just gotten married and already had a baby on the way. "Caleb has always had an old-fashioned moral code. When he got Monica pregnant, he probably married her so Emma wouldn't be born out of wedlock."

Of course, the fact that he had slept with Monica when the two of *them* had never gone beyond necking was a different kind of salt in her wound. What happened to his old-fashioned moral code when he had done that?

Desmond grimaced. "Yeah, a pregnancy can complicate things." He scratched his chin. "Must have happened pretty fast, huh?"

"You could say that," Delanie muttered. She hadn't made a Valentine for any guy since.

"Wait," Marie said. "I know it happened fast, but you always told me he cheated on you before you even left. Are you sure he actually did that? Seems a little out of character for a guy who would give up college to help his sick dad and marry a girl so his baby wouldn't be born out of wedlock." She shook her head. "I mean, it's not like that excuses him from everything— sleeping with another girl when you had only been broken up for a few months and you guys had been talking about marriage? That's not cool. But still, cheating?"

"I . . . I don't know. I thought he was. Monica was always hanging around, you know?"

Delanie frowned. Caleb being a cheater had always made sense to her before, but Marie had a point. Delanie had known

Caleb better than anyone in high school, so she'd thought, and she hadn't once got the sense he was unfaithful to her. He hadn't even *looked* at other girls. That's what had made his betrayal so much more hurtful, and why she'd had such a hard time trusting any guy she had dated since. She couldn't help but suspect that no matter how sincere and loyal they seemed, they were probably hiding something, and it was only a matter of time before she would find out what it was. Betrayal had become her expectation.

But had he actually cheated on her?

Marie shrugged. "Stranger things have happened, I suppose, but he sounds a whole lot better than Josh the Jerk. That spineless weasel doesn't care about anyone but himself."

Desmond grunted. "Did you tell her what I found out?"

"Not yet," Marie said, making a disgusted face, probably at whatever Desmond's piece of news was.

"About what?" Delanie asked.

Desmond sat up and looked down into the phone, which he must be holding between his knees, his dark eyes serious. "You remember my friend Xander?"

"Your old roomie, the lighting tech?"

Desmond nodded. "He got a job on *Trueheart*. Sorry I didn't tell you before."

He looked a little sheepish, but Delanie could hardly be mad at him for that. He had probably been trying to spare her feelings.

"Don't worry about it. What's the news?"

Desmond cleared his throat. "Josh has already hired your replacement, and they've started filming. You're not going to like who it is."

Delanie tensed. "Who is it?"

"Kaitlyn Williams. But she didn't just replace you as Maryanne. She and Josh went to a party together on the weekend, and word around the set is that they were pretty cozy."

Delanie felt like she had been punched in her gut. She didn't know Kaitlyn well, but Delanie and Josh had run into her at a house party celebrating the wrap-up of the pilot of *Trueheart* a few months ago, and Kaitlyn had then spent the entire night talking his ear off. When Delanie had later accused him of flirting with Kaitlyn, he had laughed it off, assuring her he had no interest in the glamorous beauty. Show techs were horrible gossips, so it didn't surprise Delanie that Xander had been among the first to hear about the party, then relay the news to Desmond.

Desmond looked thoughtful. "You know, I'm noticing a trend here, with you dating guys that other girls steal."

"Desmond!" Marie snapped, and he looked embarrassed.

"He's right, though," Delanie said hollowly.

She had been betrayed *again*. She had already been pretty sure Josh hadn't defended her to Crystal. Now she couldn't help but wonder if he and Kaitlyn had been seeing each other behind her back all this time. Maybe he had *wanted* her to mess up so he had an excuse to get her out of the picture and move on to his new favourite.

Just like Caleb and Monica.

She wrapped her finger in her ponytail. After what Marie had pointed out, she wasn't sure she had her story straight about Caleb. The more she thought about it, the more she realized cheating *was* completely out of character for him.

For Josh Rosenburg, though? Not so much.

On the other hand, it seemed strange that Caleb and Monica had only stayed together for a few years. Maybe he had cheated on her, too. Those kinds of habits didn't tend to go away. No matter how upstanding Caleb was in all other ways, being a cheater would be a pretty major character flaw, and one that would be difficult to overcome. Wasn't that what her mother had been hinting at that day at Nan's? Sometimes, she had to admit that her mother made a lot of sense.

But suddenly, nothing about that situation made sense anymore. Delanie was struck with an urge to send Caleb a text and ask him outright, but she shied away from it. What if she was wrong, and the situation was exactly what she had suspected all along? Did she truly want her worst fears confirmed?

"I'm such a dope." Delanie rested her forehead in her hands.

"Just because Josh is a class-A ratbag doesn't say anything about you," Marie said. "Except maybe you should have listened to me all along."

"Thanks," Delanie said dryly, meeting her friend's eye.

"Any time, girl." Marie grinned.

Delanie pressed her fingers to her temples. "If Josh is already moving on, how long before everyone else in Vancouver forgets about me? All my hard work will go down the toilet. Maybe it was a mistake to stay in Peace Crossing. I should come back, let my face be seen around town. I should be auditioning." She rubbed her hands over her face. "I need to make an apology video for my fans before I lose any more Patreon supporters."

"Whoa, whoa. Easy, little lady," Desmond said in a John Wayne drawl. Switching to a sophisticated zen-like tone, he added, "Let's just take a breath." He inhaled slowly, then exhaled, using his hands to accompany the direction of the air like he was some kind of meditation instructor.

"Des is right," Marie said. "And you should *not* make an apology video. Then the haters just pile on you more. Like what happened when you tried to manage the situation on Twitter." She arched a brow, and Delanie's face flushed with heat. "Yeah, I saw it."

"I don't know, Marie," Desmond said. "A sincere apology video might go a long way to fixing this."

"*Sincere?*" Marie scoffed. "When have you ever seen anyone make an apology video that was sincere in response to a lynching?" She shook her head, and her hoop earrings swung against her cheeks. "Those are some of the most Oscar-worthy performances I've ever seen."

"But we know Delanie *is* sincerely sorry," Desmond said. "Maybe hers would be different. I think the fans can sense that authenticity."

"Sincerely sorry for *what?*" Anger stirred in Delanie's belly, and she straightened. "I've been thinking about this non-stop for a week, and I still don't know what I did wrong. How could anyone have seen the future? But that seems to be what my fans expected me to do." She felt tears threatening again, and took a breath to banish them. "Marie's right. I'm sorry my fans are angry and that there's this huge misunderstanding, but I'm not sorry for anything I did."

"That's my girl." Marie gave an approving grin, jabbing her index finger at the screen. "That fire there—that's the Delanie that's going to get you through this."

"Maybe." Delanie's shoulders slumped. "I don't know how, though. I just feel so . . . helpless."

She had been in other situations where someone had tried to steal her power.

The girl who had bullied her in third grade.

The line chef at the café who had always made her orders last and blamed her for not putting them through at the right time to make her look bad in front of the boss.

The actor for the banking commercial she had done right after film school who had kept cornering her with sleazy come-ons.

But none of them had ever made her feel this vulnerable. She had thought her fans and supporters were on her side. This cancellation was another betrayal, potentially the worst yet.

"You know what you need to do?" Marie paused to take a sip of water and put the glass down off-camera. "You need to find yourself a date and show up at the Starlight Gala. You still have your invitation, even if you and Josh have broken up. I'll be your plus one."

"Hey, what about me?" Desmond scrunched his face.

"The invitation is only for two, and I look better in a tux. Sorry, you're out." Marie ignored Desmond's aghast expression and turned her attention back to Delanie. "We'll show Josh and Crystal and Kaitlyn and anyone else who thinks they can cut you down that you will not just lay there and take the rotten tomatoes they're slinging at you. You have no reason to be ashamed—they do. You need to show them you won't let them win."

Delanie imagined walking into the gala ballroom looking like a million bucks. The prospect of watching the smug look fall from Josh's face was tempting. But right now, he held all the cards. No matter how high she held her head, they would both know her peacocking was only to distract from the tail tucked between her legs.

"That would be easier if I had another job lined up by then," Delanie said. "Something that paid ten times more would be nice."

"Haven't you received any other call-backs?" Desmond asked.

Delanie shook her head morosely. She had finally given up on the auditions she'd done at the end of August before the *Trueheart* offer came through. If they were going to call her back for anything, they would have by now.

Marie's face lit up. "I almost forgot. I ran into Tessa Montague at the club on Friday, and we started talking about you. She said she was pretty intrigued by the work you were doing on YouTube. When I told her you were directing a community theatre kids' play, she asked for your email address. Said she might have a proposition for you."

"She did?" Delanie's heart skipped. "She's actually heard of me?" Tessa Montague was one of those eclectic artists who created films that stretched the boundaries and always made people think—not big blockbusters, more like *very successful art films*. She was one of Delanie's bucket-list directors. "Did you give it to her?"

"Of course." Marie grinned. "And I told her about the funeral and that she should wait a few days before reaching out. But you could hear from her any time now."

"Interesting," said Desmond, raising one eyebrow and tilting his head in a Mr. Spock impersonation.

Delanie shook her head. As exciting as that news was, people in the industry said that kind of thing all the time and never followed through. She couldn't lay any hopes on actually hearing from Tessa Montague, even if it would be one of the coolest moments in her career so far.

"Whether anything comes of that or not, the Starlight Gala is on the same weekend as the play performance. I don't think I would be able to take the time away to go. That wouldn't be fair to the kids."

Desmond snorted. "You'd let some volunteer gig with a community theatre play stand between you and your lifelong dream?"

"I, uh . . . well, no, of course not. But it doesn't seem like a choice I'll need to make."

Marie pursed her lips. "You know how these events go. Even if you don't have another job lined up by then, someone you meet that night could be the key to you landing something. Just like me running into Tessa. This business is all about who you know."

"True."

"Tessa will probably be there," Desmond said. "If she hasn't touched base with you by then, seeing you might remind her to talk to you. It could be the beginning of a bee-*u*-ti-ful collaboration," he said, exaggerating the syllables with a silly expression on his face.

"Also true."

Delanie tapped her fingernail against her keyboard. Some of her best opportunities had come from the people she'd met at parties. She had even met Josh at the Starlight Gala three years ago. How glorious would it be if she could take her next major step forward there, right under his nose? She wasn't one for revenge, but there was a certain satisfaction in the idea, none the less.

"You know, by the performance weekend, the director's job is pretty much done. I'll get to see the kids perform on opening night on Thursday. They don't need me to watch every performance."

Marie smiled. "So you'll come?"

Delanie nodded. "That town won't know what hit it."

And neither would Josh Rosenburg.

Chapter 10

Delanie closed her laptop and looked around at the chaos on her bed, the overwhelm setting in once more. Despite how positive she had sounded about going to the gala while talking to her friends, the idea of not seeing the kids' play through the full four-day run and missing the wrap-up party left her neck prickling uncomfortably.

She shrugged it off. *It won't be that bad. They'll get over it. They probably won't even notice I'm not there. And at least I'll be there for Nan's birthday.* Only she and her family would know opening night coincided with what would have been Molly's eightieth birthday, but it seemed important to her somehow that she would be there, watching the performance of the final production Nan had been involved in.

She placed her laptop on her nightstand, then closed the play binder. Stacking it and the script together, she clambered off the bed and took them over to her small white desk beneath the dormer window. As she set them down, she spotted the box of photo albums she had taken from Nan's on the floor beneath the desk. Carefully, she slid the scrapbook on the end—the one her mom had said she could keep—out of the box, then sat on the desk chair with her leg tucked beneath her while she opened it.

She flipped through pages and pages of Nan's successes on

the stage, pausing once more at the arresting black-and-white photograph of Nan as Anna Leonowens. Delanie had never seen *The King and I*, but she had enjoyed the Jodie Foster movie based on Anna's story. In *Anna and the King*, the Victorian-era widow had opened a school teaching the children of British officers in Singapore, then accepted an offer to give the many wives and children of the king of Siam a secular scientific British education. In the film, Anna's strong, independent nature and willingness to stand up to the king for what she wanted and believed in and his fierce protectiveness of his family and vision for his country had led to an unconventional affection and respect between the two—a romance that could never come to fruition.

Thinking about it now, Delanie's admiration for the inimitable Anna Leonowens grew. *The courage and chutzpa she must have had!* Much like the lovely woman portraying her in the photo. A woman who could have been as famous as Meryl Streep now, if only she had chosen to go to Hollywood or Broadway instead of Peace Crossing.

Had Molly realized what she would be giving up in pursuit of love? And why was it so often a choice between one or the other?

Sometimes you couldn't have everything you wanted—Delanie knew that. Anna and the Siamese king had wanted love, but hadn't been able to explore it with each other. And that was life.

But isn't that why that story is so heartbreaking?

If Anna's story had ended differently—with her and the Siamese king married, like Maria and Captain von Trapp in *The Sound of Music*—would it have been more satisfactory?

No, not with all those other wives in the picture.

But Ernie Davis had had no other wife. Molly had been the love of his life from the moment he'd laid eyes on her, as Pops had often said with a wink and an affectionate smile at Nan.

Wasn't that what everyone wanted? Someone who would be *for* you, no matter what, for life?

Delanie fingered the ripple-cut edge of the photo. Begrudgingly, she admitted that a guaranteed happy ending with one person sounded a lot more appealing right now than this striving for the love and approval of people who only cared for her as long as she did as they pleased.

But the problem was, going in, there was no guarantee. You could be stumbling along, as happy as a spring lamb, thinking all was fine with your relationship. And then something unexpected could happen, and suddenly the one thing that was the bedrock in your world crumbled to pieces, leaving you in free fall. The Ernies and Mollys of the world were the lucky ones, but most people never got what they had. And how could you know if you had found solid, life-long love or if you were standing on quicksand?

Her phone chimed, startling her from her thoughts. She set down the scrapbook, still open to the same page, and went over to her bed to retrieve the device. When she saw Caleb's name, her heart leapt. She opened the text and was even more startled by what it contained. Not the words, which simply updated her on the status of the set-building for that night. It was the heart-eyed emoji at the end that made her heart brace itself against her ribs.

Why is he sending me heart eyes? Is he trying to tell me something? The memory of the intense look in his eyes that afternoon at Cool Beans made her pulse speed up even faster.

Before she could decide how to respond, her phone chimed again.

Sorry about the emoji. I was going for the thumbs-up and hit the wrong one. My fat thumbs must be part of your horde of raving fans. I'll have to talk to them about appropriate boundaries with celebrities.

Immediately after came, *We're Canadian, boys. We don't gawk.*

She laughed, picturing him lecturing his thumbs. She sent back a laughing emoji, trying to decide if she should say more. She was in the middle of composing a message to thank him for the information about the sets when her phone chimed again.

You're doing a great job, btw.

She shifted her weight. How would Caleb even know?

She began typing as quickly as she could.

2 rehearsals and a planning meeting, all of them kind of bombed. Plus my life is spinning out of control, and I should probably be in Vancouver trying to fix it. Maybe now wasn't the best time to take this project on. Amber might do a better job than me.

This time, he sent back a GIF of a male comedian choking. Then her phone rang. Caleb.

Nervously, she answered, "Hello."

"This sounded like a topic for a phone call, not a text. I wasn't kidding about my fat thumbs. Not sure I could make them behave for something this involved."

She chuckled. "What, the lecturing didn't have any effect?"

"Less than you'd think."

"Well, they're in a smaller crowd than *you* would think."

"What?" He sounded confused.

"You know, that *horde of raving fans* you mentioned. It's less of a horde these days, more of a quiet and civilized tea party. And those fans are only sticking around because they were promised free snacks."

"They must be pretty good snacks. My thumbs have talked about it, and they've decided to stay."

"How magnanimous of them."

"What can I say? They like snacks. But they do prefer coffee over tea. Any chance there'll be some of that?"

"I'm sure I could round some up. Whatever it takes to make the fans happy." Delanie smirked, not daring to over-think what he might be saying between the lines of his quippy jokes.

After an awkward pause, he cleared his throat. "You can't

make them all happy. You know that, right?"

She hesitated. "It feels like they expect me to."

"Well, forget them. You don't owe them anything."

Delanie blinked. "You know my Patreon supporters are all I have paying my bills right now, right?" *And if I keep losing them at this rate, I'll be working at Cool Beans just to earn gas money back to Vancouver—or using up my savings.*

"Oh. Well, I suppose you owe *them* a little something. But I would be careful where you draw that line."

"Uh, thanks. I'll keep that in mind."

After another awkward pause, he said, "I looked up your videos."

She caught her breath. "Yeah?" What had happened to her clever banter now? And why did she feel like a little kid waiting for her mom's praise after her first piano recital?

"I like them. The ones I watched anyway."

"Which ones did you watch?"

"I watched that one you did about modern slavery. That was really something. And, er, both your Nathan Tait ones."

Something in his voice made her heart stick in her throat. "What did you think of those?"

"Well . . ."

She jumped in to fill the uncomfortable dead space. "My fans were right, weren't they?" She grabbed her laptop, flinging it open. "I need to watch those again. There has *got* to be something I'm missing. What did I do that was so offensive?"

"Nothing," he said. "Actually, they were both extremely well done, and I stand by my opinion that this is the stupidest cancellation I've ever heard of."

"Then why do you have that tone?"

He hesitated. "What tone?"

"*That* one. You just did it again. You had it when you said you'd watched the Nathan Tait videos. I know that tone, Caleb Toews. There's something you're not telling me."

He blew out a long stream of air. "Okay. It's just, I thought maybe you were a little hard on Nathan in the most recent video, especially considering none of the allegations against him have been proven. I went and looked it up to be sure. Nothing has been released to the public about it yet."

Delanie rolled her eyes. "Not you too. What is it with guys?"

"What do you mean?"

"My friend Desmond said basically the same thing. But there's no reason to believe Nathan didn't do it. Why are guys so quick to give other guys the benefit of the doubt, but not the women who have been hurt by them?"

"On the other hand," Caleb said slowly, "most guys never speak up when they are the victims of abuse and hurt because it's considered unmanly. Why would Nathan say those things about his wife if they weren't true?"

Delanie gaped. "To make himself seem like the victim, obviously. To get out of his current predicament. He's just using the system to get away with murder. Well, not murder, but . . . you know."

"No, I don't know, not when it comes to Nathan Tait's innocence or guilt, nor how true the accusations he made against his wife are." Caleb sighed. "That's the point, Delanie. You made a whole video painting him as the villain, when he actually *could* be the victim. Yes, he may only have come forward because of what his wife said, but if she hadn't ever gone public with her accusations, he may have suffered in silence for many more years. Don't you remember the story of Joseph and Potiphar's wife?"

"The Bible story?" She didn't remember much about it from Sunday school, but she had seen *Joseph and the Amazing Technicolor Dreamcoat*, so she knew what he was referring to—the lustful captain's wife trying to take advantage of the handsome young slave boy. When he rejected her come-ons out of loyalty to his master, she claimed he had raped her and had him thrown in jail because of her hurt pride, and perhaps a fear that he would reveal the truth.

Still, Nathan and Carmelina lived their lives in glass houses. And because of that, she had to admit, the media had had plenty of dirt to throw in either direction, most of it hearsay.

"Okay, I may have cherry-picked my sources a little. But that doesn't mean he didn't do it."

"True. But how is lambasting him in your video without knowing the facts any different than what your fans did to you?"

Delanie spluttered. "It's . . . It just is." For starters, she was pretty certain her opinion didn't matter to Nathan Tait one way or another. She had never met the man, and her following wasn't *that* big. "And, anyway, that's not the one my fans are mad about." *Only my friends, apparently. Wait . . . is Caleb a friend now?*

"No, it's not," he agreed.

The silence stretched, and the question she had been dying to ask since Marie's observation about Caleb's character slammed against the back of her teeth. How did one go about asking their ex-boyfriend whom one was now working closely with if he had cheated a decade ago without making it awkward?

Perhaps it didn't matter. It wasn't like she and Caleb were getting back together, ever. Some things were probably better left in the past.

And some things were easier said than done.

"Hey," he said, "I was thinking some more about what we were talking about today regarding Geppetto and Stella . . ."

"Yeah?" Delanie breathed a sigh of relief, glad Caleb was turning this conversation into less-fraught waters.

"I was wondering, what if we took some time to work with the main cast members individually? I mean, you'll be a much better acting teacher than I would be, but I'm happy to be there to offer observations and act as a second set of eyes. We could have them come to rehearsal in pairs a little early to go over specific scenes and work out the kinks. What do you think?"

"Um, yeah. I think that's a great idea. All of the kids would benefit from a bit more one-on-one teaching time. And that's what this play is for, right? To help the kids develop as actors and people?"

She could hear the smile in his voice. "You bet."

Someone knocked on Delanie's door, and she told Caleb to hold on, then held the phone against her chest while she invited whomever it was in.

Her mom stuck her head into the room. "Your dad and I are going to bed. Is there anything you need before we do?"

"No, and even if there was, I know how to get it. I used to live here, remember?" She suppressed the urge to roll her eyes.

"Okay, I was just checking. Goodnight, honey."

"Goodnight, Mom."

Cheryl closed the door, leaving Delanie with the distinct impression that her mom had been hurt by her response. But why? She didn't need to be fussed over like a child or a guest.

She put the phone to her ear. "My parents are going to bed, so I should probably go so I don't keep them up by talking."

"Absolutely. I guess I'll see you at rehearsal tomorrow night then. If Noel lets me out of the sweatshop backstage, that is."

"I'm sure you'll find a way to escape."

He laughed. "You don't know Noel anymore, do you?"

"Still a task-master, is he?"

"With years as the boss of his own company on him to refine the skill. Anyway, I'll call Joe's and Ainsley's parents to see if they can meet us early tomorrow. Say, half an hour before rehearsal?"

"Why them?"

"Geppetto and Stella are in the most scenes besides Pinocchio. Especially Stella. And if Joe doesn't relax a little, the poor kid is going to have an aneurism."

Starting with Geppetto and Stella was the smart choice. She probably would have suggested them, too, if she wasn't so worked up. "Maybe we should have Pinocchio come in too. He's in every scene with those two, and he has more lines to learn than anyone."

"Good idea. I'll call Ethan's mom, too."

Delanie shook her head, even though Caleb couldn't see her. "I can do that. You've got enough going on, what with Emma and work. This is my only job right now."

"It's no problem, Lanie. Seriously."

Lanie. No one had ever called her that except him, and she was suddenly thrust back to their prom a decade ago, when he was trying to convince her that they could make a long-distance relationship work and they didn't need to break up. *Lanie, can't you even give it a shot before you throw in the towel?* Caught off-guard, she relented. "Okay. Thank you, that would be great."

He didn't respond for a second, then said, "Hey, are you staying in your old room on the north side of the house?"

"Um, yeah. Why?"

"Look out your window."

"What?"

"Just do it. Look out your window right now. And turn off the lights first."

Curious, Delanie went over to the switch and flipped it off, then peered out the tall window over her desk. The tall farmyard light on the other side of the house cast some long shadows across the yard, illuminating the barn and the corrals some distance away, but it wasn't bright enough to diminish the light show that was going on in the sky above. Undulating ribbons of green, pink, and icy blue danced across a sky bright with stars. She leaned in closer, pushing the curtain aside to try and take in the whole view.

"Can you see it?" Caleb asked.

"It's beautiful," she breathed. "Wow, have I missed seeing the northern lights."

"Yeah, there's nothing quite like it. It's probably even better out there than here in town." He sounded as awed as she felt. After a pause, he said, "I'm glad you volunteered to direct the play, Delanie. I'm not sure where we'd be without you."

Her face warmed. "Oh, someone would have stepped up. Amber would have been only too happy to do the job, I'd wager."

"Oh, I'm sure. But she wouldn't have been the leader these kids needed. There's a reason you're here. Even if you can't see it yet."

Her stomach churned. There was a husky tone in his voice that reached into her innards and plucked them like guitar strings.

"Thank you. I appreciate your vote of confidence."

"You've always had it."

Warning bells started ringing in Delanie's head. She had to get out of this conversation before it started wandering into territory she had been avoiding for a decade.

"I better go. Mom and Dad's room is right next door."

"Right. Okay, bye."

"Bye."

Delanie hung up the phone and looked back out the window. The aurora had twisted and stretched, nearly blocking out the brilliant smear of the Milky Way, but she could still see the North Star shining sure and strong, just as it always had. Steady as the seasons, and the sunrise.

And Caleb's belief in her.

She flopped on her bed, staring at the rectangular spot on the ceiling that was a little less dusty than the rest, precisely the same size as a poster. She had come to Peace Crossing hoping to hide from her problems, but they had all seemed to follow her here.

"Maybe the problem is me," she muttered to herself.

No one argued with her, which she had expected. After all, that was what she'd been afraid of all along.

Then Caleb's words about jumping to conclusions about Nathan Tait came back to her.

Is that what I did with him too?

She wrapped her finger in a long strand of her hair, and her heart started pounding against her ribs. She was almost more afraid that she *had* misread the situation between them all those years ago than that she hadn't.

Because if she had been wrong about Caleb Toews, that didn't just mean that she had been unjustifiably angry at him for a decade.

It meant that there was no reason she couldn't let her heart wander back into love with him. Which was the most terrifying prospect of all.

Chapter 11

Friday found Caleb once more playing carpenter backstage at the Mackenzie Playhouse. One long wall of the vaulted rectangular workroom was crowded with locked-up racks of costumes, set pieces, and props from previous productions. Opposite that chaos hung the heavy black curtain that separated this area from the back of the stage.

Caleb and Noel had pulled their workbenches into the open space between, which happened to be the prime route for anyone coming from stage right to get over to the green room—the small room just offstage where actors did quick changes between scenes—or the stairs that led to the basement and back entrance at the far end. Of course, that's why they were both here again on a Friday night, while there were no rehearsals going on. It made it easier to work—*and it's not like either of us has a social life to speak of*, Caleb thought sardonically. Emma had gone to Monica's that afternoon, so his schedule for the weekend was free and clear, except for this and Sunday's rehearsal. Oh, and driving the grain truck for his dad tomorrow.

The plywood backdrop that would eventually represent Geppetto's workshop lay on the scarred wooden floor next to Caleb's worktable like an oversized piece of sketch paper. Samantha Crawford had already painted on a window and some tools that looked like they were hanging from the wall, but she said she would paint the workbench once the whole thing was put together. Caleb was glad he was only responsible for the woodworking—unlike his daughter, drawing was definitely not his strong suit. Nor Monica's. He wasn't sure where Emma had gotten that talent from.

Caleb carefully lined up the angle-cut end of a two-by-two brace with the mark he'd made on the bottom of the plywood rectangle that would be Geppetto's workbench. With his other hand, he jammed the end of his screw into the pilot hole he'd drilled in the brace, then lined up his screw gun. In seconds, the screw shank disappeared with the satisfying squeal of metal turning against wood.

At a separate table a short distance away, Noel measured pieces for the prop bars that would be used to "control" the marionettes of Rocco the Professor during his number—the ones played by live actors, not the wooden puppets that would share the stage with them as background props. With his height, Noel had to stoop a lot more than Caleb did, but his strong dark brown hands measured the one-by-ones with quick, sure movements, ticking off lengths with a carpenter's pencil. Whenever he didn't need the pencil for a minute, he tucked it behind his ear.

Caleb grabbed the second brace. As he lined it up, he caught sight of the time on his wristwatch—a very nice brushed stainless steel analogue one with an elastic link band his parents had given him when he had gotten his journeyman electrician certificate. *Gonna last forever, if I have anything to say about it*, his father had muttered. His father might be a spendthrift, but he believed in paying more for good quality when it would mean spending less in the long run.

Caleb frowned at his watch. *It's already nine o'clock?* With no windows in the hall, it was hard to mark the passage of time. He glanced at Noel.

"I thought you said Derrick was coming to help tonight."

Noel looked up from his measuring and shrugged. "He texted he'd be late. Maybe something happened to keep him at that house reno he was working on."

Noel and his younger brother, Derrick, had started up Butler Bros. Construction several years ago, and the fledgling business often required them to work long hours. Seeing how much effort it took to get a business off the ground, Caleb was grateful for his steady job at Martens Electric. Other than being sent out on the odd weekend emergency call, his hours were remarkably stable, which worked out well when it came to Emma or when his dad needed a hand around the farm.

"What, you mean Derrick didn't ditch us for some hot date? I'm shocked, I tell you. Shocked," Caleb said dryly. "Doesn't he know he's missing out on Peace Crossing's thriving night life?"

Noel chuckled. "What, is that wack-a-doo hypnotist back in town? Or did you mean drinks and watching hockey at the Trading Post?" He shook his head. "Can't remember the last time he went out and did that."

Caleb shook his head and adjusted his screw gun against the next screw. "Jeepers, he's a worse workaholic than you. You Butler boys, all work and no play."

Noel gave a hearty laugh. "And you're doing what right now?" He raised his brows.

"Touché." Caleb chuckled, then sank the screw into the wood. "In my defense, carpentry is my hobby, not my job. And my daughter's actually in the play. Weren't you working on the church roof next door all day?"

"I see your point." Noel extended his measuring tape further and made another mark on his piece of wood. "But I don't think Derrick's worried about what he's missing. Who has time for a night life, anyway?"

"Certainly not you until we get these sets and props all made," Caleb teased. "Much to the chagrin of every blushing beauty in town." He lined up the third brace to be attached.

Noel rolled his eyes and snorted. "Yeah, the streets out there are lined with *blushing beauties* pining away for me. It's tough being such a hot commodity. Why do you think I'm hiding in here?"

Caleb laughed and let it go. Noel had always been a bit obtuse when it came to attentions from women. Caleb could think of a handful of girls off the top of his head who may not be pining exactly, but who would be interested in his friend if Noel asked. But he knew Noel would just laugh it off if Caleb brought them up, so he kept his counsel to himself and got his screw gun in position.

Noel took his piece of wood over to the table saw. "But enough about my prospects, or lack thereof. What has it been like being around Delanie so much?"

Caleb froze, then sank another screw. He supposed it had only been a matter of time before Noel asked. Noel had known them both in high school, and he had stood by Caleb all through his troubled marriage with and amicable divorce from Monica. Few people knew Caleb better.

"It's been fine. Why?"

Noel paused, turning an arched eyebrow in Caleb's direction. "Uh-huh." He turned on the saw, put his shop glasses in place, and started zipping off pieces of wood for the bars.

Noel's question pressed against Caleb's shoulders, as well as the lie he'd given in response. By the time the noise of the saw had faded, Caleb had finished with all three braces, and they now angled into the air from the upside-down set piece like Roman spears waiting for a cavalry attack. He turned to Noel.

"It's been hard. Is that what you wanted to hear? Every time I see her or talk to her, all I can think about is how different my life would be if I hadn't stayed behind in Peace Crossing after high school."

Noel paused, piercing Caleb with his dark-eyed gaze. "Then you wouldn't have Emma."

"I know." Caleb leaned back against the worktable. "And I can never regret that. But is it weird to wish you could keep some parts of your past, and that you could have done some other parts completely differently, even if the two are mutually exclusive?"

Caleb ran his hand through his hair and hung it on his neck by the fingers, staring through the floor at an image of Delanie as he had seen her last—patiently working through scene beats with Ainsley Crawford on Wednesday night. Delanie had been in her element, and the sparkle in her eyes had almost broken his resolve to keep his distance from her. She'd been magnificent.

Noel chuckled, a deep baritone rumble. "Naw, I think that's human nature. Maybe that's why God didn't give us the ability to time travel. If we screwed up our lives that badly the first time, how much of a mess would me make if we went back and tried to only fix the parts we didn't like?"

"You have a point there." Caleb snorted. "I suppose that's why he gives us second chances, huh?"

Noel's mouth quirked. "Is that what you're hoping for with Delanie? A second chance?"

"I can hope all I want. Doesn't mean it's going to happen." He turned and heaved the workbench off the table and took it over to the plywood on the floor, propping the assembly in place near the pencilled-in guideline on the painted set piece. "Help me out with this, would you?"

Noel came over and crouched on the other side of the workbench, holding it in place on the plywood backdrop while Caleb pulled a few screws out of his pocket and stuck the pointy ends between his lips to hold them. He lined up the bench to its marked place on the wall, using a square to make sure the workbench was perpendicular to the plywood. Then he began screwing the support underneath the back of the workbench into the painted wood.

"So, does that mean she shot you down already?" Noel asked casually.

The screws between Caleb's lips gave him an excuse not to answer right away. When he had finished with the last one, he fished a few more from his pocket for the loose ends of the braces and grunted, "Not in so many words."

After three more screws had been employed, he sat back on his haunches to inspect his work. Noel let go of the now firmly attached workbench.

"What does that mean?"

Caleb met his eye. "She made it plain she's not interested. I think she's holding some kind of grudge for how things went down between us. And, frankly, I can't say that I blame her."

When he had gotten off the phone with her on Tuesday, he'd berated himself for being so confrontational about her recent video. The last thing she needed was for someone to kick her while she was down—and the comments sections of both Nathan Tait videos had been full of enough vitriol to last anyone a lifetime. But he couldn't *lie*, and she had asked him outright for his opinion. Of course, he also hadn't told her the whole truth—that in the words of her song mocking the actor's mistakes, all he could hear was how she felt about his own. Yes, she had broken up with him, but she'd made it clear she thought she was doing him a favour, giving him time to focus on his dad's health and on taking care of the farm. And that she would be happy to pick up where they had left off when he eventually followed her out to Vancouver.

Only, he never had. The truth was, they had both made mistakes. And while the rejection and heartbreak that had led to his own mistake with Monica had faded over time, Delanie's video made him wonder if she had also been wounded by the fallout.

He had thought about bringing up what had happened between them, about apologizing that he hadn't kept to his part of the plan, but there didn't seem to be much point. It was all water under the bridge, and there was no undoing the past.

That didn't mean he couldn't wish the river had taken him in a different direction.

"So you're not even going to give it a try?" Noel said casually as he collected his cut pieces of wood and took them to his work area. "You could ask her for coffee. You two are already working together on the play. It's a built-in excuse."

As if Caleb hadn't thought of that.

"It's not fair to Emma."

Noel paused, then turned to Caleb with a confused frown on his face. "How's that?"

Caleb straightened and faced his friend. "Delanie's going back to Vancouver as soon as the play is done. It's not fair to Emma to have her think something might happen between me and Delanie when it won't. She's already got a huge crush on Delanie. I don't want to break her heart worse than it already will be when Delanie leaves."

"Not fair to Emma. Yeah. That's what's going on here."

Caleb scowled. "You're not a dad. You don't know."

With anger fuelling him, he grasped the completed set piece on the floor and heaved it upright, setting it in a wheeled stand that had been used for years. When he struggled with the unbalanced weight of the workbench, Noel stepped over and helped him ease in the far side, his broad shoulders straining beneath his heavy cotton work shirt.

"Thanks," Caleb muttered, though he knew his tone didn't sound all that grateful.

"Don't mention it." Noel stepped back to survey the completed piece. "Nice work."

Caleb didn't say anything, too annoyed to speak.

"You're right," Noel added, "I'm not a dad. But my dad is a pretty great role model, and if he taught me anything, it's that you can be a good dad *and* be happy."

Caleb frowned, thinking of the tall dark-skinned man with the easy smile who had taught him science all through high school. Carl Butler was one of those men who made it look easy to be a dad. Caleb's dad, Marcus, was an excellent father, but he had been too busy with the farm to spend a lot of time with his kids while they were younger. Caleb had promised himself he would never let Emma grow up feeling like her dad didn't have time for her like he had.

"Your dad's a teacher, and so is your mom," Caleb said. "While you and Derrick and Jenny were off on family vacations with your parents every summer, I was helping around the farm. I'm not complaining about my childhood, or my dad. They were both great. But Emma's needs come first. As long as she's here in Peace Crossing, I'm not going anywhere. And I don't want to put Delanie in a position where she has to choose between giving up her dream to stay here with me or breaking up with me again so she can do what she was born to do."

"So you're going to reject yourself for her, is that it?" Noel shook his head. "Listen, most high school relationships dissolve after graduation, and with good reason. I mean, can you imagine if I had ended up with Madeleine Kennedy?"

Caleb chuckled. "She's not so bad." He hadn't seen Maddy since the last time he'd gone into Pearl's Petals to buy Monica flowers, so it had been a while. But Maddy had always been the kind of girl who held her own, which was maybe why she had already been promoted to assistant manager of the flower shop so soon after graduating. As far as he knew, she was practically running the place now.

Noel held up his hands. "No, she's not. But, man, we fought *all* the time. I'm pretty sure the angels breathed a sigh of relief when we called it quits, because the general level of peace in the universe went up three degrees."

Caleb snorted. "What's your point?"

Noel laid a hand on Caleb's shoulder. "My point is, it's been ten years since you and Delanie split up. And you've never really loved anyone else, have you?"

It was more a statement than a question, but Noel still paused for a response.

Caleb gave a barely perceptible shrug. It hadn't been for lack of trying to get over Delanie. But seeing her again had shown him how little progress he'd actually made in that department.

Noel leaned in. "Do you know how rare that is? Don't you think you owe it to yourself, and to her, to see if you guys could have something great together?"

Caleb's mouth went dry and he stared at his friend. He didn't have a good response for that.

"At the very least, you'll stop wondering what could have been." Noel clapped his shoulder. "You'll either find true love or closure. That would certainly be worth the risk to me." Noel gave a knowing nod and stepped back.

The shrill jangle of a rotary phone filled the air, and Caleb pulled his mobile out of his pocket. When he spotted Delanie's name, he swallowed.

Noel saw it too.

"You better ask her," he said, pointing at Caleb with an admonishing finger as he moved off to work on his puppet controllers.

Caleb walked away as he answered the phone, retreating to the darkness of the wings around the end of the curtain.

"Yeah, hi," he said. Why did he sound so curt? He took a breath.

"Everything okay?" Delanie asked.

"It's fine. What's up?"

"I just got a call from Amber, and . . ." She sighed. "We have a problem. And I don't know how to fix it."

"What's the problem?" He tried to remember what Amber was supposed to be tackling this week that might have gone awry, but realized it could have been any of the tasks she'd been assigned, even if they weren't due for weeks. The woman might be abrasive, but she was certainly efficient.

"Amber. More specifically, what I'm going to do about her. This is getting out of hand." Her voice trembled slightly.

A surge of anger pulsed through him. What had Amber done? "What did she say to you?"

Delanie sighed. "It's stupid. I should be able to handle this. But when I called her about Celeste coming in early to the next rehearsal so we could work the Punch and Judy scene beats with just her and Grayson, she insisted Celeste didn't need the extra practise and their family was already committing enough time to this production, and if Grayson couldn't get his act together during regularly scheduled rehearsals, Celeste shouldn't need to sacrifice to prop him up. Oh, and that if I actually knew what I was doing, the kids wouldn't need the extra time in the first place." Her voice broke on the last sentence.

Caleb's ears grew hot. The nerve of that woman!

"Where does she get off?" he blurted before he could stop himself.

"Pardon?" Delanie sounded startled.

He drew a deep breath, annoyed that he'd let Amber irk him into losing his temper. When he could speak more calmly, he said, "Sorry about that. You know her comments aren't actually about you, right?"

"Um, yeah. At least, my brain does."

He heard the tremble in her voice, but the iron underneath was even stronger. He smiled grimly. At least Delanie wasn't letting Amber rattle her too much.

"As I see it, you have a few options. One, you could talk to her about how her behaviour is affecting not only you and the production team, but also Celeste's future chances of development and true success, and hope she smartens up and things start going better from here on out."

"But she's at least ten years older than me! She should know better than this."

"She absolutely should," Caleb agreed. "But unfortunately, there isn't necessarily a direct correlation between becoming an adult and getting your puppies together."

Delanie gave an amused snort. "Getting your what?"

Caleb chuckled, his heart slowing down. "It's the phrase Monica and I started using when Emma was born. Sounds nicer than the original."

"I'll give you that." Delanie paused. "What was option two?"

"Continue to let her childish behaviour cause problems for the team and potentially ruin Celeste's potential as a capable future adult because no one ever told her mom the damage she's doing."

"Is there an option three?"

He sighed. "Ask their family to step back from the production."

"So avoid the actual conflict by shutting her out, which I'm sure would go about as smoothly as a ride up the Chin during spring. That sounds almost as bad as the first two. Besides, then we'd lose our sound guy too."

He smirked at her reference to a local logging road that was famous for being little more than a glorified deer trail, and worse maintained. *So she hasn't forgotten everything about the Peace Country.*

"I never said they were fun options."

"Thanks," she said dryly. At least she sounded calmer.

"Do you want me to talk to her?" he offered reluctantly.

"You would do that?" She sounded truly surprised.

"Of course."

Confronting Amber sounded about as fun as screwing his hand to a board. But if this was something he could do to help Delanie, he would.

"No," she said heavily. "I'll do it. I'm the director. It's my responsibility. Thanks, though. It means a lot that you offered."

A small part of him breathed a sigh of relief. He wandered back onto the workroom side of the curtain. When Noel saw him standing there, he mouthed, *Ask her.*

Caleb wanted to dismiss the suggestion. Delanie had rejected his offer to come to dinner at his parents', after all. But that *had* been a little out of the blue, and he had put her on the spot. Would he have wanted the first evening they spent together in a decade to be dinner at *her* parents'? *Not on my life. And she did just call me for advice about Amber. Like Noel said, I should at least give this a shot.*

"Say, um, Delanie?" Caleb's mouth felt like it was packed with sawdust. He moved back to the privacy of the right wing of the stage where he couldn't see Noel's furtive glances.

"Yeah?" Did she sound nervous? His heart was beating so fast, it was hard to tell.

"I was wondering, uh . . ."

"Yeah?" she prompted again.

He swallowed. "Did you want Emma to come early on Sunday too? She's got her songs memorized, but it would probably help her to work through scene beats like the others."

He punched his thigh at his own cowardice.

"Oh. Um, sure. That's a great idea." She sounded surprised. Or disappointed. "I had her scheduled for next week, but if she needs extra practise, we can start working with her now."

"Alright. I'll let Monica know."

"Great. Thanks. I guess I'll see you Sunday."

"See you then."

He ended the call and stood there with his hands on his hips, breathing deeply until his heart stopped racing.

When he went back to the workroom, Noel glanced up from his project.

"What did she say?"

"I never asked her," Caleb mumbled, snatching the scrap wood from his workspace to clean it up so he didn't have to meet his friend's eye.

He could feel Noel studying him for a few moments before he said, "Speaking of shots, you know you miss every one of those you don't take."

"Thanks for the inspirational poster, man."

"You know I got your back."

Caleb rolled Geppetto's workshop aside to make space for his next project, which was creating the prow of a little wooden boat on wheels. He had found some plans for a full-sized rowboat on the Internet and planned to use those as a guide for the prop.

If only relationships were as easy to figure out.

Chapter 12

DELANIE STOOD IN front of the first row of theatre seats with one arm crossed in front of her and her other hand touching her lips, watching the teenagers on the stage above her go through their scene.

Celeste Leclerc, her red hair covered by a frilly white cap Becca had found in the costume cage, put her hands on her hips, her whole posture exaggerated as she glared at Grayson Elcano. The slender Filipino boy had brought a jester hat from home, and the bells hanging from the floppy ends of the cap tinkled every time he moved. Not quite a Punchinello hat, but a fun touch for rehearsal. Between and slightly behind them, Ethan White, the skinny tenth-grader with the precocious attitude who had been cast as Pinocchio, looked between them with an incredulous look on his face. Two other "puppets" stood toward the rear of the stage, watching the encounter.

"Are you saying," Ethan said in a loud stage voice, "that you get to sing and tell jokes on the stage all day long, and Professor Rocco takes you anywhere you want?"

"Anywhere we want," Grayson agreed in an approximation of a Cockney accent, his voice distorted to sound like a kazoo by the swazzle in his mouth. Finding one of the small reed instruments that gave Punch's voice his signature sound on eBay had been quite a victory for Delanie.

"As long as it's somewhere *he* wants," said soft-spoken Celeste in an accent that leaned toward Cockney, though barely.

Grayson ignored her and rubbed his hands together in glee. "Ye should join us," he said to Ethan. "It's about time me 'ad someone new t'outsmart."

"Now, Mr. Punch," Celeste said, "ya know young Pinocchio here can't stay. He's got his papa to consider. And school."

Ethan gave a broad wave of dismissal. "School, shmool. Papa won't mind if I miss a little school to begin a career on the stage."

"And I can give 'im the rod as easily 'ere as they can at school," Grayson said, patting the long wooden paddle hanging from his belt.

"Don't you dare, Mr. Punch," Celeste warned.

Ethan looked toward the back of the auditorium with stars in his eyes and broad gestures. "I can see it now—they'll come from miles around to see Pinocchio and Friends."

"Pinocchio and what?" demanded Grayson indignantly.

"Tell me more," Ethan said, oblivious to the offence he'd caused. "Do you get to travel near and far?"

Grayson surreptitiously took the paddle from his belt with a mischievous look on his face. "Uh-huh."

"Do you get to meet interesting people?"

"Uh-huh."

Grayson moved the paddle into position behind Pinocchio's behind, which Ethan seemed not to notice, too caught up in looking toward his pie-in-the-sky visions of fame and fortune. Celeste did, however, and she raised her hand to object, but not before Pinocchio cut her off.

"Do you get to meet the queen?" Ethan enthused.

Grayson looked incensed. "The queen? Why would a scoundrel like me get t' meet the queen? Ye young rascal." And he pretended to smack Ethan on the bottom, chasing a jumping Ethan all around the stage while Toby the Dog, another puppet character in the supporting cast played by a firecracker of a girl named Laura, chased Punch and barked.

Delanie chuckled, then looked nervously at Amber, who stood observing the scene from the aisle to her right. The woman's crossed arms and pinched expression reminded Delanie of their looming confrontation, and she swallowed. She had stopped by the Leclerc residence to talk to Amber about her behaviour yesterday, but had been deterred by the stern demeanour of Amber's husband when he had opened the door. The tension in both Luc Leclerc and Amber when she'd come to the door had been palpable, and Delanie had lost her nerve and come up with an excuse that she had stopped by to ask a question about the play instead.

I can't avoid that conversation forever though.

More than the obvious tension, Amber's behaviour had rung some alarms—she hadn't even let Delanie in the door, but had come and stood outside in the chilly autumn air on the step without a sweater on, closing the door behind her. And then she'd acted impatient for Delanie to leave, glancing furtively toward the living room window as though she were afraid someone was watching. Her husband?

Ever since Delanie had seen the way Amber and her husband had behaved, she couldn't help wonder if there was something more going on at the Leclerc residence that would explain Amber's inconsistent, erratic behaviour. After all, if someone as high-profile as Nathan Tait could have been abusing his wife behind closed doors while living in a glass house, how much easier would it be to get away with such things within the squat, solid bungalows of a small town like Peace Crossing? People were friendly enough in this town, and it wasn't like gossip was unheard of, but they mostly let their neighbour's business be their business.

Delanie's attention was caught by Celeste waving her hands and yelling for Mr. Punch to stop chasing Pinocchio. Grayson froze, then turned to look sheepishly at his "wife."

"Yes, darling?"

"Mr. Punch!" Celeste said, her fists on her hips. "Ya can't go beatin' the poor boy every time he says somethin' foolish. You'll scare him off! He's not the policeman, you know."

In the background, the boy playing the policeman puppet, dressed in a British bobby's hat, popped his head above a cloth-covered table with an alarmed look on his face, then saw Mr. Punch turn toward him with his paddle raised and ducked down again before he could be seen. During the play, the policeman would be inside a traditional Punch and Judy puppet booth to add to the jolliness of the situation.

"I was just havin' a bit o' fun," Grayson said.

"I'm not sure Pinocchio would consider that fun," Celeste said, crossing her arms. "Would you, Pinocchio?"

Ethan rubbed his behind, his face contorted, then caught Grayson's warning glare. "No, no. It was pretty fun," he said hurriedly and unconvincingly.

Celeste frowned. "Are you *sure*?"

Ethan hesitated, glancing at Punch's slapstick.

Grayson leaned toward him and said in a stage-whisper, "Ye want t' stay or not? Or maybe ye'd prefer to go back t' school?"

Ethan plastered on a fake smile and looked at Celeste. "*So* fun. *Barrels* of fun. I could barely *stand* how fun it was." Wrapping his arms around his belly, Ethan gave a long, loud laugh, in which Mr. Punch joined him. When Celeste rolled her eyes and turned away from the two foolishly laughing puppets, Ethan rubbed his tender bottom once more and stage-muttered with a sidelong glance at Grayson, "Just not fun enough to do again."

Grayson made a threatening move with the slapstick, and Ethan jumped aside with a high-pitched yelp, eliciting a chuckle from Delanie. A titter of laughter rose from a few of the younger kids sitting around the theatre who had finished rehearsing with their group and had come back into the auditorium to wait.

Celeste shook her head and turned back to the audience, rolling her eyes. "That Mr. Punch, always beatin' people with his slapstick. When will he ever learn?"

Grayson swaggered up beside her. "Learn? Do ye see 'ow everyone laughs when I do that?" He gave a sweeping gesture at the audience. "If ye ask me, that's the way to do it!" he said with an exaggerated sing-song lilt on the last phrase—Punch's signature line. Grayson dropped character and looked at Delanie uncertainly. "And that's when the music starts, right?"

Delanie smiled at Punch's squeaky swazzled voice asking Grayson's question. "You got it. That was great, you guys. We made a lot of progress today."

The kids, catching the signal that it was time to break up, dropped character and turned to listen in more casual poses. Grayson slid the swazzle out of his cheek and tucked the small reed device into its plastic storage case, which he'd fished from his pocket.

"Keep working on those lines," Delanie said, "and get those lyrics memorized. We're going to start blocking the songs next week, and I want you off book by then. It's time for the big song rehearsal with the rest of the cast, so go take a quick bathroom break and come back to the hall as soon as you can."

After a round of acknowledgements, the kids shuffled down the stairs that led into the auditorium at stage left. As the group moved past her, Delanie called Celeste aside. The girl came over, looking anxious.

"You're doing well with your lines, Celeste, but you need to project a bit more. It was tough to hear you even from here, and your voice needs to go all the way back there." Delanie pointed at the back of the theatre.

Celeste nodded, her shoulders bunching. "I know. I'm so sorry. I'll do better." She looked like she might cry, reminding

Delanie of the tension she had felt at the Leclerc residence the day before.

"Hey, no. That wasn't to make you feel bad. Here, let's try something. Come stand here next to me."

Delanie planted her feet at shoulder width facing the back of the hall. Celeste mimicked her pose, though with less confidence.

Delanie smiled encouragingly. "Great. Now, what's your best friend's name?"

"Zoe," Celeste said.

"Okay, I want you to pretend Zoe just walked up the stairs at the back there, and you want to say hi to her. How would you do it?"

Celeste glanced at the back of the theatre with a dubious expression, but Delanie kept her gaze fixed on the girl's face.

"Hi, Zoe," Celeste said half-heartedly.

"I don't think she can hear you," Delanie said kindly. "Put your hand on your diaphragm, like this." She put her hand on her own midsection, and Celeste copied her. "Now, feel it get firm and full when you breathe in?"

Celeste nodded.

"You need to *push* that air out when you call your friend, like this." Delanie pushed in on her diaphragm as she called, "Hi, Zoe!" to the back of the theatre, and a few parents who were having a conversation in the back row glanced their way.

Celeste glanced uncertainly around at the kids gathering in the seats, then looked at the rear of the auditorium and straightened her neck. "Hi, Zoe!" she called, louder this time.

Delanie grinned. "Much better. Tell her that you had a burrito for lunch."

Celeste gave an embarrassed giggle. "I never eat burritos."

"Pretend," Delanie said gently.

Celeste nodded, then resumed her erect posture. "I had a double-bean burrito for lunch. What did you have?"

Delanie relaxed, patting Celeste on the arm. "That's the way to do it!" Delanie said, mimicking Punch's squeaky catchphrase.

Celeste giggled again, and Delanie smiled.

"If you use that voice when you're on the stage, they'll be able to hear you over at town hall, which is exactly what we want."

Celeste nodded, looking embarrassed but pleased. "Thanks, Miss Fletcher."

"Anytime. Seriously." Thinking of her suspicions, she added, "If there's, uh, *anything* I can do to help you, you let me know, okay?"

Delanie didn't know if the fervency of her meaning would come through her words, but she didn't dare say anything more, in case she was wrong. And even if she was right, she didn't want to embarrass Celeste by saying something so openly.

Celeste nodded with a confused expression on her face. "Thanks, again. I, um, better run to the washroom before the song rehearsal."

"Sure."

As Celeste walked away, Delanie looked up to see Amber standing nearby, watching with a tight expression on her face. Delanie braced herself for the expected tongue-lashing for helping her *perfect, talented* daughter. But instead, Amber looked thoughtful and came a few steps closer, watching her daughter leave.

"Thanks for doing that. I think it will make a difference," Amber said.

Delanie blinked, then remembered to smile. "You're welcome."

Nodding stiffly, Amber moved past her up the aisle toward the back hall after Celeste.

"Well," said Caleb's voice behind her, "that was unexpected."

Delanie nearly jumped out of her boots. She whirled toward the double doors at the front left of the hall that led backstage to see him standing there with two metal travel mugs in his hands. *How long has he been standing there?*

"What do you mean?"

As he walked toward her, he took a sip from one of the mugs and then nodded at Amber. "Her, showing gratitude. Better mark it on the calendar."

Delanie rolled her eyes. "Oh, she's not that bad. Cut her some slack."

"Weren't you the one who was calling me, desperate for advice, not two days ago?" He gave an amused snort and held out the other mug toward her.

"What's this?"

"Latte with three sugars and some cinnamon on top, just the way you like it."

She blinked. "Cool Beans is closed on Sundays."

He gave her a small grin. "I didn't get it from Cool Beans."

She popped the top on the mug and inhaled the aromatic steam. It smelled like heaven. "Where did you get it, then?"

He gave her an impish grin. "I'll tell you after you try it."

"O-kay."

She hesitantly took a sip, watching him over the rim of the cup. The hall was getting noisier as kids shuffled in from their various chorus group rehearsals to practise the big group numbers.

"Mm. Tastes even better than it smells," she said, loud enough to be heard over the din. "Okay, spill the beans. Is there a new coffee shop in town no one told me about? Or does Tim Hortons have something new on their menu?"

He gave a self-satisfied smirk. "Nope. I made it."

She gaped at him, speechless.

He chuckled. "I got an espresso machine a few years ago. It's become a bit of a hobby of mine. Sometime you'll have to come over so I can make you one with fancy latte art on the top. It all gets messed up in a travel mug."

"Well, Mr. Toews," Delanie said playfully, choosing to ignore the fact that he'd just invited her to his house, "aren't you just full of surprises?"

"I have my moments."

Caleb took another sip of his coffee, and the look in his eyes made Delanie glance away. Her stomach had gotten all fluttery, and she was pretty sure it had nothing to do with the creamy caffeine in her mug.

Violet made her way to the front of the room, along with their pianist, Edith, who proceeded to settle herself at the small electric piano on the auditorium floor near the stage. Celeste came in and sat with the other senior high students, and Amber stood in the back near the stairs with her arms crossed, her expression stern.

"How did it go with Amber, by the way?" Caleb said quietly from right beside her.

Delanie jumped again, startled by how close he was. Taking a breath to gather herself, she glanced up at him. His brows were furrowed in concern.

"It hasn't yet. I'm looking for the right moment."

"I know what that's like," he muttered. He cleared his throat. "Say, uh, I know I already made you coffee, but would you like to go out for coffee after rehearsal? I mean, you could have tea or water or, um, something else if that's too much caffeine. I could even buy you dinner, or whatever you want. If you want. Emma's with Monica this weekend, so it would be a perfect time to, er, catch up."

Delanie's heart had sped up with each word. She almost chuckled at his awkward delivery, but she was much less unprepared this time than when he had asked her to his parents' for supper. And much less unwilling, she had to admit.

"Um, sure."

Caleb met her gaze and blinked. "Yeah? I mean, great."

He smiled, and Delanie's breath caught in her throat. He'd always had a great smile. And those eyes—amber brown accentuated by the green of his plaid flannel shirt. He was the same old Caleb, and she kind of loved that. Except, apparently, he was now a hobbyist barista.

"Caleb?" came a woman's voice from up the aisle.

Delanie turned to see Monica and Emma coming toward them. She wasn't sure if she was disappointed or relieved at the interruption.

"Hi, Miss Fletcher!" Emma said with a wide grin as Monica moved close to Caleb to talk to him without having to shout.

Tearing her gaze away from Monica and Caleb, who looked close enough to kiss, Delanie leaned over to talk to the little girl and pasted on a smile. "Hi, Emma. How did rehearsal go downstairs?"

"Great! I was practising my scene with Luigi and Claudia, the one when they capture Lucy to try and make her tell them where Pinocchio is, but then she tricks them and gets away. It's so much fun!" She bounced a little.

Violet looked up from the notes she had been reviewing at her conductor's music stand and smiled at the little dark-haired girl. "Emma is doing a great job with her lines *and* her songs. Lucy is a tough role, but she's working hard, and it shows."

Delanie smiled. "That doesn't surprise me at all."

Beaming, Emma went to sit in the front row with the other younger kids. Delanie turned back to Monica and Caleb in time to see him nodding in response to something she'd asked.

"Of course I can take Emma, no problem," he said. "Oh, wait." He glanced over at Delanie guiltily. "Monica got called in to work, and Dave is out of town. She needs someone to watch Emma for a couple of hours."

"Oh!" Delanie blinked. "Of course. We can have our coffee another time."

Monica looked sharply at Delanie, who took another sip from her mug—which was branded with the Martens Electric logo—and turned away.

"Thanks, Caleb," she heard Monica say. "I should be there soon after eight."

"Anytime."

Delanie glanced back at Monica in time to catch a piercing stare thrown in her direction before the woman turned up the aisle to leave.

Caleb came over. "I'm sorry, Delanie. I really wanted to spend some time with you."

"No problem," Delanie said with a dismissive wave. "It's your daughter. Not like we'd had this in the works for weeks or anything."

His frown looked somewhat pained. "No, but . . . say, do you want to come over for supper with me and Emma? It might just be pizza by the time we get out of here, but we could play a board game after. She's been getting into *Settlers of Catan* lately."

"She plays *Settlers of Catan* already?"

Caleb nodded. "She's good, too. Careful, or she'll kick your keester."

Delanie chuckled, then bit the inside of her cheek. The irrational sense of rejection she had felt when Caleb had so quickly changed his plans for the sake of Emma shifted into something more akin to fear—what did it mean that he wanted her to come over and hang out with the two of them all evening?

Still, the only socializing she'd had for the last week had been over video chat or with her parents. As fun as it had been to watch *The King and I* with her mom the night before, a night away from her parents—and a distraction from her self-recriminating thoughts—sounded like a wonderful idea. And Caleb *sounded* like he truly wanted her to come, that he wasn't just offering out of guilt.

"Sure. I'd love to."

"Yeah?" Caleb's face lit up again, leaving no doubt that the invitation had been sincerely given. "Cool. Um." He glanced at

Emma, who was tapping her feet up and down to a fast-paced song only she could hear, then back at Delanie, looking like he was trying to stifle a grin—and losing the battle. He nodded for no particular reason. "Right. I better go see how Noel's doing backstage."

"And I have a rehearsal to lead." Delanie indicated the now-crowded auditorium, hoping she didn't sound as breathless as she felt.

"Yeah. Cool," Caleb said again, then spun and strode off through the double doors to return to his set-building.

Delanie watched him go, her heart bouncing as rapidly as Emma's toes.

Chapter 13

DELANIE LAID TWO small blue sticks along the lines on the colourful game board and gazed triumphantly around Caleb's snug dining nook at Caleb and Emma. "There, a road. Now I can finally build another town thingie."

"Sorry, Miss Fletcher, but you're too late," Emma said, her lips stretched in an excited grin as she handed several cards to her dad, the banker, and laid down some pieces of her own. "I just won."

Caleb gazed at the board, counting, while he rubbed the dark beard he'd been letting grow in. He laid his cards down. "Congratulations, Chickadee."

"What? Already?" Delanie peered at the girl's impressive sprawling empire of interconnected red wooden pieces. She had played *Settlers of Catan* enough to know what she was doing, but she was by no means an expert, especially at the *Cities and Knights* variation. Still, it seemed like she had just started gaining momentum, so how could Emma already have enough points to win?

Emma pointed at her pieces on the game board as she summed up her points. "Ten, eleven, and two for the longest road is thirteen. See?" She grinned proudly, then glanced at Delanie. "Next time, you should try to turn your villages into cities earlier. It helps a lot."

Delanie laughed off the girl's unsolicited advice and began collecting her pieces. "I'll keep that in mind."

While Emma's focus was on gathering her pieces and dropping them in a little plastic bag to put away, Caleb rolled his eyes for Delanie alone to see. "She gets that from her mother," he whispered.

Delanie chuckled.

"What did you say, Daddy?" Emma blinked at him innocently.

"Nothing, kiddo." Caleb repressed his smile. He stood and helped Delanie sort out the remaining game pieces. "Your mom should be here soon. Why don't you go make sure you have everything you're taking over there? Miss Fletcher and I can clean up."

"Sure." His daughter obediently hopped out of her chair.

As though on cue, a light knock sounded on the door. Delanie glanced toward the street through the living room picture window and saw a minivan sitting on the street curb, its lights glowing red in the deepening dusk.

Emma ran to open the door and greeted her mother, who wore the brick-red button-down shirt uniform of a cashier at the local grocery store, Miller's Market, under a pilled cream cardigan.

"Guess what!" Emma exclaimed as Monica came inside. "Miss Fletcher came over for supper. I totally beat her and Daddy at *Settlers of Catan*."

Monica smoothed Emma's hair with an indulgent smile before casting a tense glance at Delanie and Caleb. "I'm sure you did. You've gotten so good at that game. Hurry up, now. It's getting late."

"Okay, be right back." Emma raced away down the hall toward her room.

"No running," Caleb called after her, and she moderated her step a little.

"I'll finish here," Delanie said quietly to Caleb. She could sense Monica's chilly attitude from across the living room, and suddenly felt like an awkward third wheel. "You go see Emma off."

Caleb's brow furrowed. "If you're sure."

"It's almost all put away anyway."

Caleb nodded, then went over to talk to Monica. Delanie tried not to listen in, but from what she did hear, they were mostly talking about Emma and that week's schedule. By the time Emma returned with her pink fall coat on and her mint backpack over the shoulder, Delanie had put the lid on the box. She left it in the middle of the table and went to lean on the wall dividing the galley kitchen from the living room, trying to stay out of the way.

Monica glanced over at her. "I was sorry to hear about your grandmother."

Surprised, Delanie mumbled, "Thank you." Glancing down while trying to think of something to say, she noticed the large sparkling diamond on Monica's left hand. "Congratulations on the engagement. And the baby."

Monica looked taken aback. "How did you—?"

"Emma let it slip." Delanie gave a small smile. "Don't worry, I haven't told anyone."

Monica gave her daughter a look of consternation, but Emma was focused on putting her shoes on and didn't notice. Monica glanced back at Delanie, her smile softening. "Thank you. I appreciate it."

Emma hopped to her feet. "Okay, Mom. Ready!"

"Okay, sweetie."

Emma threw her arms around Caleb's waist and he hugged her awkwardly around the shoulders while standing. They said their goodnights, and moments later the door had closed behind Monica and the vivacious girl. Caleb went to the living room window and waved at Emma, who stood on the sidewalk below waving madly. Then the girl raced toward the minivan after her mom. He stood watching until the minivan had driven away, then turned to face Delanie, who had awkwardly watched the whole scene from the arch between the dining nook and the living room.

Delanie was suddenly acutely aware that it was just the two of them in the house—she was alone with Caleb Toews for the first time in ten years. Her pounding heart and dry mouth told her it was time to go.

But, surprisingly, a larger part of her didn't want to leave.

"Say, I know it's a little late for that latte I promised," Caleb said, "but would you like a steamed hot chocolate?" He grinned. "I really want to show off my barista skills."

Delanie's chest warmed. He didn't want her to go, either.

"Sure. I'd love that."

He met her gaze with that intense look that stirred the butterflies in her ribcage. She drew in a deep breath.

I might be crazy to stay. But why do I feel like it would be crazier not to see where this might lead?

CALEB METHODICALLY FILLED the frothing jug with hot chocolate ingredients, hoping the familiar movements would ease the tension now bunching his shoulders, courtesy of Monica. She hadn't come right out and said she didn't approve of Delanie being here, but she didn't have to—he knew that look well enough. But Monica had left *him*, not the other way around. If he chose to spend time with Delanie again now that the opportunity presented itself, Monica would have to get used to it. He hadn't complained about Super Dave, after all. And why should he? Dave was a good guy.

Then again, he and Dave didn't have the history that Monica and Delanie did.

While Delanie stood by and watched, Caleb finished steaming the milk and cocoa mixture in the stainless-steel jug, then released the button on his shiny home espresso machine and withdrew the jug from the steam wand. In smooth motions that were the result of long habit, he wiped down the wand, purged it with a burst of steam, and then poured the drink into a large homey stoneware mug, gratified at the perfect amount of froth bubbling to the top.

"Your order, m'lady," he said in a posh British accent, handing it to Delanie with a little bow.

She laughed—that laugh he had missed so much—and took a sip.

"Mmm, delicious."

When she pulled the mug away from her mouth, it was his turn to laugh.

"What?" she asked.

"You know it's good when it leaves a froth moustache," he said, searching for a napkin or something she could wipe it off with.

Touching her lip, she chuckled. "Oh."

He considered letting her use the cleaning cloth, but decided that would be both unpleasant *and* unsanitary, so he settled on ripping a piece of paper towel off the roll hanging beneath the top cupboard. She took it from him and gingerly dabbed the creamy brown bubbles away.

"Could you show me how to do it?" she asked, gesturing at the empty mug he'd brought out for himself.

"Sure," he said, pleased. He quickly rinsed the frothing pot and dried it, then handed it to her. "First, you put in two rounded teaspoons of cocoa."

"Alright." She picked up the metal scoop and the cocoa tin and followed his orders.

Caleb walked her through his hot chocolate recipe, looking over her shoulder as she did the steps.

"Okay, before we turn on the steam, let me explain how to do it," he said, moving over to the machine. "First, place the jug beneath the steam wand so the wand is just below the surface of the milk. You want it to pull in a little air for a few seconds. And put the wand in off to the side so the milk will spin around in the pot."

"Like this?"

She held the jug beneath the wand, but he could tell the wand was too deep. Without thinking, he overlaid his hand on hers to move the jug a little lower.

"That's more like it."

She glanced at his hand, then up at his face over her arm, and he became aware of how little space there was between them and the warmth of her slender fingers beneath his. Feeling his face grow warm, he dropped his hand. "Okay, that looks good. Now pull the jug down and we'll do it for real. You always want to purge the wand after you have it in milk and wipe it down to keep it clean, but you also want to purge it right before you use it to get rid of excess water."

He was about to show her what he meant when she set down the jug and copied the purging steps he'd done earlier. He grinned.

"Well, Delanie Fletcher, you always were a quick study."

She smiled, obviously pleased. "I do alright."

She went through the remaining steps to steam the chocolate milk in her jug, with him offering pointers only when needed. Less than a minute later, she was handing him a mug full of frothy chocolate to sample.

"Did I do okay?" she asked.

He took a satisfying sip. "Better than my first time." When her expression became anxious, he quickly shook his head to reassure her. "It's good. Really. A little too much foam, but that will come with practice. It tastes perfect."

She relaxed. "Oh, good." She took the frothing jug over to

the sink and ran some water into it.

"I'll take care of that later," he said. "Why don't we go sit in the living room?"

"Sure." Delanie set the pitcher in the sink and picked up her mug of chocolate.

Did she sound nervous, or was that his own pounding heart tainting his perception? How long had he dreamed of what he would tell Delanie if he ever got the chance? Now that he had the chance, what would he actually tell her?

He followed her into the living room. She sat on the reclining rocking chair near the window, so he chose the couch, slightly disappointed that she hadn't sat where he could sit next to her. *Don't rush this, Caleb. If this is meant to be, it's worth taking your time.*

But Noel's words from the other day stuck in his mind—*you miss all the shots you don't take.* Cheesy as his friend's advice was, this might be his only chance to set the record straight with Delanie. He didn't want to waste it. Even if nothing happened between them after this, at least he would have cleared the air.

But before he could open his mouth, she asked, "Caleb, do you believe in second chances?"

His heart raced. Did she mean for them, or something else?

"Of course," he said carefully. "How are people supposed to get better if they have to be perfect the first time they try something? If we didn't have space to make mistakes, we would never achieve anything."

"Hmm." She frowned and looked out the window while she took another sip of her hot chocolate. He knew she could probably see the tree-lined dike bounding the river at the end of the street, and beyond that, the twilight would be bathing the hills on the other side of the Peace River in reddish gold. He resisted the urge to go over and look. He wanted to give her space. Besides, it would be hard to top the view he already had.

One of her hands fidgeted with her phone.

"Is this about the thing with YouTube?" *And Josh?* But he kept that last thought to himself.

She sighed and turned to face him, glancing at the dark screen of her phone.

"Yeah. I'm trying to decide what to do about it. My friend Desmond thinks I should make an apology video for my fans, and Marie says no way, that will only make things worse. I'm not even sure what I should apologize for, but if I don't do something soon, I think I'll lose some fans who may have been supporting me up until now. It's been two weeks already, and I've barely said a peep about anything." She sighed. "I just don't know what to do. What do you think?"

He took a sip of his drink to buy himself time to think. He had never been in a situation like Delanie was in—and hoped he never would be—but he could imagine the strain she had been under as she wrestled with how to move forward. How could he possibly advise her on this?

Then again, hadn't he been about to ask forgiveness for the mistakes of his own past? Wasn't this just another type of relationship that needed to be repaired?

"I would be honest with your fans. That's all you can do. They trusted you. The ones who started the mob—well, those weren't really your fans, so I wouldn't worry about them. They were just there for the show, and when that show became your destruction, they either joined in on the stoning or got out the popcorn and watched."

She gave a sardonic snort. "Yeah, that's a fair assessment."

"But for the rest, the ones who are maybe feeling a bit lost and confused and wondering what happened and why you aren't saying anything about it, I would tell them the truth. Don't remain silent. That only leads to more hurt, and it will be harder to come back from that later."

She looked at him sharply, and his conscience twinged. He had *wanted* to reach out to her before, but the timing had never seemed right. Would she hear his regret in his words?

"Thanks, Caleb," she said at last, studying him with those dark eyes. "I think you've gotten smarter since I knew you last."

The vulnerability in her gaze made his breath shudder.

"Delanie, I . . ." His voice cracked, and he cleared his throat, searching the carpet for the right thing to say.

"Caleb, I'm sorry," she said.

He looked up at her in surprise. "For what?"

She put her mug on the side table next to the chair and leaned back, wringing her hands in her lap.

"What I did to you. The expectations I had. It was stupid. I mean, I broke up with you, but I somehow believed you would want to follow me to Vancouver so we could pick up where we had left off? I never once considered how you would feel about that. I was so focused on what I wanted that I didn't think about what you wanted. Or needed. No wonder you chose Monica over me."

Tears glistened in her eyes, melting Caleb's fears in the face of her pain. "Delanie, I didn't—"

"And Emma. She's great. I mean, I'm sorry it didn't work out between you and Monica, but you got a pretty amazing bonus out of that choice, didn't you?" She smiled through her tears and wiped them away, sniffling.

"Yeah, I did." He grabbed a box of tissues from the side table next to the couch and took it over to her. She took several tissues from the box, smiling her thanks, and he set it on the table next to her mug, then slowly went back to the couch and sat down.

He closed his eyes and took a breath, then opened them. *Now or never.* "Delanie, I wanted to follow the plan. But I screwed up."

Her gaze snapped to his. "What do you mean?"

"I was lost after you left. Things were so uncertain with my dad, and I had a lot to do with the farm. Mom was so stressed out that I was helping with the younger kids too. It was just a lot of responsibility for an eighteen-year-old to handle. A few months after you left, I was feeling especially bereft, so I went to this party with some of our friends from school. There was alcohol, and I thought, *Why not?* You know I had never even tried beer before, and I've barely touched it since. But that night with the alcohol buzzing through my system was the first time I'd felt okay in a long time. I drank so much that I don't remember most of it. I do remember Monica being there. She was being inappropriate, but I let her. It felt good to be wanted." He swallowed. "Six weeks later, she told me she was pregnant. And I did the right thing. I married her."

He watched her face the whole time he spoke, expecting to see hurt and betrayal. Instead, he saw relief.

"You mean you hadn't been seeing her before?" Delanie said, her eyes damp again.

He shook his head. "No. It was one time, one epic night packed full of mistakes. And it changed everything."

She covered her mouth, the tears streaming down her face. "I thought . . ." She shook her head, dabbing at the tears with her tissue. "I thought you were cheating on me." She leaned back, biting her lip. "All this time, I thought you had lied to me about why you didn't come to Vancouver. But you didn't . . . ?"

The raw emotion in her voice hauled him off the couch so he could take her hand. Squatting on the floor in front of her, he said, with as much emphasis as he could muster, "No, never. Delanie, you were my world. I wanted to marry you and live happily ever after. *You* were my dream girl." He paused. *Moment of truth, bro.* "Still are," he added.

She searched his face, her eyes still bright with unshed tears. She leaned forward and he met her in the middle, their lips colliding with the need to communicate a decade of pain and regret and longing. With his lips on hers and his hands tangled in her hair behind her head, none of that seemed to matter.

He wanted this kiss—this moment—to last forever. But as his body awakened with feelings he had long ignored, he pulled away.

Don't rush this, he reminded himself again. *Take your time and do it right.*

He took a breath and took her hand again. "That was . . . wow." He shook his head in wonder and cupped her jaw in one hand. "I missed you, Delanie Fletcher."

She searched his soul, her face only inches away. "After all this time, I can't believe it. I . . ." She leaned back, looking away. "I can't do this. I have a life in Vancouver, Caleb. I have to go back there. And you have Emma, so coming with me isn't even an option this time. What are we doing?"

She was right. All of her objections were the same ones that had kept him from reaching out to her after he and Monica had divorced, and that had been screaming at him ever since he had seen Delanie chatting with his daughter in Mackenzie Playhouse a little over a week ago.

But right now, he didn't care.

"Aren't you the one who believes that things always work out in the end?" he asked. "Maybe it's time you had a little faith."

She looked at him pleadingly. "I don't know, Caleb. I'm not sure I can go through that heartbreak again. Getting over you was hard enough the first time."

He pressed his lips together and glanced out the window. Dusk had receded to the deep velvet blue of night. Above the river, high enough that the street lights couldn't overwhelm it, glowed the North Star.

"Look." He pointed out the window and got to his feet, pulling her up to come stand next to him at the window. "First star of the night. Make a wish."

She gave him a long, uncertain look, then glanced at the pinpoint of white light before closing her eyes for several long seconds. He stared at her, drinking in her presence, her beauty, knowing she couldn't feel uncomfortable about his gaze if she couldn't see it.

Then her eyes fluttered open, and she blushed. "Were you looking at me the whole time?"

His face warmed. "Maybe," he mumbled.

"Didn't you make a wish?" she asked.

He shook his head. "I don't need to. My wish is standing right here."

He pulled her into him and enveloped her in his arms. She stiffened, then relaxed and wrapped her arms around his waist, leaning into his chest.

"I have a confession to make, Lanie," he said. "I never got over you. Not for a single second."

After a pause, she said, "A wish isn't enough to overcome all the obstacles between us."

"No. But it's enough to make me believe we could. This time, I have no intention of letting you go anywhere without me. Whatever happens, I want to give us a fair shot."

"But what about Emma?"

"We'll figure it out."

She pulled her head back and looked up at him again. This time, their kiss was gentle and slow and sweet. The kind of kiss that says, *There's no need to hurry. We've got time.* A kiss that encompassed all of eternity and was still over too quickly. It promised that whatever the future might hold, they would face it together.

And he intended to make good on that unspoken promise.

He just had to figure out how.

Chapter 14

DELANIE KNELT ON Nan's carpeted basement floor in front of a cardboard box of old paperbacks. She finished writing *Put'n'Take* on the side with black permanent marker, then slid the marker into the back pocket of her jeans next to her phone. After closing the box, she picked it up, lifting with her legs as she stood. The rumpus room that had stored most of Pops's things for the last decade or so was nearly empty, save for a few other boxes waiting to be labelled and taken upstairs. Delanie had found a few small treasures to take back to Vancouver with her, but, mindful of her and Marie's small apartment and the limited cargo space in her car, had managed to put all but the most tempting of prizes into boxes to be passed on.

I guess Caleb could bring some things with him later.

She pushed the thought aside. Since that night at his place almost two weeks ago, she and Caleb had only had one date. He had taken her to dinner, followed by a romantic walk along the dike under the stars. Other than that, they hadn't been alone once, unless you counted a few stolen kisses behind the stage curtain at rehearsals. And they hadn't talked about what would happen when she had to leave Peace Crossing and go home to Vancouver. She wasn't ready to mar the joy of their newly restored relationship by bringing it up again just yet, and she sensed that neither was he. Deep in her heart, she feared there wasn't a real solution, and the thought made her brace for the worst.

No. He said we would figure it out. I'm sure he'll think of something. Maybe Dave and Monica will move to Vancouver too?

The thought was ridiculous, and she wasn't even sure she would want her old rival there. But if it meant she and Caleb didn't have to break up again, she would get used to it. After all, there was no way Caleb would move to Vancouver if Emma couldn't come too. While that was the right priority, she couldn't help feeling a little jealous—just once, she wanted Caleb to choose her first.

As she tramped up the last few steps of the narrow stairwell, the back of a slim woman in a delicate floral-print cotton top and light blue work slacks came into view in the kitchen. Caleb's mother, Adelaide, was bent over the sink, her hands covered with bright yellow rubber gloves, rinsing a rag in the soapy water it contained. When she heard Delanie coming, she glanced over her shoulder, her short greying brown wedge cut barely stirring with the motion.

"I'm nearly finished wiping down the cupboards. I'll start on the dining room walls next."

"Awesome," Delanie said, grunting a little with the weight of the books as she moved past Adelaide toward the living room. "Thank you so much for coming to help. I know you have plenty to do at home."

Caleb had mentioned that his dad's health had been acting up again lately, which was why he had been so preoccupied. He'd been spending his free time helping his dad bring in the harvest, which he did every year, but with his dad struggling so much, he'd barely been getting out of the tractor for rehearsals during the past week. So Delanie had been surprised when his mom had volunteered to help with the final stages of clearing out Nan's house. She suspected her mother's dramatics might have been a factor in Adelaide's decision and felt a twinge of embarrassment. *Stop it. That's between the two of them.*

Adelaide smiled, making her sky blue eyes sparkle. "It's my pleasure. I'm only sorry I couldn't have done more."

Delanie smiled. "You're doing plenty, trust me. I hate washing walls."

She set the box on top of another one also destined for the local Put'n'Take, wedging it between the faded rose-print couch—now sans slipcover—and the wall, then straightened and stretched.

She could hear her mother humming as she cleaned the bathroom down the hall. Delanie recognized the tune as a worship chorus from her days going to church as a teenager. The sound was comforting and familiar, a reminder of the unwavering faith in a place beyond death that kept her mother going even in difficult times. Delanie knew that's where her mom thought Nan and Pops were now, and was struck by a longing to know if that were true. She adored the thought of them back in each others' arms again at last. Instead of a song from church, though, the idea reminded her of the poignant Irish love song "Danny Boy"—*you will bend and tell me that you love me, and I shall sleep in peace until you come to me.*

The sound of wheels crunching on the gravel outside drew her to the living room window. Her father's bronze half-ton pickup eased to a halt, its rear end facing the sidewalk from the entrance.

"Dad's back!" Delanie called toward her mother.

"Wonderful," Cheryl responded. "Can you ask him to take the microwave with this load? That old beast isn't going to do a thing for the house when it's staged."

"Sure."

Delanie glanced around the transformed living room. The furniture was all still there, but the shelves crammed full of books had been emptied and wiped clean, ready to be artfully filled with plants and sculptures. The gallery of family photos had all been taken down, leaving a stark wall pock-marked with nicks. They would need to fill the holes and paint before the realtor would start showing the house, and, more than likely, that blank space would be filled by some cheap print bought from Walmart to increase appeal. Several piles of boxes waiting to be taken to final destinations filled the gaps between the furniture. It made Delanie sad to see all the reminders of Nan stripped from this place—it was like she was dying all over again. She sniffled and wiped away a tear.

Her dad came in the door, closing it behind him. When she sniffled again, he turned toward her in concern.

"What's the matter, Sweet Pea?"

She shook her head. "It's just . . . this place feels so empty and devoid of personality now, like we're taking Nan's spirit away, not just her things."

Her father encircled her shoulders with one strong arm and pulled her into his barrel-chested frame so he could kiss her temple. "I understand. It's hard letting go of the past sometimes. But you know we carry Nan with us in our hearts, right? We don't need her things to remember her."

"Of course." She wiped another errant tear. "I'll be fine. It just hit me, that's all. Mom wants you to take the microwave this time."

"What the queen wants, the queen gets," he said affectionately. "You okay?"

She nodded, and he smiled. Releasing her, he headed into the kitchen to retrieve the appliance.

Delanie's phone buzzed long in her back pocket, and she pulled it out, smiling when she saw Marie's face on the screen. She swiped to answer the call. "Hey, girl. What's new?"

"What's new with me? Nothing much. *You*, on the other hand," Marie said. "Holy Toledo, girl, Desmond showed me the video. It's amazing. I knew you would pull it off."

Delanie sat on the couch, relieved warmth blooming in

her chest. Thanks to Caleb's sage wisdom and a great deal of thought, she had finally found the words to smooth things over with her fans, and she had recorded it on her phone in her room yesterday morning. Then, several hours later—after it had finished uploading to the cloud on her parents' painfully slow rural Internet—she had sent it off to Desmond to edit. He had texted an hour ago to say it was done and ready to go, and she had given him the go-ahead to publish it to her YouTube account. Nothing fancy, no skit, just her talking to the camera. It was about as raw and authentic as she'd ever been on her channel, and she was more than a little nervous about how it would be received.

"Thanks," she said. "I'm glad you think I did okay."

"Not just okay. You nailed it. No pandering, no butt-kissing, you just told it like it is. You remembered who your people are, and those people are going to love it. The rest can go crawl back into the holes they were spawned in."

"I hope so." Delanie caught herself chewing a nail. She tucked the offending hand behind the arm holding her phone.

Marie's voice took on a playful tone. "So, speaking of new, how are things with Caleb?"

Marie had been victorious when Delanie had told her what Caleb had revealed about the situation with Monica all those years ago. *I knew he hadn't cheated,* she'd crowed. And ever since Delanie and Caleb had started seeing each other again, Marie had been insatiable about digging for more information about him.

"He's still fine." Delanie grinned. "You know, maybe you should come to Peace Crossing and meet him. You could come up for the play performance. Then you wouldn't have to keep grilling me for information."

"I'd love that! Then I would get to see all your hard work. And see all those amazing kids in my designs." She paused. "Isn't that the same weekend as the Starlight Gala though? I thought you were coming here."

"Oh. Right."

"You still want to stick it in Josh-the-Weasel's face, don't you?"

"Yeeaah . . ." Though that seemed less important now that she and Caleb were together again.

"And talk to Tessa Montague?" Marie prompted.

"Definitely." Delanie stuck the fingernail back between her teeth, then pulled it out and started twirling her finger in her ponytail instead. "If you came up a few days before, you could watch opening night with me and then we could head back to Vancouver together. It would be nice to have an extra driver, especially since it will be a marathon to make it back in time for the gala."

"You mean Caleb's not coming back with you?" Marie teased.

"I, um . . ." Delanie struggled to find answers she still didn't know herself. Just then, her mother gave a loud squeal, and Delanie jumped to her feet. "Sorry, Marie, something happened to my mom. Gotta go."

She ended the call without even waiting to hear her friend's goodbye and ran down the hall, meeting her father and Adelaide, who had run from the other end of the hall, outside the open bathroom door. Bill was staring through the door at his wife with an expression of mixed confusion and concern.

"What happened?" Delanie asked. She peered into the room and saw her mother holding her phone in her hand, her mouth agape.

"I've just had a call from Murray Jones, the head of Peace Valley Community Theatre."

Delanie's heart leapt to her throat. Had something happened to the hall? "Was it about the funding for the new sound board?" She hoped it was that, and not that the ancient wiring had caused a fire that sent the hall up in flames.

"He didn't mention that," Cheryl said, then paused, drawing the moment out.

"For the love of Pete, Cheryl, what is it?" Bill asked.

Cheryl met Delanie's gaze. "Murray and the board want the family's approval to name the main stage of Mackenzie Playhouse after Nan. It would be the Molly Davis Memorial Stage." Cheryl's eyes brimmed with tears. "Isn't that wonderful?"

Delanie's hands flew to her mouth. "Oh, my . . ." She rushed into the narrow bathroom and threw her arms around her mother, tears flowing down her cheeks. Then, jumping up and down like Emma would, she turned and embraced her father and Adelaide in turn as Cheryl did the same with the other, while both of them offered congratulations.

Delanie plucked a tissue from the box on the counter and dabbed the moisture from her eyes. "Nan would have loved this."

Bill snorted as he relaxed his hug around his wife, though they each kept one arm draped around the other's waist. "Are you kidding? Your grandmother would have been so embarrassed, she probably wouldn't have even attended the ceremony. They likely would have honoured her years ago, while she was still alive, if she weren't so bull-headed about this kind of thing."

"Oh, stop," Cheryl said, playfully swatting her husband's arm. "She would have been thrilled."

Adelaide chuckled. "I don't know. I noticed that dusty box full of awards that Delanie hauled out of the basement earlier. Molly wasn't one to rest on her laurels or put them on display. She would rather have been out doing something useful than talking about the things she already did. Do you remember how she reacted when she got that Lifetime Achievement in the Canadian Performing Arts award? Didn't you have to practically hog-tie her to get her to Edmonton to accept it, Cheryl?"

Cheryl laughed. "That's true, I did. She kept grumbling about how she shouldn't get an award like that until she'd actually lived her lifetime—and she was already sixty-eight. Granted, she lived another twelve years and never stopped serving the arts community, but that was my mother for you."

"Huh. I guess you're right then, Dad." Delanie hadn't even known Nan had received most of the plaques and awards in that box, which was now being stored in her parents' basement instead of Nan's. It seemed at every turn of this project, she was learning something new about her grandmother. "But it's wonderful anyway. When are they going to announce it?" she asked her mother.

Cheryl released her husband's waist and glanced at her phone as though it held the answer. "Well, I'll have to check with my siblings, of course, but I can't see any of them saying no. Murray said they thought they might do it after opening night of the play. Seems fitting, don't you think, since that's her birthday?"

Delanie's chest expanded, and more joyful tears threatened. She drew a deep, happy breath. "I think it's perfect." And if her ducks would keep lining up in a lovely little row, it would only be one high of what promised to be a very exciting weekend. Her phone vibrated with an incoming text—Marie asking if her mom was okay. "Excuse me," she said, retreating down the hall.

"Are you texting Caleb?" Adelaide called, her voice playful.

It had been impossible to keep their relationship status a secret, thanks to Emma, but Adelaide had given Delanie a warm hug and well-wishes when she had arrived today, reassuring her that she bore her no ill will for what had happened before.

Delanie's own mother had been more reserved in her congratulations when she had heard the news. In fact, Cheryl probably would have objected, but Delanie, anticipating as much, led with the information that Caleb had definitely not cheated on her. Cheryl had made a surprised sound in her throat, and when Delanie had told her they were dating again, she had said nothing other than, "And are you happy?" To which Delanie had replied in the affirmative, and Cheryl had simply said, "Okay, then."

Delanie supposed that was about as good as she could expect from her mother, even if she had hoped for more—like an apology. After all, Cheryl had been the one to plant the notion of Caleb's cheating in the first place. But while Delanie was tempted to blame Cheryl for ten years of unnecessary pain, she had soon realized there wasn't much point—she had been as quick to believe the worst of Caleb as her mother had, even though she should have known better. And whether Caleb cheated or not, his actions would have still hurt—actions which he had already apologized for. No sense beating a dead horse. Best to just move past it.

"No," Delanie said to Adelaide, "my friend Marie. To let her know my mom's okay. I didn't know why you were screaming," she explained to her mother, then hit send on the text.

She turned away to hide her embarrassment at Adelaide's good-natured teasing. As though she and Caleb were teenagers who had never been in a relationship before.

In some ways, though, it did feel a bit like being teenagers again. Like she wasn't quite sure what the rules were.

Bill shook his head and retreated down the hallway to return to his duties.

"But you're coming to Thanksgiving dinner on Sunday, right?" Adelaide asked.

"Oh." Delanie turned to face her again, uncertain how to respond. "Caleb mentioned it, but I, um . . ."

Cheryl's expression filled with hurt shock. "I thought you told me you would be home for Thanksgiving dinner since the play rehearsal is on Monday. Savannah's coming home on Saturday and everything."

"No, of course I'll be home," Delanie assured her. She turned to Adelaide. "Sorry. Thanks so much for the invitation, but I should spend that time catching up with my sister. The funeral weekend was so rushed."

Adelaide smiled. "I understand, and I'm sure Caleb will too. It would have been lovely to have you so you could reconnect with everyone though."

Delanie thought of Caleb's four siblings and their families all crammed into the dining room of the Toews farmhouse and cringed internally. What would they all have to say about her and Caleb's restored connection? "Sorry. Another time, maybe."

"Of course. There's always Christmas. That might work out better—since Monica has Emma this weekend, she'll get to be with us when you come."

Delanie blinked. Christmas? She could barely think beyond the end of October. She'd been so caught up in the play, and in fixing things with her fans, and in trying to get back into the good graces of important people in the film industry in Vancouver that it had never occurred to her this thing with Caleb would mean deciding where to spend the holidays. For potentially every holiday for the rest of their lives. At this point, they weren't even sure how they were going to make it work once she went home in a few weeks. And how was that fair to him? Or Emma? Or any of his family?

"O-of course," she stammered with a stiff smile.

Cheryl gave Adelaide a sharp gaze. "Maybe Caleb should come to our place this weekend then. If Christmas is already spoken for, I mean."

Adelaide pressed her lips together. "I suppose that makes sense," she said slowly.

"Um, I'll ask him." Delanie looked between the two women, taking in Adelaide's pensive expression and her mother's victorious smile. Just what she needed—to be the cause for more tension between them. "I have to go get some more boxes for Dad to take on this load. Excuse me."

With that, she fled back down to the basement. Sorting out

Nan's things had been a massive chore. But it suddenly looked like a cakewalk compared to sorting out the mess she had made of her love life—*all because I jumped to conclusions.* Even if those conclusions had been prompted by her mother's overt suggestion in the first place. She thought of the hubbub around her Nathan Tait videos and chewed the inside of her lip. Just because she had made that mistake with Caleb didn't mean she had been wrong about the actor. And even if she was, would that resolve the uproar her fans had created because of it?

She snorted. *Hardly.*

But still, something niggled inside her chest. What if she *had* been wrong? Even if she hadn't been, what gave her the right to stand in judgement of him and his personal life? Could she truly claim to be so much better than Nathan after dumping Caleb and going off to Vancouver without a moment's thought about the devastated boy she had left behind?

And what would happen when she had to leave Peace Crossing again? Would he come with her this time?

Will he choose me first?

She shook her head and wiped away another tear. How could she even think such a thing? He wouldn't leave Emma, and she didn't want him to. Which meant . . .

Which meant she would soon have a choice to make. Again. And what would she choose this time—love or her dreams?

Can't I have both?

Opening another dusty box of her grandmother's things to check the contents, she found several shoe boxes inside. Lifting the lid of one of them, she discovered loose photographs that must not have made the cut for Molly's albums. On top was a black-and-white photo of Nan and Pops in their middle years, standing next to some people Delanie didn't recognize but whom they had obviously cared enough about to record the moment with. The other woman's closed eyelids explained why the photo languished in this box instead of being secured in one of Nan's albums.

"Oh, Nan," Delanie said in despair, gazing at yet more evidence of a life well lived. "I wish you were here to tell me what to do."

But the only response was the doubt inside her own heart.

Chapter 15

DELANIE HURRIED TO open her parents' front door as fast as her black patent pumps permitted. Caleb stood on the covered stoop in a wool-lined denim jacket, hunched slightly against the biting wind. His amber eyes lit up when he saw her, and warmth bloomed in her chest. Thick grey clouds covered the sky from horizon to horizon, threatening snow, and the stiff breeze pushed brown leaves over the mostly green lawn, moaning through the needles of the large spruce in the centre of the yard. On the far edge of the lawn, a tall, bushy hedge obscured the view of the gravel road beyond.

Delanie smiled warmly as Caleb came in the door. "I'm so glad you could make it," she said in a low voice, closing the door behind him. "It'll take the heat off of me for the afternoon."

He swept her with his gaze, taking in her Thanksgiving ensemble. She smoothed the vintage floral apron she wore over her black sheath dress—the apron, a treasure from Nan's collection; the dress, one of the few nice outfits she had with her. A French twist contained her long blond waves.

He leaned over to kiss her. "You look nice."

"Thank you." Her face warmed. Maybe he hadn't noticed that it was the same dress she had worn at Nan's funeral. Or maybe he didn't care. She pointed at the heavy-looking black cloth grocery bag he held. "Is that your contribution?"

Caleb passed it into her waiting hands. "As requested."

While Caleb took off his jacket to reveal a button-down black shirt and striped pumpkin-orange tie, Delanie peeked inside the bag. Sure enough, there were the jar of dill pickles and the bag of dinner rolls her mom had assigned Caleb when he'd asked what he could bring. But underneath the rolls was a circular container covered with aluminum foil.

"What's this?" she asked, feeling the container through the bottom of the bag.

He grinned, hanging his jacket on one of the entranceway hooks. "I'm sure Cheryl was only trying to keep expectations low for the bachelor when she gave me grocery-store items, but I thought I'd bring a little something of my own to contribute."

Delanie raised a questioning eyebrow. "The suspense is killing me."

He leaned close to her and whispered, "Pumpkin cheesecake. My specialty."

His breath on her ear sent a shiver up her spine. She grinned at him and shook her head.

"You're just full of surprises, aren't you, Caleb Toews?"

"I try. I would have made the rolls, too, but Dad needed some help on the farm yesterday, and I ran out of time." He put his boots on the mat beneath his coat and followed her into the kitchen.

"Look who I found," Delanie said, setting the bag on the butcher block island. "And he came bearing gifts."

She withdrew the pickles and buns, and Caleb pulled out the cheesecake. Savannah stood at the counter on the far side of the kitchen whipping potatoes. Her cute black-and-silver knee-length dress was protected by a frilly gingham apron—another one of Nan's—tied around her long, slender waist, and her dark brown hair spiralled down her back from a high ponytail. She turned off the mixer and glanced over her shoulder at the newcomer. "Hey, Caleb. Nice to see you."

Cheryl came over from the stove where she had been stirring the gravy, holding out arms clad in a boldly printed chiffon bat-wing blouse. Caleb just had time to set the cheesecake tin down on the island before Cheryl encased him in a hug as though he were a long-lost son.

"Welcome, Caleb. We're thrilled you could join us."

He recovered quickly from his surprise, patting her on the back and darting a confused grin at Delanie.

She returned an equally uncertain smile, then exchanged glances with her sister, whose eyes bulged in a *didn't see that coming* look. Since when did their mother approve of Caleb Toews?

Bill came in from the dining room, still adjusting his tie. "Is it time to carve the turkey yet? Oh, hi, Caleb."

Caleb inclined his head. "Mr. Fletcher."

Bill came over and shook Caleb's hand. "Call me Bill, son."

"Yes, sir. Bill."

As Bill went to the turkey-cutting station Cheryl directed him to, Caleb gave Delanie an embarrassed look. She stifled a snort of laughter. Some changes were hard to get used to. Like calling your high school girlfriend's father by his first name.

Dinner proceeded smoothly, and Caleb soon fit in like one of the family. He never tried to ingratiate himself to her parents, but he took such a genuine interest in each person at the table that they couldn't help but open up to him. Surprisingly, Savannah seemed the most reserved, watching and listening to the conversation while she quietly ate her meal. But when he commiserated with her about the long hours she worked as a medical intern, saying it reminded him of harvest time on the farm without the relative peace of sitting in a tractor cab or getting to watch the sunset, even Savannah warmed up to him.

Delanie watched him laugh and joke with her family as though he had always been a part of it and wondered what

Thanksgiving would have been like if she'd brought Josh Rosenburg home to dinner. *He would have stuck out like a sore thumb.* And the more Josh would have tried to ingratiate himself to her family, the worse he would have made it—the Fletchers had very little patience for flattery, which was almost the only language Josh spoke.

Looking back on their relationship now, she could hardly believe she'd dated him for as long as she had and hadn't noticed. *That's three years I'll never get back.* When had she lost the knack of noticing when someone was a fake? Had the superficiality that often pervaded the film industry permeated her so completely? Or had she just been that desperate to impress someone that she took whatever she could get?

She gave Caleb a sidelong glance, taking in his rugged profile as he listened to her father tell a funny story one of the guys at the machine shop had told him yesterday. Was it fair to compare Josh to Caleb? After all, how much better would Caleb fit into her world in Vancouver, with its parties and press conferences and weekends spent thrifting before a night at the theatre? Could she truly picture him feeling at home there? *Maybe. I hope so.*

She fidgeted with her fingernail under the tablecloth. He had wanted to come with her once. Why wouldn't he be able to make a home there now?

"So, Caleb," Bill said, changing the subject, "Delanie tells me you're considering a move to Vancouver. That's a big change."

"What?" exclaimed Cheryl, blinking first at her husband, then Caleb, then Delanie. "Moving to Vancouver? Since when?"

"Nothing's been decided yet," Caleb said, giving Delanie a look of consternation. "I've got my daughter to consider, and I still need to figure out how I'm going to make that work."

"We're taking it one step at a time, Dad." Delanie glanced at Caleb apologetically. *Sorry,* she mouthed. When her father had asked her how she and Caleb planned to date long distance, she'd mentioned her hope that Caleb might move to Vancouver if things worked out. She hadn't thought he would bring it up before she and Caleb even knew what they were doing. Would Caleb think she was pressuring him?

"That's sensible, Caleb," Bill said. "I admire your sense of responsibility."

Cheryl pierced a glazed baby carrot, glaring at it as though it might try to escape. "In my day, the woman didn't expect her beau to move across the country for her. *She* was the one to make concessions."

Delanie gaped at her mother. "I guess it's a good thing the world has progressed past *Mad Men* then, isn't it?"

Cheryl transferred her glare to her daughter. "Is it so crazy to think you might want to stay here in Peace Crossing? After all, what have you got to go back to? A tiny apartment and no job? A fickle mob who ruined your career over something someone else did?"

Delanie's jaw dropped. "I . . ."

But she had no words to follow the one she had managed to choke out. Savannah had frozen with a forkful of turkey slathered in cranberry sauce halfway to her mouth, watching the proceedings with tense interest. Caleb met Delanie's eye, his jaw working. Delanie wanted the floor to swallow her up.

"Now, Cheryl," Bill began, but his wife cut him off.

"No, Bill, she needs to hear this." Cheryl's gaze swivelled back to Delanie. "It's time you woke up and grew up, Delanie. You're busy chasing dreams, and in the meantime, life is passing you by. So you go back, and what? In another ten years, you may have had some success, but, most likely, you'll be looking back at another decade of jobs that didn't quite turn out how you wanted them to. And who will be there for you then? Who will look after you? If you leave Peace Crossing this time, you're throwing your life away. And I don't want to watch it."

She glanced around and saw everyone staring at her in

open-mouthed shock. "Excuse me."

Cheryl pushed her chair away from the table and retreated to the hallway. Her footsteps thumped up the stairs, followed by the sound of a door slamming.

Delanie's face burned, and tears prickled behind her eyes.

Bill swallowed, then turned to Delanie. "Sweet Pea, you'll have to excuse your mother. Since Nan died, she's been a little—"

Delanie stood abruptly, cutting her father off. "Sorry, Dad. I just . . . I just need some air."

Caleb had risen to his feet when she did, and as she fled to the front hall and ripped her coat from a hanger in the closet, she heard him excusing himself and following behind her. She thought he would try to talk her into coming back to the dining room. So when she felt him take her coat and hold it up behind her so she could put her second arm into it instead, she glanced over her shoulder in surprise.

"Thanks." She turned to face him as she buttoned.

"Do you want to go for a drive?" he asked quietly.

She gave him a weak smile. "I'd love that."

CALEB KEPT BOTH hands on the steering wheel, occasionally glancing across the dark truck cab at Delanie. She hadn't said a thing since he'd helped her up into the truck—a tricky climb in heels and a slim skirt. She had only stared through the window at the thick, fluffy flakes that had started falling during dinner. He turned onto the highway and headed toward town. She glanced his direction, and he offered her his hand. Giving him a strained smile, she slid her slender fingers between his and they rested their hands between them on the console.

When Caleb pulled up in front of the dark Mackenzie Playhouse on a street that was completely deserted of cars,

Delanie blinked at him in surprise.

"Haven't we been spending enough time here lately?"

He quirked his mouth at her. "I thought it might be a good place to calm down."

Delanie hesitated, then nodded. "Okay."

She clutched his arm through his coat as they made their way to the door through swirling snow. There wasn't any ice on the ground yet, but he didn't think she was leaning on him because of treacherous conditions. And he liked being the one she wanted to lean on when she was upset.

After they unlocked the door and went inside, he led the way into the main auditorium and turned on the lights, then climbed the steps to the stage and turned on a rack of floodlights. The stage was empty save the painted backdrop hanging from the scaffolding above that displayed the Act One background of an Italian village street. Delanie came to stand next to him and wove her fingers between his as she surveyed the piece.

"Samantha's done a great job with the painting, hasn't she?"

"Yeah. I hear Ainsley has been helping her."

"Like mother, like daughter."

"Indeed."

They stood there in silence, and Caleb wondered if Delanie was thinking about her own mother, and how much alike the two of them were, or weren't. For his part, Caleb could see the same stubborn determination in both women . . . but he doubted Cheryl had ever exercised hers in pursuit of anything riskier than her eccentric fashion choices. Not like Delanie, who only saw mountains as hills she hadn't climbed yet.

Delanie pulled away and walked to the centre of the stage. "Do you remember our first kiss?"

Caleb's heart stuttered. "How could I forget?" It had been Grade Eleven, and he'd already had a crush on Delanie from afar for at least a year. "I could hardly believe my luck when I got cast as Harold Hill in *The Music Man*. But when you got cast as Marian?" He shook his head. "You know, I was able to play glib-tongued Harold just fine, but I never did have his knack with words in real life."

She grinned. "Your lips communicated pretty well without them."

Caleb chuckled as he remembered how he had snuck their first kiss while hiding in plain sight. In one scene, they were supposed to kiss, which actually meant they would lean close together while he shielded their faces from the audience by holding up his straw hat. One night during rehearsal, frustrated that he had been unable to tell Delanie how he felt about her, he'd given her a quick peck on the lips behind the hat.

"I believe you were standing right about here." He guided her a few steps over from where she was. "And I was here." He positioned himself in front of her and placed his hands on her hips.

She tilted her head to look up at him, draping her arms around his neck. "This seems about right."

He lowered his mouth to hers for a kiss decidedly longer than the first one they had shared.

When they broke the kiss, she grinned. "Little did you know all those times when we sang *'Til There Was You* during rehearsals, you had stolen my heart for real." She moved her arms to encircle his waist beneath his open jacket, then leaned her head against his chest.

He wrapped his arms around her, the wool of her red pea coat soft against his skin. Quietly, he started singing and swaying with the music. "There were bells on the hill, but, um, something, something, ringing . . ."

She chuckled, and he fumbled through the next line, her sweet voice joining in on the title hook of *'Til There Was You*. Since he had forgotten most of the lyrics, he switched to humming, and they swayed back and forth on the stage for several minutes. As they reached the last bars, he heard her sniffle. She pulled back, her face contorted in pain and remorse.

"Not my dancing's fault, I hope," he said, trying to lighten the mood. He was rewarded by a smile breaking through her tears, and she shook her head, wiping her face and ducking away from him. He stepped toward her and lifted her chin so she would look at him. "Your mom's wrong, you know."

She studied him, then pulled away, wrapping her arms around herself. "That's the problem. She's right. Everything she said to me, I've been thinking for weeks. What am I doing with my life, Caleb?"

She went over to the front of the stage and sat down, her legs dangling over the edge. Caleb joined her, looking out at the dimly lit auditorium and the rows upon rows of folded red theatre seats.

"You know what Mom's reaction was when I told her I want-ed to go to acting school?" Delanie didn't wait for him to reply before continuing. "She tried to get me to become a teacher first so I would have something to fall back on."

Caleb snorted. "My dad wasn't exactly fired up about me be-coming a screenwriter either."

Looking back on it now, though, he wasn't sure how much of that had been his own dream, and how much had been Dela-nie's. He loved Peace Crossing. He would be quite content to live there until he died, if circumstances permitted. She had been the one who couldn't wait to *escape*, as she had put it.

"But at least he never tried to stop you. It's not like he got sick on purpose." Delanie sighed. "Ever since I was a little girl, long before I was Marian the Librarian, all I ever wanted was this." She gestured around the empty hall. "To be on the stage and bring people joy through the stories I helped tell. I thought by now, I'd have won an Oscar at least."

She gave him a wry grin, and he chuckled.

"But things haven't quite worked out the way I planned," she continued. "Maybe it's time I grow up, like Mom said."

"You know, maybe you're right."

Her gaze snapped to his and she blinked. "Pardon?"

"You do need to act like a grown-up."

As her brow furrowed, he quickly explained. "One of the things Monica and I have agreed on as co-parents to Emma is that we will encourage her to develop whatever she shows an interest in. But sometimes that means she needs to commit to things, like a full year of voice lessons at a time, and she doesn't get to quit just because it gets hard or she's not progressing as quickly as she wants. Because when she grows up, we want her to know that she can accomplish anything she sets her mind to, as long as she doesn't give up. *That's* what grown-ups do. They keep going, even when things are tough."

Delanie pursed her lips. "But they also know when it's time to stop pursuing a fruitless effort. That's probably the harder skill to develop."

He nodded. "True. But are you at that point? I mean, it's not like you've accomplished nothing in the last decade. These things take time." *No matter what your mom says.* "And there *are* people who believe in you and support you. Like your patrons, right?"

She nodded, wiping away another errant tear. "Yeah, that's true. Some of them even came back this week after I posted that video."

"See? It's not just me who believes in you."

She tilted her head up at him, her brow furrowed. "Why do you?"

"Why do I what?"

"After all these years, and after what I did to you, why do you still believe in me so much?"

He swallowed, staring into the dark pools of her eyes. "Because of who you are on the stage. You . . . you come alive while you perform, Delanie. I mean, you're always full of life, but when you're performing, it's like you glow with your own light. The first time I saw you huffing at me as an exasperated Marian Paroo, I knew this was what you were meant to do. You're a natural."

"Is that why you never tried to stop me from going?"

He stroked her jaw with the back of his fingers, relishing the soft curve. "Did you want me to?"

She glanced down. "No. I would have been furious if you had tried. I was so focused on my plan, I couldn't imagine doing it another way."

"That's why I never tried to stop you. And that's the determination that's going to make sure you succeed. This is just a temporary setback."

She scooted closer to him and he wrapped one arm around her. She leaned into his shoulder. "But what about you? Did you talk to Monica about Emma yet?"

His throat closed. "Uh, no. There hasn't been a good time." And he still wasn't sure what he was going to say. It was no more fair for him to ask Monica to let him take Emma to Vancouver with him than it would be if *she* left Peace Crossing and wanted to take Emma. He couldn't do that to her. But what he *would* do, he still didn't know.

She nodded. "Well, there's no rush, I guess. I mean, we've only been dating for a couple of weeks. It's too early to make rash decisions."

His breath caught. "Are you having second thoughts about us?"

She turned her head to look up at him. "No. Of course not. I just . . . I don't want to put you in a position where you have to choose between us. Between me and Emma, I mean. I know Emma will always come first, and that's the way it should be. But you have to know something—my Nan gave up her career to marry Pops and move to Peace Crossing, and I think she always regretted it. I don't want to live with that same regret."

He looked at her, his heart breaking with the certainty that she was right—Emma held the primary place in his heart. But it seemed that Delanie's career held that place in hers. And neither one of them wanted the other to change their priorities.

Or did he? The thought of Delanie going back to Vancouver without him again made his chest ache. But could he bear leaving Emma behind to make sure he and Delanie lived happily ever after?

"I don't want you to give up your dreams for me, Delanie. You would always resent me for it, and that's not what I want from you." He pulled her close to him, tucking her head beneath his chin. "I'll talk to Monica. We'll figure something out. I told you, I don't want to lose you again."

"Okay." The only sound was their breathing. Then, "Caleb?"

"Yeah?"

"I don't want to lose you either."

She lifted her mouth to his for a kiss. Then she laid her head against his shoulder and they cuddled on the stage until their posteriors ached, while Caleb contemplated if there actually was any way out of the impossible situation they found themselves in.

He was startled by Delanie sitting up suddenly, her attention focused on the small window leading to the sound booth at the back of the hall.

"What is it?" he asked, following her gaze in concern but finding nothing out of the ordinary. He looked back at her to see her eyes sparkling almost as much as when she was performing.

"I just figured out how we're going to fix our sound board and wiring issues."

"And how's that?"

She turned to him, her face alight. "We're going to make a fundraising video. We'll get the kids to help us, and I'll post it on my channel and tell all my patrons about it. Maybe we can even use one of the songs from the play—then the kids won't have to learn something new." She looked up at him, her whole body emanating joyful, positive energy. It was as though the conversation with her mother hadn't even happened. "I just have to talk to the parents. Oh, Caleb, this is going to work, I know it." She noticed his expression and pulled back, trepidation tainting her joy. "What?"

He shook his head in amazement, then leaned over and kissed her. "That's my girl," he said against her lips.

Smiling, she leaned into his kiss and wrapped her arms around him. And they didn't pull apart for a very long time.

Chapter 16

CALEB SAT NEAR the back of the dimly lit Mackenzie Playhouse theatre during Sunday rehearsal, relishing the break from constant activity. In one hand, he held a Butler Bros. Construction travel mug—a gift from Noel—that contained a homemade cappuccino to combat his exhaustion. His other hand rested on the spiral notebook balanced on his knee. The page was half-filled with a list of play-related tasks for the week in his scratchy handwriting, and his pen remained poised but still above it.

Harvest had been wrapped up earlier in the week, but he had spent the day before helping Delanie shoot her music video with the kids. The constant push of being on the go had taken its toll, and he fought his heavy eyelids. But in only two more weeks, the play would be over. He could survive this hectic schedule for that long.

Only two more weeks and Delanie will be going back to Vancouver.

He pushed the thought away. No sense dwelling on the future at the expense of enjoyment of the present.

Onstage, his daughter quipped a line, then seamlessly started into her solo, supported by a chorus of townsfolk and the accompaniment of the handful of musicians set up on the floor in front of the stage. Emma had exceeded even his expectations of her abilities, and from what she had told him, he wouldn't be surprised if acting and the theatre became a lifelong passion of hers. Especially with Delanie's input and influence, and under the continued guidance of Violet Butler. The spritely music teacher stood in front of centre stage where she could direct both the kids singing above her and the musicians crammed into the narrow space between the stage and front row on either side of her.

Delanie stood in the third row, her back to him, with a clipboard tucked against her hip. She was watching everything intently, occasionally stopping the action to give directions to a kid who went the wrong way or for the group to check their sight-lines so no one blocked anyone else from view of the audience.

Caleb watched her, pride filling his chest. She had been so nervous about doing this, but she had risen to the challenge as much as Emma had. Even Amber seemed to be giving Delanie more respect these days, begrudging though it might be. Maybe that was due to how Celeste was killing it in her role since Delanie had been helping her out. Amber had even agreed to Celeste being part of the music video, which meant all the main cast kids—and even a few of the chorus kids—had participated. After the full day of shooting and reshooting the big musical number from the finale yesterday, the kids were super confident. Not only with their number, "Every Star that Shines", but in their parts and with each other. It was nice to see—even if Caleb wasn't the only one whose energy seemed a little low this afternoon.

He took another sip of coffee. There were few things more satisfying than a well-made cup of cappuccino, but seeing people he cared about live up to their potential was one of them.

Someone slid into the seat next to him, and he turned to see Monica settling into the chair.

"Hey," he greeted her.

"Hey." She looked at the stage, her attention on Emma. "She's doing great, isn't she?"

"Better than. She looks like she was born to be there."

Monica nodded, continuing to watch Emma sing and dance, but her gaze seemed to be looking right through her.

"Everything okay?" Caleb said. "You look distracted."

She glanced at him with a tight smile. "Actually, there's something I need to talk to you about."

His gut clenched. What now? "Okay, shoot."

Monica gave Emma one last glance, then twisted to face him. "Dave got a call from his mom last night. His dad isn't doing so great. She was wondering if Dave would consider moving home to help run the body shop and eventually take it over."

Caleb's chest tightened. "Move home? Doesn't his family live in Ontario?"

Monica nodded. "Brampton." She fidgeted with her engagement ring. "We talked about it, and he said yes. We're moving."

Caleb's heart reared and kicked him in the throat. "And what about Emma? She needs her mom, Monica. You're going to leave her behind?"

She shook her head. "That's why we need to talk. I . . . I want to take Emma with me, Caleb. I hope you understand."

Heat flooded through Caleb. Monica wanted to take his daughter and move to Ontario? He put his travel mug in the chair's cup holder and turned to face her. "She needs her dad too," he said through gritted teeth. "How can you do this to her? To me?"

His conscience pricked him—hadn't he been considering asking her a similar question about Emma, except to move in the opposite direction? But right now, all he could think about was that Emma might be moving across the country, away from him. And Brampton was a lot farther away than Vancouver.

"You could come too," Monica suggested. "I'm sure there are plenty of electrician jobs out there."

"The trades don't pay nearly as well out east, and you know it." He clenched his jaw and stared at the stage. Emma finished her song and Delanie directed the kids to move offstage so the next scene could be run. "This is about Delanie, isn't it? You're upset that we're together again, so you're giving me an impossible decision."

Monica gave him a hurt look. "You think I'm making this up just to break up you and Delanie? Come on, Caleb, you know me better than that. I know you might find this hard to believe, but I do actually want you to be happy. And if that's with Delanie, then that's the way it is." She glanced toward Delanie. "You two were practically written in the stars, much as I hate to admit it."

"Sorry, I'm just . . ." He floundered for words. "I'm not sure what to say. I was already facing a hard choice, but it has now gone from hard to impossible."

"What do you mean?"

"Delanie. Emma. Mom and Dad. I'm worried about Dad—he hasn't been doing so well again lately. This harvest was hard on him, I could tell. I had thought I could make things with Delanie work for a while by us travelling back and forth regularly so I could still see Emma and help at the farm, but that was a stretch even between Vancouver and Peace Crossing. Ontario might as well be on another planet. And you just want me to lay down and let Emma go?"

Monica's face hardened. "I'm not giving her up either, Caleb. You're a good dad, and I want you to continue being part of her life. But I'm her mom. You and I both know that if you fight this, the courts will award her to me. I was hoping we could find an amicable solution without having to resort to lawyers. We've always been able to resolve things in the past."

"Most things," he said, looking at her sideways. If their conflict resolution skills were truly up to snuff, he couldn't help but think they would still be together.

Then again, he couldn't have pretended emotions he didn't have—he wasn't that good of an actor. He had cared for Monica, but he'd never loved her—not with a whole-hearted, I'd-do-anything-for-you sort of love. Not the way he loved Emma. Or Delanie. And Monica had sensed it. When she had told him she wanted a divorce, he'd tried to convince her to stick it out for Emma's sake, but in his heart, he couldn't blame her for leaving. And they had been able to work out a peaceful co-parenting solution he'd always been happy with.

Until now.

Now, his blood ran cold when he realized Monica was right. If he fought this, she would end up with Emma anyway and it would only cause bad blood between them.

"It doesn't sound like I have much of a choice," he muttered.

She gave him a look of mixed regret and resolve. "No. I'm sorry, but you don't. I was hoping you would see it my way, but I'm taking Emma, either way."

She paused to watch the show, then sighed.

"I'm sorry, Caleb. I really am. But Dave is my family now. His baby deserves to know its father too. And maybe this actually works out better for both of us."

"How could that be?"

She shrugged. "If you were already planning to fly back and forth between Vancouver and Peace Crossing, flying to Ontario instead will probably cost half as much and take the same amount of time, or maybe less, without the additional hop from Edmonton to Peace Crossing in the mix."

She was right. Local flights were expensive and layovers were time-consuming. In some ways, this might make his decision easier—he could move to Vancouver with Delanie and the end result would be much the same as if he had stayed here.

But the thought of his daughter being most of the way across the country from him felt like agreeing to let Monica rip out his heart and take it to Mars. Maybe he should consider moving to Brampton after all, and fly to see Delanie instead. But that left his dad stuck with the farm alone again, and with the way Marcus's health had been regressing lately, Caleb couldn't do that to him.

"Did you ask Emma what she wants?"

Monica frowned. "I hardly think that's a fair burden to give a nine-year-old. Choosing between her parents? I had hoped we could come up with an arrangement first and just tell her."

"Are you afraid she'd pick me?" He knew he sounded childish, but anger and the fear of losing his daughter had made him petty.

Anger flashed through Monica's eyes. "I'm not going to ask her to pick anyone. It's not her decision. We're her parents, we get to decide what's best. And I hope you'll see that what's best is for her to stay with her mother."

Caleb clenched the pen in his fist. "But what if it's not? I'm not her only family here, Monica, which was something I'd already been factoring in while wrestling with my *other* decision. She has two sets of grandparents here, plus all her friends and a school she loves. And this." He indicated the theatre with a wave. "Small towns present opportunities that big cities do not."

"And the opposite is also true. You know that." Her expression softened. "Nothing about this is easy, Caleb. But the hard choice is often the right one. You of all people should know that."

He pressed his lips together, a maelstrom in his chest. When he said nothing else, Monica stood.

"I should get back downstairs to help make fairy crowns."

He grunted a response, and she retreated down the row and headed toward the stairs at the back of the hall.

He returned to watching the love of his life direct the rehearsal. Emma was sitting in the front row of the side section of seats with her head down, working on a friendship bracelet that was pinned to her tights. She glanced up and saw him looking at her, responding with a happy wave. He smiled and waved back, and she went back to her knot-tying.

Caleb felt like he was being torn in two. No matter what he chose—follow Emma, or follow Delanie—he would be leaving half his heart with the other. And who would help with the farm if he left? Neither of his brothers-in-law were farmers. They wouldn't have the first clue. And Isaac had never wanted to be a farmer. As soon as he had finished his engineering degree, he'd gotten a job with an oil company and had worked out of their Calgary headquarters for the last three years. The last thing he would want to do was give that up to move back to Peace Crossing so he could milk cows and bale hay.

Caleb pressed his palms into his eyes. *Why, God? Why can't anything be easy for once?*

Chapter 17

DELANIE SAT AT her parent's kitchen table with her laptop open before her, her heart pounding with excitement. After supper had been cleaned up, her parents had gone to the next room to watch TV, and she had decided to catch up on email while she waited for Caleb to pick her up for a coffee date at Tim Hortons. She read Tessa's email again, hardly daring to breathe.

Dear Ms. Fletcher,

Marie Daramola gave me your email address and said it would be fine to contact you this way. She mentioned your work with your local community theatre, a subject about which I am also passionate. I am working on a new project to benefit community theatre groups and develop young actors that I think you would be perfect for, and I would love to have a meeting to discuss the particulars. The project is experimental and the budget won't be large, but if all goes well, it could lead to future work for both of us.

I look forward to hearing back from you soonest.

Sincerely,

Tessa Montague

Balcony Pictures

P. S. I admire how you handled the recent furor over your Nathan Tait videos. This industry needs more people with that kind of backbone. Stand up and be seen, I say. Bravo.

P. P. S. I noticed your campaign to raise funds for a new sound system at your local theatre. My donation will be forthcoming promptly, and I shall be sure to tell my friends.
  P. P. P. S. I am sorry for the loss of your grandmother.

Delanie breathed deeply a few times to calm her racing heart and took a sip of water. She could hardly wait to tell Caleb about this.

Quickly backing out of Tessa's email, she clicked on the email notification that had come in right after from her fundraising platform and gawked at the number. Not only would they now be able to afford a new sound board, but for that amount, plus the funds that had been steadily coming in since Desmond posted her latest video, she could talk to Murray about finally replacing the medieval wiring that caused so many problems with feedback and hum during performances. Clicking back into Tessa's email, she hit *Reply* and added her agent, Sandra Sanderson, on the carbon copy line.

Dear Ms. Montague,
  Thank you so much for your generous contribution to my fundraiser. It will go a long way to improving the facility in my hometown of Peace Crossing. I would be thrilled to discuss your idea with you. I have long been an admirer of your work, and would welcome a collaboration, especially for a cause so close to my heart. I have looped my agent into this thread, and she can arrange a meeting at your earliest convenience.

She stopped and chewed her nail, trying to think if there was more to say. After a sentence explaining that she was still in Peace Crossing so the meeting would have to be done online, she signed her name, then added a post script of her own.

P. S. Thank you for your condolences, and for your encouraging words. I know you understand how risky creating art based on controversial opinions can be, so it means a lot coming from you. And please call me Delanie.

She read it over again. Then, holding her breath, she clicked *Send.* Bursting with excited energy, she texted Marie and Desmond the good news in their group chat.

The return text from Marie was almost immediate. *Oh my gosh! I knew she'd come through. That's amazing!*

Delanie had just typed her thanks followed by a few starry-eyed emojis when Desmond texted, *Good job. Another steak and champagne night soon?*

Delanie laughed and shook her head. Trust Desmond's brain to go straight to the celebration party.

We should have something concrete to celebrate first. Will keep u posted.

Desmond sent a thumbs-up, and Marie sent a GIF of a baby dancing.

Her phone blared the opening bars of "There's No Business Like Show Business", and she blinked at the name *Sandra Sanderson* in surprise. It seemed a little late for her agent to be at work. Then again, it was an hour earlier on the coast where Sandra was, and Sandra did seem to be a bit of a night owl. Maybe she had something to say about the offer.

"Hello?" Delanie said.

"Well, that's an interesting proposition," Sandra said without preamble. "Came at an interesting time too. I was about to call you even before I got the email notification."

"You were? Why?"

"All kinds of *interesting* things have happened today. I got a call from Joshua Rosenburg that he's been trying to get a hold of you, but you haven't been returning his calls? Not that I blame you, mind you. But it turns out, he did have something to say besides making excuses for himself."

Delanie leaned back in her chair, her gut tensing. "And what was that?"

"Turns out the folks at *Trueheart* want you back. According to Rosenburg, they have *reviewed the situation, and they admit to being too hasty in their judgement.* Which is a first for me. What did you say to him anyway?"

Delanie's head started spinning. She could have her role as Maryanne back? What was happening?

"I, uh, didn't say much. Mostly, I broke up with him and have been ignoring him ever since."

Except that one time a couple weeks ago when she had accidentally answered the phone without looking at the caller ID. After getting frustrated when Josh kept trying to convince her they could work it out between them—he had even claimed that Kaitlyn Williams meant nothing to him—she had told him she was dating someone else. Could he have been so determined to get her back that he'd actually gotten her job back for her?

She frowned. "Haven't they started filming *Trueheart* already?"

"Yeah, but the replacement wasn't working out. They're willing to reshoot her scenes with you if you could start on Monday."

"I see." Josh had probably dumped Kaitlyn as casually as he'd started dating her. What had Delanie ever seen in that human toadstool?

But she didn't have to date him, or even like him, to work with him. A role on *Trueheart* would still be a fabulous career boost—but it was shooting on location near Kamloops, a good eleven-hour drive from Peace Crossing. It wasn't like she could just commute until she was done with the play. "I have commitments here for two more weeks. Are they flexible at all?"

"I don't know, hun. They're already sliding you in late. But I'll ask 'em, if that's what you want me to do."

"Yes, please."

"And what about the thing with Montague?" Crinkling plastic came through the line, and Delanie imagined Sandra unwrapping a candy and popping it in her mouth. Her agent was addicted to caramels.

"Please set up a video chat meeting for anytime during the day this week. I'll think about the *Trueheart* thing, but I'm not sure I'm ready to run back the instant Josh snaps his fingers."

"Good for you, hun." Sandra's words were slightly garbled by the candy. "But also, you know what an opportunity this is. I wouldn't waste it, if I were you."

"I'm aware," Delanie said dryly.

"Okay. I'll let you know how it goes."

"Thanks."

"And Delanie?"

"Yes?"

"Way to beat the mob, hun."

The line went silent, and Delanie pulled the phone away from her ear, watching the screen as her agent's photo faded to black.

"Huh."

Sandra was right. It *had* been an interesting day. She had spent most of it texting back and forth with Amber and Caleb and reviewing last-minute things for the play. With the performance dates coming up fast—opening night was only ten days away—it seemed like there was way too much left to do. Maybe when Marie came next Wednesday, she could help with the last-minute prep work.

Delanie swallowed. The impending performance meant her return to Vancouver—or Kamloops—would be here before she knew it. Which meant she and Caleb should talk about what they would do after she left. She wondered if he might come out just for the gala, even if he couldn't stay in the city long. It would be fantastic to see Josh's face when she walked in with her new man on her arm.

She shook her head. Josh was in the past. And if she worked with him again, it would be because it was a good decision for her career and nothing else. But she wasn't sure she wanted to. After the email from Tessa and the talk with Sandra, she wondered if her name might have less of a black mark in industry circles than he had led her to believe. And what kind of project did Tessa have in mind?

"Caleb's here," called her dad from the living room.

"Thanks, Dad," Delanie called back.

She closed her laptop and moved it to a side counter, then hurried to put on her coat and boots at the front door. By the time Caleb stood knocking on the stoop, she was ready to go. She let him in with a smile and a quick kiss, then popped her head into the living room.

"I'll be back late. Please don't wait up."

Cheryl, who had barely said two sentences to Delanie since Thanksgiving dinner a week ago, glanced sideways at her and nodded before turning back to the show, her arms wrapped around a pillow in front of her chest.

Bill glanced at his wife with a sigh, then gave his daughter a warm smile. "Have a good time, you two."

"Thanks, Dad." Delanie looked at her mother, her chest tight. "Bye."

"See you, Mr. and Mrs. . . . Bill and Cheryl," Caleb finished, then opened the door for Delanie while rolling his eyes at himself, which made her giggle.

Despite the tension that seeped out of the house behind her, she couldn't help but bounce a little as she took Caleb's hand and followed him out to the truck.

"That's a big smile," he said as he helped her into the cab. "What's up?"

"I've got some big news," she said.

He raised his brows. "Yeah? Sounds like we'll have a lot to talk about."

He closed the door and went around the front of the truck to the driver's side. He seemed tense, and there was something reserved about his manner.

Delanie bit her lip as she watched him climb behind the wheel, her stomach sinking. She couldn't shake the feeling that she wasn't the only one with something important to say, but whatever was bothering him wasn't going to be good news. Maybe he had decided that long distance wasn't going to work after all. That Emma and his life here were too important for him to leave behind. Would this coffee date be their prom night all over again?

Her heart sped up with the revving of the engine. As he pulled out of her parents' driveway and turned toward town, she drew a deep breath.

It could be nothing. But after all the good news she had just received, why did she feel like she should brace for the worst?

Chapter 18

CALEB FIDGETED WITH the paper Tim Hortons coffee cup on the table before him, listening to what Delanie was sharing about her new job prospects with a sinking heart. When she finished telling him about the email from Tessa Montague and the call from her agent, she smiled.

"So, what do you think?" She took a sip of her hot chocolate.

What do I think? I don't want you to do any of that. I want you to say you'll go wherever I go so I don't have to decide between being near you and being near Emma.

He cleared his throat. "Those both sound like great opportunities. I can see why you're so excited."

"Yeeah . . ." She frowned at her red paper cup. "I guess I mean, which one do you think I should pursue?"

Caleb glanced through the window next to their booth. The sun had long set, but tall lampposts illuminated the parking lot, and their orange light gleamed off the few vehicles and the wet asphalt. A few small puddles from the light rain earlier in the day collected in the low spots, but offered him no wisdom. He turned back to Delanie.

"Do you have to choose between them? You don't even know what Tessa wants yet. Maybe you can do both." He sighed. "And I suppose if you have to leave early to start filming *Trueheart*, Amber and I can hold down the fort without you.

And Anne Erickson is out of the hospital now. If we're stuck on something, we could talk to her or Violet."

"Leave early?" She swallowed. "I mean, I guess . . ." She chewed her thumbnail, her brow furrowed. "I suppose you could come out to Vancouver later on the weekend to meet me. But if I leave early, Marie wouldn't come, and she wouldn't get to see the kids in her costumes." She sounded like she was thinking out loud.

"What weekend are you talking about?"

"Oh!" She focused on him. "It's the annual Starlight Gala, a big shindig to fundraise for Vancouver's homeless shelters, and I meant to ask if you would like to come. It's next Saturday night. Black tie. Lots of important people." She grinned slyly. "I have this great dress I think you'll love."

The thought of Delanie in an evening gown did sound appealing. But—

"Next Saturday night? During the performance weekend?"

"Yes. The announcement to honour Nan will be on Thursday night, and I'm planning to drive out on Friday with Marie. You could come with us. I think she's gonna love you." She smiled brightly.

"But we would miss four of the five performances." He frowned. Emma would be devastated. "And what if something goes wrong while we're gone?"

She sighed. "I'll admit, the timing isn't great. But once we get to opening night, our job is pretty much done—everyone knows what they're supposed to do. The parent volunteers can run everything without us. For that matter, Amber could probably run it herself. She's organized enough." She pursed her lips. "It's what she's wanted all along anyway. Besides, you literally just said I could leave early to go back to work and it would be fine."

"Yes, but I didn't mean . . ." He huffed in frustration, his gut a hard ball.

"What?" She leaned forward. "What didn't you mean?"

He looked at his cup. "I didn't mean I wanted you to."

Her lips curved slightly and she placed her hand on his. "I don't want to leave early either. But this is my chance. Going to that gala will show everyone in the industry that I didn't just lay down and let the mob slay me, that I'm still standing strong on my own two feet." She squeezed his hand. "And I want you to be there with me. I have a friend I'd like you to meet. He's interested in your script, and—"

"What?" Caleb's throat closed. He had sent Delanie his most recently finished script, an *Indiana Jones*-inspired action-adventure, in confidence. He had never meant for anyone else to see it. "Did you send that script to someone else? Without asking me?"

She stopped short, staring at him. "Yes. It's really good, Caleb. I sent it to a director I know, someone I went to school with, and he loves it. I wanted to surprise you. I . . . I thought you'd be happy. This could be your chance to do what you always wanted to do—to start your career as a screenwriter." Her eyes grew moist. "Are you mad at me?"

Seeing her on the verge of tears, he softened, ashamed that he'd let his anger get the better of him. And someone was actually interested in that script he'd only written to fill the long nights alone? Go figure.

"No, I'm not mad. I know you did it with the best of intentions. I just . . ." He ran his hand over his beard. "I'm not so sure that's the life I want anymore, Delanie. I have Emma now, and there's Dad and Mom and the farm to consider. There's a lot of uncertainty in the arts, as you know. And I actually like my job."

"You do?"

He smiled. "Yeah. I get to fix people's problems all day and work with my hands. I get most of my evenings and weekends off. And it's a steady paycheque. Those are all pretty appealing things."

"Well, I suppose you could get a job as an electrician in Vancouver. People use electricity there, I've heard. Did you talk to Monica about Emma yet?"

"Yeah. About that . . ." He rubbed both hands down his chin and drew a breath to steel himself against the reaction he knew he would get to what he was about to say. "Monica's moving to Brampton, Ontario with Dave, and she's taking Emma with her. Which means I might have to move to Ontario."

When he looked in her eyes, it was about as bad as he had expected. Her expression had gone as hard and flat as granite.

"So you're choosing her over me again."

"Her, who? Emma?"

"No. Monica." Delanie's face grew red.

He shook his head. "No, Delanie. I'm not choosing *anyone* over you. But Emma is my daughter. I thought you understood that she's my priority."

Tears brimmed in her eyes. "It doesn't matter. There's always someone else who's a priority over me. Emma, Monica, your dad. I just want you to choose me first for once, Caleb."

He gaped. "And what about you? When have you ever chosen me or the people you care about over your career? You're not even staying until the play production finishes."

A tear slid down her cheek, and she leaned closer, lowering her voice. "I thought you wanted me to pursue a career as an actress. You told me you believe in me."

"I do!" he said too loudly, attracting attention from the workers behind the counter and the people a few tables over. He took a breath and spoke more calmly. "I do. And I don't want to have to choose between you and Emma, but unless you want to come to Ontario with me or Monica changes her mind, I'm going to have to. And it sucks. But I don't want you to have to choose either. I just don't know what to do. I can't figure out a way to make this work." He took her hand. "But I promise you, Delanie. I will. *We* will. This time, we have to."

She studied him, then shook her head and pulled her hand from his. "No, Caleb. We're just lying to ourselves. There's no way we can be together without one or both of us giving up something we love. And I don't want that. I don't want either of us to resent the other for what we gave up to be together." She gathered her purse into her lap. "Maybe it's time we just called this thing off for good."

Caleb's heart slammed into this throat. "So you're just going to leave again? Go to Vancouver without me?"

"Yeah, I guess I am." She looked at him sadly. "At least we tried."

"Did you, though?" He narrowed his eyes at her, his old wound bleeding and raw. "I should have known you wouldn't give us a fair shot. Maybe you're right, Delanie. Maybe we *have* been lying to ourselves."

Her jaw fell open and she stared at him. She looked like she wanted to speak but couldn't, just like she had when Amber had confronted her during that first meeting. This time, though, he wasn't going to help her out. After a few seconds, she got up and slung her purse over her shoulder.

"Goodbye, Caleb."

She got all the way to the door before she turned around. When she reached him again, she said with a stony expression, "I came with you. Would you take me home now, please?"

In any other circumstance, he would have laughed. But not today.

Today, his laughter was drowned by the pain pouring from his broken heart.

Without a word, he grabbed his keys and followed her out the door.

Chapter 19

"I CAN'T BELIEVE Josh Rosenburg wants you back," Desmond said.

His and Marie's faces spanned Delanie's laptop monitor. The laptop itself was currently perched on her legs, which, in turn, were extended in front of her on her bed and covered with some very comfy pink microfleece lounge pants. She was glad her friends couldn't see the worn and faded pink bunny slippers she also wore, which she always left at her parents' for when she visited—and because they were actually pretty hideous, what with one of them missing an eye and the other one needing a popped seam repaired. But desperate times called for desperate measures. She probably should have cared more that her friends had caught her in her PJs at one o'clock on a Friday afternoon, but she couldn't muster the energy. Ever since her disaster of a coffee date with Caleb on Tuesday, she'd been lucky to get her hair into a messy bun unless she was leaving the house.

"I can," Marie said. "I just can't believe Delanie's going to do it."

Delanie made a face. "It's not like I'm going to date him again, Marie, just rejoin the cast of *Trueheart*. It's my best shot at getting back to where I was when this whole mess began. After everything that's happened, I kind of think I have to, don't you?"

"You most definitely do not," she snapped. "And I think you need to question whether you even should. Going back says *I don't have any options but to tuck tail and return to the hand that bit me.*"

Desmond rolled his eyes. "And not going back says *I prefer eating ramen every night for the rest of my life to acting like a mature adult.*"

Delanie gave a hollow chuckle. Desmond's comment poked the welt left by Caleb's words about giving up too quickly, something she'd been wondering if she had done once again on Tuesday. She had gotten used to being the mature one in her dating relationships. But would a mature adult have demanded Caleb give up a life with his daughter in order to support her in her career in the arts?

On the other hand, would a mature adult demand that I give up that career to be with him?

"Either way, it's too late," Delanie said. "I've already talked to Josh, and I've signed the contract. Again. Sandra even negotiated a bigger trailer for me this time. And a fuel allowance so I can go back and forth to Vancouver on my days off. She even arranged a perpetual supply of Starbucks lattes for me on set. Don't ask me how they plan to make that happen."

She chuckled. *Always ask for at least one outrageous thing,* Sandra had told her. There were more useless things she could have asked for, but she didn't want to push her luck. Thinking of lattes reminded her of Caleb's barista hobby, and regret needled her. Maybe she should have asked for an espresso machine. Using Caleb's had been kind of fun.

"I'm leaving here Sunday morning and driving out to Kamloops so I can be ready for work on Monday morning," she added.

Marie blinked, but Desmond grinned.

"Cool," he said. "Does that mean we get to do martinis next Friday night? Marie, there's that place I've been wanting to show you, remember?"

"Wait," Marie said. "What about *Pinocchio*? And Caleb? And your Nan's big award announcement? I already bought my plane ticket."

Desmond yanked his head back in surprise. "What? Marie got invited to all that and no one said a word to me?"

Delanie pursed her lips. "Sorry, Des. You would have been welcome to come too, but now it doesn't matter. And I'm sorry for the plane ticket, Marie. I'll pay you back." She sighed. She would have to tell them eventually. "Caleb and I broke up."

Desmond made an appropriately sympathetic face, but Marie gave a shocked frown. "What? Delanie, what's going on out there, girl? I thought you two had worked everything out. You sounded so happy."

Delanie swallowed the lump that had formed in her throat, adjusting her kitty tank top while she regained her equilibrium. "I thought we were. But I guess there are some differences that just can't be overcome."

"Like what?"

"I told you he has a daughter, right? Well, his ex-wife is moving to Ontario and taking Emma with her, and Caleb is planning to move out there now too. I thought Caleb and I would have been able to work something out if he only had to come back to Peace Crossing every few weeks or something. But Ontario . . . that's another story."

"There's a film industry in Ontario," Desmond said helpfully. "Why don't you move too?"

Delanie had already considered doing just that—for all of half a second before deciding against it. Even she didn't want to be that far from home. "It's too far from my parents and sister," she was surprised to hear herself say. "Besides, my network is all in BC. And now, so is my job."

"A job you might be better off without," Marie pointed out, her eyebrow raised. "I hate to agree with Desmond on this, but you might find something even better in Toronto. Or the thing with Tessa might open some new doors. And then you wouldn't have to miss the culmination of all your hard work."

Delanie stared blankly at Marie. "What do you mean?"

"The play? Plus the Molly Davis Memorial Stage announcement? C'mon, girl, you can't tell me you actually want to miss that."

"No, of course not. But if missing it means I have a regular paycheque coming in—for actually acting—then I think it's worth it. Nan would have understood."

"Mm-hmm. And what about the kids? Do they understand?"

"I . . . I haven't told them yet. I'll have Amber tell them on Sunday."

"After you've left?" Desmond gave his head a shake of disbelief. "Delanie, that's cold."

Delanie tamped down her annoyance and guilt. She had thought about telling the kids last night at rehearsal, but, if she were honest with herself, she had chickened out. "What difference does it make when I tell the kids? The end result is the same."

"So it would appear." Marie's tone was laden with meaning, but Delanie couldn't decide what her friend was trying to imply. "And Caleb? Have you told him?"

Delanie shrugged lightly. "He knows." He'd practically suggested it.

Desmond's brow puckered, and he ran his hand over his slicked hair. "I don't know, Delanie. Are you sure about this?"

No. Not that she would admit it with Marie all up in her business. Not this time. "Reasonably."

Marie hesitated, then shook her head. "I'm just going to say it. Delanie, I think you're making a huge mistake."

"Oh, there's a surprise," Delanie muttered.

"What's that?" Marie frowned.

"Nothing," Delanie said.

"Oh, no, I'm pretty sure it's something. Out with it."

On the other edge of the screen, Desmond shifted uncomfortably but said nothing.

Delanie sighed. "It's no big deal, I guess. It just seems you think I'm making a huge mistake pretty often. It would be nice if you were a little more supportive of my choices."

Marie looked affronted. "I *am* supportive of your choices, when you make the right ones. Like going back home to help your mom, or taking your grandmother's place as director of the show. And signing on to *Trueheart*—the first time. In hindsight, I may have been wrong about that one." Marie frowned. "But I can't support you throwing away the career you could have, or your future happiness, because you're afraid to take a chance on the one guy you've ever truly loved."

Delanie froze. "Wh-what did you say?"

Marie leaned toward the screen. "Do you know how many times you've told me about your Nan giving up on her career for love, and how that's not going to be you?"

"Not that many—"

"You've mentioned it enough, and *Caleb* enough, for me to know that the guy has never stopped mattering to you. You love him, Delanie, admit it. If you didn't, then you wouldn't be fighting so hard to avoid following in your grandmother's footsteps. And what would be so bad about that, anyway? From everything you've told me, your grandmother had a full, rewarding life, and never actually gave up her career in theatre. It just shifted a bit. Otherwise they wouldn't be naming a stage after her." Marie paused, but before Delanie could respond, she said, "You know, if it weren't for a woman just like your Nan, I would never have come to Vancouver for costume design. And you wouldn't have come here either. When you talk about Molly, you always talk about what she didn't do. But you forget to talk about what she did."

Delanie's mouth was dry, and she couldn't think of a single

rebuttal. Why did her brain always do this when she needed words the most? Ever since she had been cancelled, it seemed she just froze up when people confronted her. She shook her head, missing the old, more confident version of herself.

"Marie," Desmond said, "maybe we should talk about this another time."

Delanie whole-heartedly agreed. Never would also work. "It doesn't matter. I've already signed a contract. I'm sorry to have disappointed you." She flopped back against her pillows and crossed her arms—which put the faded rectangle of Nathan Tait's missing poster directly in her line of sight. Annoyed, she sat up again.

Marie's tone softened. "I'll never be disappointed in you going for what you want, Delanie. I'm just not sure you're being honest with yourself about what that is."

Delanie opened her mouth, but all that came out was a choked sound. Abruptly, both Desmond's and Marie's faces froze, and a few seconds later, the call ended. A notification about her unstable Internet came up, and she slammed the laptop closed. She sent a quick text to the group chat that the call had dropped, then turned off her phone before Marie could reply.

She'd had quite enough of an earful for one day already. And she wouldn't be able to get a single word of it out of her head.

I don't love Caleb. Not the kind of love that makes you give up your dreams to be with someone.

But the words rang hollow in her heart. Not for the first time that week, she buried herself under her blankets and cried.

Chapter 20

CALEB PULLED UP in front of his parents' farmhouse and turned off his truck. His parents' faithful Golden Retriever, Shorty, hobbled down the steps and past his mother's tidy flower beds with the field-rock edging to greet him. Ever since he and Delanie's fateful conversation at Tim Hortons last week, Caleb had done nothing but think about what she'd said. And since Emma had gone to Monica's on Friday, there had been even less to distract him. He hoped a conversation with his parents would help clarify his muddled thoughts.

As he came in the back door into the kitchen—after a thorough neck scratch for the dog—his mother greeted him with a cheery smile and a hug. She was already dressed for church.

"Caleb, what a nice surprise! Not often we see you out here this early on a Sunday—not after harvest is over, anyway."

"I haven't seen you guys much lately. And I miss your coffee." Caleb kissed her cheek, then stepped away to take off his denim jacket and hang it on one of the hooks by the door.

"Do you want some eggs? I just finished making your father's. The pan should still be hot."

"No, no, Mom. I ate at home." He spotted the coffee pot on the percolator warming burner with a full serving in the bottom. "Mind if I have that, though?" He pointed at it.

Adelaide beamed. "Of course. You go sit down. I'll bring it over."

Caleb made his way through the kitchen to the breakfast nook on the far side, taking note of a few new rock-based projects-in-progress sitting on the peninsula that separated the kitchen from the nook. After Marcus got sick, he had started using the ubiquitous rocks that seemed to spring up from the ground here to make all kinds of things—he said keeping his hands busy when his body required the rest of him to be inactive is what had kept him sane. Marcus had made a wide array of projects, from painted fairy garden decorations to modern-looking candle stands, most of which he'd given away to friends and family.

Once Caleb got close enough to the nook to see past the upper cabinets, his father's slight frame came into view. The thinning grey hair on top of Marcus's head was visible as he bent over a farming industry magazine laid on the circular wooden table, occasionally putting a bite of scrambled eggs from the plate next to it into his mouth.

"Hi, Dad."

Marcus looked up, his amber-brown eyes crinkling in a smile. "Caleb! Good to see you, son."

He set down his fork and stood to give Caleb a firm hug, something he'd also started doing after he got sick. After ten years, Caleb was almost used to it.

As Marcus sat down, he winced, but that wasn't terribly unusual these days, either. Caleb pretended not to notice and took the chair on the far side next to his father.

"What brings you here so early on a Sunday?" Marcus asked, closing his magazine and pulling the plate of breakfast directly in front of him.

Caleb ran his hand through his hair, gathering his thoughts. His mother brought over his coffee and set it on the table before him, along with some cream and sugar and a teaspoon, and he smiled his thanks.

"I've got a bit of a dilemma that I'm hoping you two can

help with."

"Oh?" Adelaide picked up another mug from the butcher block island top for herself, then came and sat across from Caleb next to her husband. "Everything okay?"

No. No, it most definitely is not.

"It's not Emma, is it?" Adelaide prompted, worry in her eyes.

"No, she's fine. It's not about her. Not exactly." He poured some cream in his coffee and stirred. "But it kind of is."

"C'mon, son," Marcus teased gruffly. "Out with it. I'm not getting any younger."

Caleb drew a deep breath, then launched into his explanation—about how he'd been trying to figure out how to make sure he got to see both Delanie and Emma on a regular basis, but then Monica declared she was taking Emma to Ontario. About how Delanie had broken up with him without even trying to work anything out. About how he thought he would have to move to Ontario too, but he was worried about the farm.

As he spoke, his mom listened with sympathetic murmurs of acknowledgement, and Marcus quietly ate his eggs and bacon, though Caleb knew he was paying just as much attention. When Caleb mentioned the farm, Marcus's head snapped up.

"What about the farm?"

Caleb shifted uncomfortably. "You know. If I'm not here, who's going to help you out?"

Marcus cocked his head. "You're not the only able-bodied man around these parts. And I'm not that feeble just yet." He frowned at Adelaide. "Have you been talking to him? Is that why the boy almost killed himself to bring in the harvest with us this fall? I told you, I'm fine."

"So you keep saying," Adelaide said. "But if Caleb is concerned, it's not because of me. I'm not the only one with eyes around here." She took a sip of her coffee, studying the wood grain of the tabletop.

"No one thinks you're feeble, Dad," Caleb said dryly. "But you and I both know how much work it is running the farm. I know Oliver helps out, but he wasn't born to it like I was. I just don't want to leave you in the lurch if I end up moving somewhere else."

"Well, I appreciate your concern, just like I have appreciated all your help over the years." Marcus sighed, pushing away his empty breakfast plate. He crossed his arms on the table in front of him. "The truth is, I've started wondering if it might be time for me to pass the farm on to someone else. The problem is, I feel too young to call it quits here and too old to consider a career change. But I know even you don't really want to take over for me. Maybe it's time to sell." He sighed. "Never thought I'd say that. I thought I'd keep working the fields until someone pulled my stiff, wrinkled corpse from a tractor seat."

Caleb stared at Marcus in shock. "Are you sure, Dad?"

"No, not really. But sometimes, reality makes your choices for you. Now, don't you two get all mother-hen-like, but this year's harvest was harder than usual on me too. I'm not as young as I used to be."

"But . . . where will you live? What will you do?" Caleb glanced at Adelaide, but she just kept drinking her coffee, watching the two of them. She and Dad had obviously had this conversation already.

"I'll still drive logging trucks in the winter for a while, I imagine," Marcus said. "And we've got a decent savings put aside. Your mother keeps telling me I should sell some of my rock art, but I don't know about that."

Caleb glanced at his mother, then back. "I think that's a great idea."

Marcus shook his head as though he didn't want to entertain such a foolish notion. "Point is, we'll be fine. But I thought you came here to talk about where *you're* going to live, and what you're going to do about the pickle you find yourself in."

"I did, but . . ." Caleb had so many worries and questions in the face of this new development, he wasn't ready to move on yet.

"Son, we'll be fine," Marcus said. "God's never let us down yet. I don't think he intends to start now."

Adelaide took Marcus's hand and squeezed it, and he returned her affectionate smile. Then she turned to Caleb.

"Besides, you've already given up enough of your own happiness for us and this farm. I think it's about time you started chasing after your own future instead of ours."

Caleb swallowed. He wanted to object to his mother's observation about the happiness he had given up, but the words stuck in his throat. Yes, Emma made him happy. But his mother was right—he had been using his daughter and his parents and this farm as an excuse for not getting on with his life for too long. He'd even hidden behind his feelings for Delanie. It was time to stop living in the past and make the right decision for his future.

Which, now that he and Delanie had broken up, was to be the best dad he could be.

"So you're okay with me moving to Ontario?" he asked.

Adelaide tilted her head and regarded him over her mug. "It's not what I'd selfishly want, obviously, but if that's what you feel you have to do." She set her coffee cup on the table and leaned forward with an earnest expression. "But consider this: no matter where you and Emma end up, she'll always be part of your life. She's your daughter, and I know you. You'll make sure she knows you're there for her, no matter how many miles lay between you at any given moment. But what happens if you let Delanie go this time? I know how you feel about her. If you let her walk away, you're not likely to get a third chance. And you'll spend the rest of your life wondering what you two could have had."

Caleb glanced at his parents' conjoined hands. That's what

he'd always wanted—a marriage as solid as theirs, the kind he knew would last a lifetime and outlast any disagreement. And every time he had pictured that imagined future, where *he* was holding hands with his wife of thirty-five years or more, it was always Delanie's face he saw.

"She dumped me, though. Twice. I'm starting to get the message she doesn't think we're worth fighting for."

"Or," Marcus said, raising his brow, "maybe she just wants to see if *you* do."

Caleb stared at his father, thunderstruck. *I just want you to choose me first.* She had told him that outright. How had he not heard it before?

He tossed back the last of his coffee and stood. "Thanks, Dad. Thanks, Mom. I gotta go."

His mother chuckled as he bent over to kiss the top of her head. "Where are you going?"

"The Fletchers. You're right, Dad. You've always been the smartest guy I know." Caleb swung his jean jacket on. "See you at church, but I might be a little late."

The last thing he heard before he closed the door behind him was his father calling, "Good luck, son!"

Caleb gunned the engine all the way to the Fletchers. They lived on the opposite side of Peace Crossing, and the miles had never passed so slowly. But when he pulled into the yard, Delanie's little coupe was missing.

He pulled out his phone to send her a text, then hesitated. Texts and phone calls were too easy to ignore, and he wanted to have this conversation in person. He hopped out of the truck and climbed the stairs to the front door, then knocked.

Cheryl answered the door. She had her coat on, and Bill stood in the entrance behind her, putting his on too. They were probably about to leave for church.

"Caleb! What's going on?"

"Good morning, Cheryl. I'd hoped I could catch Delanie.

Do you know where she is right now?"

Cheryl's face clouded. "She left early this morning, on her way to Kamloops for that acting gig. Didn't she tell you?"

"She left already?" Caleb resisted the urge to smack the door frame. "Do you happen to know where she's staying tonight?"

Bill came up to the door. "I think she planned to drive straight through today. She needs to be on set tomorrow morning. That's why she left so early."

"What time was that?"

Bill looked at his wristwatch. "Oh, about three hours ago now, I'd say."

A three-hour head start? Well, he would drive all the way to Kamloops if he had to.

"Okay, thanks." He smiled, then rushed back to his truck.

"Caleb?" Cheryl called as he was climbing in the cab. He looked up to see her standing on the stoop.

"Yes?"

"She's staying at the Thompson Motor Inn. I'll be praying you catch her." Cheryl smiled knowingly.

"Thanks, Mrs. Fletcher. Happy Sunday!"

"And a happy Sunday to you too."

As Caleb backed up and turned around, he hit speed dial on Monica's number.

He needed to tell Emma why she wouldn't see him at rehearsal this afternoon. Then he would call Amber. Delanie was right—Amber Leclerc probably could have run the entire production herself. For the sake of the kids, though, he hoped she wouldn't have to. Not this year, or any year soon.

"Not if I have anything to say about it."

He turned west on the highway and hit the gas.

Chapter 21

D<small>ELANIE TAPPED HER</small> key card on her motel room door and
pulled her suitcase into her room, gratefully kicking off her
shoes and letting her toes sink into the plush carpet. It had
been an excruciatingly long day of driving. Letting her suitcase
stand upright, she hooked her hands over her shoulders and
rubbed, trying to work out the knots, and glanced around the
room.

For a budget motel, it could be worse. The room was nice
and clean with an airy aesthetic. And she would take the func-
tional little suite with its small kitchenette—including a full-
sized if narrow fridge—over a spa room in a fancier hotel any
day. Even though a soak in a hot tub would feel pretty good
right about now, if the motel had had one, it would have been
closed at this time of night anyway.

An enormous basket wrapped in cellophane sat on the small
dining table next to a manila envelope. She spied bananas, ap-
ples, chocolates, coffee beans from one of her favourite Victoria
roasters, and an oversized mug. She went over and opened the
plain white folded card tied to the top—*Delanie, Glad to have
you back. Josh.*

"'Have me back.' Of all the entitled . . ."

She let the rest of the sentiment remain unsaid. She was too
tired to waste that kind of energy on Josh Rosenburg. Besides,

she was being oversensitive now—it was just an expression. She really needed sleep.

She glanced in the envelope and confirmed that it contained her call sheets for the next few days. That could definitely wait. She rolled her suitcase to the closet and heaved it onto the suitcase rack inside, then unzipped it. Laying on top of her clothes was Nan's scrapbook, the one her mother had let her keep. She still hadn't had time to look through the whole thing. Pulling it out, she tossed it on the table next to the basket.

Behind the cellophane, a bottle of red wine and two wine glasses caught her eye. In lieu of a soak in a hot tub, a glass of wine sounded pretty good right about now. She set to work untying the ribbon binding the cellophane wrap together.

After she'd poured some wine—with help from a cheap folding wine corkscrew she found in one of the kitchenette drawers—she pulled out her phone to text Marie that she had arrived safe. Then she noticed she had missed a text from Amber earlier.

Dress rehearsal went well. The kids were sad you weren't here, but most of them understood. Celeste says good luck with your new job. Also, Luc ordered the new soundboard today. Should get here just in time for opening night.

Delanie smiled. When she had stopped by Amber's place yesterday to drop off her play binder and the cheque for the soundboard Luc was ordering for the theatre, she had expected the same odd treatment she had received the first time she had gone there. Instead, Amber had surprised her by inviting her in. And that wasn't the only surprise.

No one else had been home, and Delanie had hesitantly accepted Amber's offer of tea, figuring it would be good to have a little fortification while she went over the last-minute items with the assistant director. As they were wrapping up, Amber met Delanie's gaze.

"I just want to thank you for all you've done for Celeste. I . . . I know I haven't always been easy to get along with. We've had a lot going on here for the last few months, and I think the stress affected me more than I realized."

"Oh?" Delanie said carefully. "Was your husband upset about how involved you and Celeste were with the play?" *Is that why he had gotten so involved too—to keep an eye on them?* Delanie tried to keep her tone casual, but hoped Amber would sense that Delanie was willing to listen if she wanted to talk. She hadn't had many personal interactions with Luc, but when she had, he had always seemed a bit stand-offish. It had been hard to get a read on him.

Amber arched her brows. "Why would Luc be upset?"

"Oh, I, uh . . . Things just seemed so tense that day I met him, I wasn't sure what was going on."

Amber frowned thoughtfully. "Right. I think you came by the day we were moving Mother into long-term care. She doesn't do well with change these days, and I think she was having a bit of a fit at seeing her things go out the door—we wanted to set up her space before we took her over there. I'm sorry I didn't invite you in. I just didn't want you to have to see that. Bad enough that we had to deal with it. And, I'm sorry to say, Luc doesn't handle that kind of stress well." She leaned forward and dropped her voice, even though there was no one else there. "Please don't take it personally. It just takes him a while to warm up to people."

Delanie blinked, glad she hadn't come right out with her suspicions earlier. "Is your mother, um . . ."

"Senile? You could say that." Amber gave a half-hearted smile. "Her dementia has advanced pretty quickly, and it's been . . . hard."

"I'm so sorry," Delanie murmured. "I had no idea."

"No, we haven't talked about it much. Things have been better since she moved, though. I still go to see her every few days, but she loves it at the senior's home. She's made a bunch of friends—and she gets to make them again every day." She smiled wryly. "It's been better for the kids too. My mother can be . . . harsh. And appearances are important to her. My boys didn't notice it as much, being younger, but I don't want Celeste to have to deal with some of the things I did growing up. I'm actually glad my mother's not here all the time now." Amber scrunched her eyes as though fearing Delanie's response. "Does that make me a horrible person?"

"No, not at all. Dealing with parents can be difficult."

Delanie suddenly saw Amber in a new light—her controlling nature, her fears about Celeste looking foolish. If Delanie had a mother like that, what would she be like? Dealing with her own mother's meddling and dramatics was bad enough.

"I'm so sorry for everything you've been going through," she added. "Thank you for sharing that with me."

"Well, I thought you deserved to know." Amber lifted her mug to her lips for a sip of tea, and her hands trembled. "There's, um, something else," she said, then took a sip.

Delanie's throat closed again. "Okay," she asked more than said. What could have made Amber so nervous all of a sudden?

Amber put her mug on the table and wrapped both hands around it, staring at the amber liquid. Then, as though steeling herself, she drew in a breath and met Delanie's eye.

"I owe you an apology. After I heard you were going to direct the play, I went and looked you up. Of course, I wasn't expecting the gong show I found on your social media feeds, but it made me question whether you should be the one in charge of the play, leading all the kids."

Delanie's chest tightened, her heart speeding up. "Amber, no, you don't—"

"I do. Please let me finish." Amber set her jaw.

Delanie gave a small nod. She felt like she already knew what Amber was going to say next, that the woman would outline her reasons for her belief in Delanie's incompetence. That was the last thing she wanted to hear, but if saying it aloud helped Amber in some way, she could bite her tongue, no matter how uncomfortable it would be for her.

Amber swallowed. "But my doubts about your abilities were just an excuse. I was jealous, there's no other way to say it. When I heard Molly passed away, I had planned to volunteer to direct the play. But before I even got the chance, I heard you had been appointed. I thought someone should have at least asked me first—you don't even live here."

Her voice broke a little, and Delanie resisted the urge to stop her again. That certainly explained why Amber had had a chip on her shoulder right from the start.

"I'm ashamed to say that I actually participated in your public massacre," Amber continued. "Not in a big way—I just liked some comments and maybe left a few of agreement—but it was enough. I was wrong to do it. And I was wrong about you."

Delanie's heart pounded in her ears, and heat pulsed through her veins. She hadn't expected that. She swallowed, searching for something to say. But Amber wasn't done.

"I want you to know I deleted the comments I made." She put her mug aside and folded her hands in front of her. "For the record, I think you've done a great job with the play. Truly. I have learned a lot from you, and I know now why you were put in charge. You have the same joy for theatre that Molly had, and the same ability to infect others with it. I'm only sorry you won't get to see the kids perform."

Something in Delanie's chest let go, and she drew a deep breath. After how Amber had acted, the fact that the woman had been humble enough to clear the air in this way left Delanie a little stunned. She thought Amber might be sweetening her words a little for effect, because Delanie hadn't done much for the kids that someone else couldn't have done—but she wouldn't ruin Amber's confession by arguing about the woman's opinion. Her mother had taught her how to graciously accept an apology.

"Thank you. That means a lot."

"No, thank *you*. Celeste has really blossomed this year, and I think it's in large part due to the extra help you've been giving her to develop her acting." Amber brightened. "I talked to Violet, and she's going to start giving Celeste voice lessons next week."

Delanie smiled, her heartbeat returning to normal. "That's wonderful! I'm so glad to hear that."

"It wouldn't have happened without you."

Remembering the grateful look on Amber's face, Delanie took a sip of wine, then swirled it around in her glass, watching the legs trail down the sides. Celeste wasn't the only one who had bloomed during the last two months. Delanie felt like she knew so many of the kids personally. Helping them develop their talents on the stage had been one of the most satisfying things she had ever experienced. She thought of the dress rehearsal she'd missed that day and pushed aside her regret with another sip. Everyone had probably done just fine without her.

Still, it was too bad Sandra hadn't been able to convince Crystal McLean to give her even one more week before starting work. And since the production would be playing catchup with her scenes, there was no way she would be able to take extra time off this weekend to go back to Peace Crossing and see the play. She would have to wait until the videographer Amber had hired was finished editing and producing the videos—though watching a recording was bound to be a poor substitute for being there. At least she had the video she'd made with the kids to tide her over.

She glanced at Nan's scrapbook, debating between going through the last few pages and pulling up the fundraising video to watch. But the wine had started to do its job, and she had to get up early to drive out to the set in the historic town of Barkerville. What she needed was a good night's sleep. Instead of indulging her sentimentality, she pulled out the call sheets and looked over the scenes she would be shooting tomorrow.

After downing the last swallow of wine, she went and hopped in the shower. Fifteen minutes later, she was asleep.

DELANIE WOKE UP to her phone jangling a show tune. She reached for it, confused. She was certain that wasn't the ring tone she had chosen for her alarm.

When she picked it up and stared at the screen through bleary eyes, she realized that's because it wasn't her alarm. Someone was calling her.

Caleb.

She thought about cancelling the call, but then noticed it was after midnight. If he was calling her this late, it must be important. Had something happened to Emma?

She answered the call and put the phone to her ear. "Hello?"

"Which one are you in?" he asked.

She propped herself up on her elbow. "What are you talking about? Caleb, what's going on?"

"I'm outside your motel. I found your car, but I need to know which room is yours."

"What?"

She sat bolt upright, then hopped out of bed and went to the window, pulling the curtain aside so she could see the parking lot. Sure enough, there stood Caleb, surveying the rooms with his phone to his ear. He saw her peeking through the window of her second-floor room and started for the stairs.

"Caleb, what are you doing here?" She dropped the curtain and went to the door, opening it just as he reached it.

"I had to tell you something," he said, pulling the phone from his ear.

"What did you have to say that couldn't have been said

on the pho—"

Her next words were cut off by his lips. He wrapped his arms around her and kissed her like he had been thinking about it all day. And, since it took almost eleven hours to drive here from Peace Crossing—not counting any stops—he probably had.

She awkwardly tossed her phone on the bed and melted into his arms, into the kiss she had missed so much in the week they'd been apart. Then she remembered why she'd been missing it and pushed away from him, stepping back.

"No. Caleb, we broke up. Why did you come here? Did you think you could run into my arms like in some rom-com and stifle all the reasons we broke up with a passionate kiss, and everything would be okay?"

"Yeah. I mean, no, of course not. But that would have been romantic, right?" He gave her a crooked grin, and she almost relented. Almost.

To cover her discomfiture, she stepped back, crossing her arms and arching a brow.

When she said nothing, he cleared his throat and shuffled his feet. "Right. Well, I do have something more to say, actually."

"I'm listening."

He rubbed his eyes, and she saw the weariness in his shoulders. Whatever he wanted to say must have been pretty important for him to drive all this way to say it. She relaxed a little, and even let her heart hope. Had he come to apologize? Had he changed his mind about moving?

"Do you remember Maisie's puppies?" he said.

She blinked. "Maisie . . . your old dog?" Why was he talking about the dog he'd had as a teenager?

"Yeah, her. Do you remember what happened to her?"

Now that he mentioned it . . . "Didn't she get hit by a car when her puppies were only a few weeks old?"

"Yeah. Dad didn't think they would make it. But Rachel, Abigail, and I took turns getting up to hand-feed them through the night for weeks. Mom looked after them during the day while we were at school. And they all did just fine, except one little runt." He paused, his gaze looking back in time.

Delanie frowned. "Why are we talking about this?"

He focused on her. "I wouldn't give up on the runt, even after everyone else said I should. I went on the Internet and tried to figure out what was wrong with him. Dad wouldn't pay to take him to the vet, but the vet had to come out to look at a cow, so I asked her what to do and did what she told me. No one else would help with him anymore, so I did it all.

"Eventually, when he started doing better, Rachel and Abby offered to help again, but I wouldn't let them. I was sure I had to be the one to help him, that if I didn't supervise it all, he would die when I wasn't looking. And in the end, Shorty made it. My parents still have him, and he's still happy and healthy, if slowing down a bit these days."

He smiled, looking down as though the dog was sitting right there. Then he glanced up.

"I, on the other hand, came down with a nasty cold that took a month to get over. I missed all of volleyball season."

Delanie sat on the bed, her back aching and the weariness creeping back over her. "What's the point of all this?"

He sat next to her and took her hand. "The point is, Lanie, that I take care of those who need me, even to my own detriment. Even when others might have lightened the load, if I would let them. And even if it means missing out on my own happiness." He looked her in the eyes. "It wasn't you that I wouldn't let myself choose first. It was me. Because *me* always wanted to choose *you*. I just had too many puppies to take care of."

Delanie frowned, not sure she understood the metaphor. "Does this mean you're willing to move to Vancouver with me? Or"—she gestured around the room—"wherever?"

"I am." He looked around the room. "Though it might be

a bit tricky to hold down a steady job in *wherever*, so we have
some logistics to work out."

"What about the farm? And Emma?"

"My parents are thinking of giving up the farm anyway, even
if I stay in Peace Crossing. And Emma . . ." His eyes clouded,
then cleared. "I'll always be her dad. I'll just have to get used
to doing it remotely most of the time from now on. A decade
or so sooner than I'd hoped, but it was bound to happen eventually."

Delanie could hear the catch in his voice. She stared into his
eyes, which were dark brown in the dim light of the room, trying to see into his soul. "Is this really what you want?"

"If it wasn't, do you think I would be here?" He raised his
brows, then tilted his forehead toward her. "Yes, Delanie. This
is what I want. To spend every day of the rest of my life loving
you, if you'll let me. I choose you first."

Her heart leapt. How she had longed to hear those words! No
wonder he'd driven a whole day to get to her.

But . . . was it what *she* wanted? To know he had given up
the treasure of his heart to deal with the hot mess she knew
herself to be, when she wouldn't have done the same in return?
Wouldn't she always wonder if he regretted his choice?

"I . . ." Her heart thudded against her ribs, and every word
she'd ever heard flew out of her mind. "I don't know what to
say."

"I'm not going to lie, I was hoping you would say something
similar in return."

"I mean, I want to. But I'm not sure you've thought this
through. Those logistics you skipped over *matter*, Caleb. It's
not like you'll ever find a discount flight from Kamloops to
Brampton, and I'm going to be living here for the better part
of the next three years, at least. And what if something happens
to your dad? Not to mention, you can't just get a new job every
time I do. I know you. You're a guy with deep roots. And living

with me, living like this"—she gestured around the room again—"means tearing those roots up over and over again. We could get a house in Vancouver, I suppose, but would you want to live in Vancouver full-time if I can only see you on weekends? I just can't believe you would be happy long-term, no matter what you say."

"So what are you saying?" he asked, and the disbelief in his eyes almost broke her.

"I'm saying . . ."

She searched for the words. She knew he meant what he said. But she also knew to the depths of her soul that she wasn't worth the price he was willing to pay. He would come to see that eventually. She swallowed, sucking some moisture back into her sandpaper tongue.

"I'm saying I can't. I can't let you do this. Not for me." She swallowed her doubt. "I'm saying no."

He stared back at her for a long moment, his nostrils flared and his jaw working. "So you were lying at the coffee shop, then. This wasn't about my choices at all. It's about yours. It's always been about yours. Well, you know what?" He stood, his hands clenched. "I'm done trying to figure out your rules, Delanie. You keep changing them. You want someone to give you the moon, but when they do, you say you can't accept it."

Delanie stared at him with tears streaming down her cheeks, his words like lashes on her soul. Especially since she knew she deserved every one. "I'm sorry, Caleb."

He jerked his gaze away. "I'm sure you are. But you know what I think?" His eyes pierced her, his amber irises as dark as molasses. "I think you're so stuck on your plan, you're too scared to make room in it for anyone who might love you." His shoulders slumped. "Bye, Delanie. I hope you find your happiness."

Before she could think of something to say in return, the door slammed behind him.

She pushed herself back on the bed and pulled her knees to her chest, wrapping her arms around them as she sobbed. She wished the bed would eat her whole, that it would hide her from the truth in his words. *You're too stuck on your plan to make room for anyone who might love you.*

Was he right about her? Was the real reason she had turned him down because she was afraid? Afraid of making room in her plan for love? She crawled beneath the covers and stared wide-eyed up at the ceiling. She tossed and turned until just before dawn, when she finally crawled out of bed to get ready for work.

All through the sleepless night, she still hadn't managed to convince her shattered heart that she had done the right thing.

Chapter 22

DELANIE DRAGGED HERSELF through her motel room door, exhaustion permeating every bone in her body. It had been another long day on set—and it was only the second one. She felt like she had worked for sixteen hours instead of only twelve.

She was used to long hard days, and they didn't usually bother her. Maybe it was the fresh air—many of her scenes were shot outdoors. Even though temperatures here were still in the warm mid-teens during the day, it wasn't the same as working in a studio, or even outdoors in the mild, lush Lower Mainland. Yes, it was probably the exertion and fresh air draining her. Not the perpetual dull ache in her chest.

She had barely had time to change into lounge pants and put on her slippers—the ragged pink bunnies she'd brought from her parents'—turn on the TV, and settle on the small couch with her next day's script pages in hand when someone knocked on her door. She got up and peeked through the window. Josh stood on her doorstep, looking around with his hands on his hips. Despite his day having been just as long as hers, he looked as though he had just stepped out of the shower, trendy-casual in a jean jacket, white T-shirt, and jeans over a body he obviously found time to train at the gym on a regular basis. Rolling her eyes, she went and opened the door.

"Hey, Josh. Is there something we need to talk about?"

He rubbed his nose. "You could say that. I was hoping I could take you to dinner to discuss it."

She cringed internally. Going out again was the last thing she wanted to do right now. Especially with Josh. "Is it urgent? We could talk about it at work tomorrow."

He looked over her I'm-staying-in attire. "We could order in, I suppose."

The thought of inviting Josh into her space, such as it may be, made her skin crawl. She hesitated, then shook her head. "No, I need to eat anyway. Give me five minutes."

He grinned and took a step toward the door. "Okay. I'll—"

She closed the door before he could push his way inside. Taking hints was not Josh Rosenburg's strong suit.

Four minutes later, wearing jeans and a blouse and with her hair brushed, she opened the driver's door of her car, which was right beside Josh's.

He rolled down his passenger window and leaned over. "Hop in with me."

She leaned down to look in the window. "No, I'll follow you. Where are we going?"

He blinked, then named a restaurant.

"See you there," she said, and got into her vehicle.

She closed her door and started her car before he could object further. Looking back at him, she saw him give her a long look before he shrugged, rolled up his window, and reversed out of his space.

The restaurant he had chosen was trendy and modern, and they were seated at a small table in the corner, not too close to anyone else. She would have preferred something a little more out in the open, but the hostess probably thought they were on a date. She hoped Josh didn't think that too.

Caleb would love this place. She pushed the thought aside, blinking back the moisture that threatened to spill from her eyes. She had given up the right to think about what Caleb would love. She would have to get used to it.

After they placed their order, Josh leaned back in his chair with a grin on his face—the one she used to think was charming and sexy, but which now struck her as a little arrogant and smug. What had she ever seen in this guy?

"So, how did things go in Hicksville?" he asked. "Your aunt died, right?"

Delanie drew a steadying breath, her stomach curling in annoyance. "My grandmother, actually."

"Sorry about that. I bet she was a fine woman if she was related to you." He propped his elbows on the table with his hands folded and studied her as if she were the most interesting woman in the world.

"She was. She's the reason I became an actress."

"Is that so?" He arched a brow. "A fine woman indeed." He paused. "I heard you've been talking to Tessa Montague. That's quite a connection to have."

"How did you hear that?" Delanie and Tessa hadn't even managed to make their schedules mesh to have a meeting yet. She couldn't imagine who would have told Josh that they'd been in contact.

Josh shrugged. "Word gets around. Does she want you for a movie or something?"

"I don't know yet."

He grinned. "Well, good luck. And I would love to meet her, if you think to mention me."

Delanie curled her hands into fists under the table, but kept her tone sweet. "So, Josh, what did you want to talk about?"

"Getting right to the point, I see." He glanced down, and Delanie was gratified to see she had thrown him a little off-balance. Good. It was time he was the one on unsure footing between them.

He placed his hands on the table. "Well, no sense beating around the bush. Delanie, I'm going to level with you. I missed you. I haven't been myself since you've been gone. I was hoping we could pick up where we left off, before things went . . . sideways."

She narrowed her eyes. "I wasn't the one who broke things off."

"Actually, you were."

She frowned, remembering. "You're right. I was. But only after you fired me."

"Delanie, I told you. That wasn't my decision. I'm sure you can see why Crystal was concerned about bad publicity tanking the show."

"I thought there was no such thing as bad publicity."

"Sometimes there is. People a lot bigger in this industry than you have been fired for a lot less in recent years."

"I'm aware." She folded her hands together under the table, restraining the urge to bite her thumbnail. No way was she going to let Josh see how nervous she was. If she didn't set the record straight right now, she would regret it for the rest of her career—and possibly her life. "But the thing is, I didn't actually do anything wrong, and no one at the studio had my back—not even you, and you were my boyfriend."

Josh gaped. "How can you say that? If it weren't for me, you wouldn't be back on the show."

"Convenient that that only happened *after* Kaitlyn Williams proved her lack of ability to act."

Though she'd heard a rumour that Kaitlyn had chosen to leave, even though she would have been in breach of contract. Delanie didn't know if it was true, but if it was, maybe the woman had more self-respect than she'd thought.

He narrowed his eyes and sat back. "I can see you're determined to paint me as the villain."

She fidgeted with her roll of cutlery. She had to tread carefully. This man was still her boss, and they would have to work together for a long time. "No, Josh, not a villain. People aren't so cut and dried as that in real life. I'm sorry for lashing out at you. It was out of line. I've had a very trying week, and I'm tired."

He nodded knowingly and placed his hand over hers. "It's alright," he said, his tone magnanimous. "Everyone makes mistakes. Fortunately, I'm big enough to overlook this one too."

She stiffened, staring at him. Then she tugged her hand from his and placed it in her lap again. This time, her hands were wringing with restrained anger, not anxiety. "Thank you," she got out.

"That's just the kind of guy I am. That's why we work." He gave her that ultra-charming grin again, and she choked on the words crowding the back of her throat.

Fortunately, they were interrupted by the arrival of their food. Delanie took a swig of water, wetting her dry mouth and trying desperately to gather her thoughts. Maybe Marie was right . . . again. Rejoining the show might have been a bad idea.

Lord, please give me the words.

She must be desperate. She was actually praying. Her mother would be thrilled if she knew.

Josh set to work on his prime rib with gusto, then looked up and noticed Delanie still staring at her plate of red snapper, her roll of cutlery gripped in her fist.

"Everything okay?"

Everything is most definitely not okay. I should be in Peace Crossing for the final dress rehearsal tonight. I should be there with Caleb, and Emma, and the rest of the kids. With people who care about me. With a man who was willing to overlook me breaking his heart to spend the rest of his life with me, who never made me feel like I was at fault for things I never did. And who forgave the mistakes I did make from the bottom of his heart, not the front of his too-perfect teeth.

She drew a breath and met Josh's gaze. "Josh, I'm grateful to be back on the show. It's a good opportunity, and I recognize that. I also think you're a talented director. But you and I need to get something straight. We're not going to be together. Ever. I've learned a lot in the last two months, and one of the biggest lessons is that I deserve better."

He stared at her, his face stony. "You don't mean what you just said."

"I do." Her heart thundered against her ribs, but she refused to look away.

"No, you don't. You can't. Because you wouldn't say something like that to me and mean it. Not when I'm the guy who could fire you again in a heartbeat. And I don't even need to tell you what I could do to your career. I've got connections too, you know."

Her stomach clenched. *What am I doing?* She no longer believed Josh had the ability to ruin her career, but one thing she did know—Josh Rosenburg thought he could do whatever he wanted to people he perceived as weaker than him. After only two days of watching him making subtle come-ons and inappropriate comments to every semi-attractive woman on set, she wouldn't be surprised if Kaitlyn *had* left. And if she were going to come out of this unscathed, she had to make sure he knew she wasn't the wilting flower he had fired two months ago.

Under the table, she eased her phone out of her small purse and hit the record button she kept on her home screen for the dictation app she used to practice her lines into. "All I said is that I don't want to date you. I think we could still work together just fine."

He set down his fork and sat erect. "If you think you're better than me, then I don't see how."

"I never said I thought—"

"No? What do you think *I deserve better* means, Delanie?"

"It means, I, uh . . ." How *could* she answer that without digging herself into a deeper hole? And after how she had treated Caleb two days ago, did she even believe that was true?

Josh snatched his napkin from his lap and dabbed at his mouth, then tossed it on the table. "You know what? Never mind. If you want to throw your career in the trash and light a match to it, that's on you. Seems like that's been your entire mission in life lately. I should have realized you can't save someone who doesn't want to be saved. I can't believe I actually saw potential in you. Goes to show that even I make mistakes."

Ice frosted Delanie's spine. She felt naked on a stage while the world was throwing tomatoes—just like she had after she'd been cancelled. She opened her mouth to answer, but no words came.

Then a gentle voice she hadn't heard before whispered to her heart.

Don't believe the lie. Your worth doesn't depend on this man's opinion of you.

Faces of people who loved her and believed in her filled her mind. Marie. Desmond. Sandra. The kids in the play. Emma. Even her mom and dad.

Caleb.

And not a single one of them gave half a crabapple what Josh Rosenburg or anyone else thought about her.

"I never asked you to save me, Josh," she heard herself say. She didn't know where the words were coming from, but now that she had started, she couldn't stop. "And somehow, I think you need me more than I need you. Fire me if you want, but you don't have as much power as you think you do. And I'm sorry I ever let you have any power over me. Believe me when I say that it won't happen again."

He glared at her, his nostrils flaring. Then he set his jaw. "You're done. I want you out of your motel room by tomorrow afternoon."

She stared at him and swallowed.

"Fine." She grabbed her purse from the back of her chair and stood. "It's been a pleasure working with you, Mr. Rosenburg.

I wish you the best."

He ignored her, instead picking up his cutlery and slicing off another bite of meat.

When she got to her car, she composed a brief text to Sandra and attached the recording. Then she tapped another text to Josh that read, *A parting gift from your greatest mistake.* She attached the recording, but before she hit *send*, she paused.

"No. I won't stoop to his level."

She hit *delete* and put the phone back in her purse. There were other ways to handle this.

As she drove away from the restaurant, she felt freer than she had in a long time. Cranking the music, she smiled and tapped the steering wheel to a pop song promising better days ahead. She didn't know what she was going to do for work now. But she did know where she was going next.

She had a kids' musical in Peace Crossing to direct.

And the love of her life to apologize to.

Chapter 23

DELANIE SAT IN her car, the ache of another long day on the road tightening her shoulders, and stared up at her parents' front door. Going in there meant telling her mom that she had been fired from *Trueheart* again. That her grand plan to fix her life hadn't lasted three days. It meant facing the smug judgement in Cheryl's eyes.

"So I'm just going to sit here?" she said aloud. "After driving eleven hours?"

She snorted and rolled her eyes at herself. She climbed out of the car into a light layer of snow and pulled her suitcase from the hatchback.

Her father met her at the door, already wearing his coat and boots. "I thought I heard a vehicle. What are you doing home, sweetheart?"

When she threw her arms around him and held onto him like her life depended on it, he wrapped her in a strong hug.

"Hey, now. It will be okay." He stroked her hair.

"Delanie?" came Cheryl's voice.

Delanie released her father and stepped back to see her mother staring at her in shock from the kitchen entrance.

"Why are you back so soon? Did you get some time off already?" Her face brightened hopefully. "Did you talk to Caleb?"

Delanie smiled and sniffled at the same time. "You could say

I have time off. A *lot* of time off. I got fired again."

"Why?" Bill asked.

"Because I wouldn't date Josh, the director."

"Your ex-boyfriend?" Cheryl frowned in disapproval, but not of Delanie. She came over and silently wrapped her daughter in a hug. "He didn't deserve you anyway."

"I know," said Delanie into her mother's shoulder, smiling through tears that now flowed freely, streaming as much from her mother's surprising sensitivity as the sting of the loss of the career opportunity.

Cheryl released her. "You take off your coat while I go put on a kettle for tea."

Delanie nodded. "Okay, Mom."

Cheryl smiled, then disappeared back into the kitchen.

Bill gripped her arms and met her gaze. "You know you can stay here as long as you need to, right?"

"Thanks, Dad." She smiled at him.

He gave a firm nod as though putting the final seal on an agreement, then released her. "I was just on my way out to the shop to change the oil in your mother's car," he said apologetically. "Do you want me to stay?"

Delanie waved him off. "I'm fine. That's all my news, anyway."

He frowned briefly. "It is? Hmm. Okay. See you when I get back in." He kissed her temple, then, with one last look, went outside.

When Delanie went into the kitchen, the electric kettle was at a hard boil, but her mother was nowhere to be seen. The button on the kettle popped, and Delanie poured water into the brightly striped ceramic teapot waiting next to it. She inhaled a fruity herbal—not her usual poison, but probably a smart choice for this late in the evening.

She had just finished transferring the teapot, mugs, and fixings to the sturdy farmhouse table and sat down when her mother bustled into the room, carrying a large worn shoebox.

"Sorry that took me so long," she said. "I forgot where I put this."

"What's in there?" Delanie peered at the familiar-looking box. Where had she seen it before?

Cheryl set it on the table and pushed it toward Delanie with a nostalgic smile as she sat down. "Love letters that Nan and Pops wrote each other. I found them in one of the boxes we put in the basement. I thought you might want to have them."

Curious, Delanie removed the lid and peered inside. The letters had been bundled into neat packages of a dozen or so and tied together with brown string. They filled the box from end to end.

"That's a lot of letters. I didn't realize Nan and Pops had been apart this much."

"Oh, yes. It was before they were married. There were a couple years where Mother was touring with a theatre company in the States when she and Dad corresponded quite a bit."

Delanie pulled out the first bundle and reverently untied the string, then carefully opened the yellowed envelope—addressed to Molly Wright, care of a theatre in Washington—and withdrew a single folded page covered in her grandfather's expansive cursive. It was dated the sixth of September, 1954.

"This was two years before they got married, wasn't it?" She showed her mother the date.

"Approximately."

Delanie began reading aloud.

Dearest Molly,

I hope this finds you well and happy. I haven't been able to stop thinking about you since we parted ways last month. I want you to know that I haven't give up on us yet. I know you think we can't be together because I'm a farm boy from northern Alberta and your life is on the stage, and maybe you're right. All I know is that

I never lived until I saw you smile, and I don't want to go back to the person I used to be. Give me a chance, Molly. If you hold any affection in your heart for me at all, write me back. I can't help but think we could be so much more than star-crossed lovers whose time has come.

Yours,

Ernie Davis

Delanie stared at the page, re-reading it silently to herself.

"As you can see, she wrote him back." Cheryl indicated the box, chuckling.

Delanie put the page on the table. "I had no idea they had a time in their courtship where they didn't know if they would end up together. The way Pops always told it, it was a done deal from the moment he saw her."

Cheryl smiled and picked up the teapot. "For him, I think it was. Mother took a bit more time and convincing."

"Apparently." One more thing she and her grandmother had in common. Delanie pushed her mug closer to her mother so Cheryl could pour her tea. "Did you know Caleb drove all the way to Kamloops to see me?"

"Did he?" Cheryl took a sip of her tea, and the look she gave Delanie over the rim of her mug was too innocent.

Delanie snorted and shook her head. "Of course you did. You're probably the one who told him where to find me."

Cheryl pursed her lips and shrugged. "Maybe. I seem to recall something about that, now that you mention it." Her exaggerated tone and studiously blank expression belied her innocence.

"It's okay, Mom. I'm not angry."

"Well, why would you be angry?" Cheryl gave up her pretence and leaned forward eagerly. "That's the most romantic thing I've ever heard of . . . except maybe my dad writing letters for two years to a woman he'd only known for a few days to convince her to marry him. I mean, your father does okay in the romance department, but his gestures are more ordinary."

"Like changing the oil in your car for you?"

Cheryl smiled, affection shining in her eyes as she glanced in the general direction of the shop. "Yes. Like that." She focused on Delanie. "I've been dying to know what happened with Caleb. Is he the reason you came here instead of going back to Vancouver? Is that why you told that Josh fellow no?"

Delanie shook her head, overwhelmed by her mother's sudden gush of words. "Slow down, Mom. I would have told Josh no, no matter what. He's an entitled jerk, it just took me a while to see it. Him firing me because I wouldn't date him only proved it." She bit her thumbnail. "I turned Caleb down. I came back to finish with the play."

Cheryl sat back in her chair, her face aghast. "You . . . you turned him down?"

Delanie nodded miserably, looking into her mug. "It made sense to me at the time, but I think I made a big mistake." She waited for her mother to start haranguing her about her future, but Cheryl surprised her.

"Why?" Cheryl asked gently.

Delanie met her mother's gaze, tears pricking the back of her eyes. "Because I thought I had to choose between him and my career. I didn't want him to resent me for making him choose me over Emma. Did you know Monica's taking Emma to Ontario, and Caleb is going to move there too?"

Cheryl nodded. "Adelaide told me at church."

"But if I'm going to be away from home for months at a time on a job, that home could just as easily be in Brampton, couldn't it? And I could get jobs there too, just like Desmond said."

"Who is Desmond?" Cheryl asked.

Delanie waved the question away. "My friend. It doesn't matter. The point is, I messed up, and I don't know how to fix it."

Her tears spilled over at last, and she wiped them away. Her mother plucked a paper napkin from the holder in the middle of the table and handed it to her.

"Thank you," Delanie said, taking the napkin and dabbing her cheeks.

Cheryl waited until she'd collected herself before speaking. "Delanie, one thing I've learned is there are very few mistakes we make in this life that can't be fixed. Do you love Caleb?"

Delanie nodded. "I do. Heaven help me, I do."

Cheryl smiled. "I'm pretty sure Heaven did have something to do with it. And anyone with eyes can see how he feels about you. Don't you think a man who loves you that much would be willing to forgive you for taking a little extra time to figure out what your heart wants?"

Delanie blinked at her mother, absorbing her words. All the way back to Peace Crossing, she had repeated her arguments for why she and Caleb couldn't be together, but everything she told herself had fallen flat. After all, plenty of other actors and crew members worked away from home for months at a time on location, and they managed to maintain relationships and have families. She had told Caleb it wasn't fair to him to subject him to the lifestyle her job would demand—but, in her heart, she knew her real reason had nothing to do with what he would or wouldn't be able to handle. He had already loved her for the decade they'd been apart. What made her think a few months apart at a time would ever change that?

"You're not just saying that because you secretly hope I'll settle down and give up acting?"

Cheryl's eyes widened. "Whatever gave you the impression I would want that?"

Delanie snorted, looking away. "Only everything you've ever said to me."

"Explain yourself," Cheryl said sharply.

Delanie sat back in her chair and drew a deep breath. "Mom,

you've never been happy that I wanted to be an actress. I mean, you never stood in my way, but I know you would rather I had gone into teaching, or med school like Savannah, or even into office administration like you. Basically anything that would have let me stay close to home."

Cheryl took a long sip of tea, then set down her teacup and regarded her daughter steadily. "Delanie, I'm sorry if I've ever given you the impression that I don't support your dreams. That wasn't my intention. I only wanted you to be able to support *yourself*."

Delanie frowned. "Then why did you leave all those college brochures out for me? And why did you keep trying to hook me up with every available bachelor you could find?"

Cheryl shook her head, studying the box of letters. "Ah. Now I see." She met Delanie's gaze again. "Would I like to have the peace of mind of knowing you're securely looked after? Of course I would. Whether that's by your own means or someone else's, I just want to know you'll be okay. But most of all, I want you to be happy." She gave a small smile and leaned toward Delanie. "And I've never seen you as happy as you are when you're on the stage."

She leaned back and took a sip of tea, then put down her mug with a thud.

"That's why I put you in all those music and dance lessons," she continued, "and why I made sure you got to be in the play every year. It's why I never stopped you from pursuing acting, no matter how afraid I was for how your life might go if you chose a career in the arts. You've always been determined and brave. Your father helped me see that if I let you go, you would find your way eventually. And he was right. I'm sorry that the things I did hurt you. And, um, I know I was a little harsh at Thanksgiving. With losing Nan, I'm afraid I haven't been quite myself lately. But even then, I was only trying to help."

Moisture sprang to Delanie's eyes, and she blinked it away.

Cheryl took her hand. "Honey, I'm so proud of all you've accomplished. I know this TV show thing didn't work out how you planned, but there will be other opportunities. This isn't the same world my parents lived in. It's a lot smaller, and there are more options. You're not limited by the same things they were. It's okay to love acting and to love Caleb. You don't have to choose." She chuckled. "Call me a romantic, but I believe true love does find a way. Just like it did with Nan and Pops."

Delanie stared at her mother, her heart swollen and pressing against her ribs. All this time, her mom had only been worried about her? She swallowed, tears still pricking her sinuses. "Thanks, Mom. You have no idea how much that means to me."

"Oh, honey." Cheryl leaned forward and cupped Delanie's jaw, her eyes bright with moisture. "You've always been a shining star to me. And you're going to find your way through this mess, just like you always do."

Delanie's cheeks were wet again as she and her mother leaned into an embrace.

"I love you, Mom."

"I love you, too, sweetheart."

Just then, Bill came back into the kitchen. Taking in the sight of his crying, hugging wife and daughter, he spun on his heel and went right back out.

Delanie and Cheryl pulled apart, laughing through their tears.

"Crying has never been Dad's thing," Delanie said.

"Nope," Cheryl agreed, and took a sip of her tea. "Good thing he looks cute in a ball cap."

Delanie laughed. She had no idea why her mother would find that attractive, but it didn't matter. Her parents had made their relationship work despite their differences.

And, for the first time, she had real hope that she and Caleb could do the same.

Chapter 24

CALEB SAT BEHIND the small table that served as a ticket booth in the upper foyer of Mackenzie Playhouse, chatting with the trickle of early-arriving patrons as they climbed the stairs and handed over their tickets. He had just unlocked the front doors on opening night, and not many people had arrived yet—including Raelene Elcano and Caleb's brother-in-law Oliver, who were supposed to be manning the ticket table. Caleb glanced at his watch, wondering what was keeping them.

He looked up to see a willowy Black woman in striking silver eyeliner and a brightly patterned wrap dress beneath her wool coat accompanied by an East Asian man in a burgundy sports jacket and skinny jeans climbing the creaky stairs. Caleb smiled and greeted them as he took their tickets, then looked at their seat numbers and pointed at the seating chart on the table before handing the tickets back.

"You'll be right here. Go up the stairs to the right, down two rows, and then into the centre section. The usher will help you." Caleb pointed at the double doors leading into the main hall, gesturing to the right as he explained.

"Thanks," said the woman.

"I haven't seen you two around here before," Caleb said. "Are you visiting a cast member?"

"In a sense," the woman said with an amused smile. "We're

Delanie's friends."

Caleb blinked and did a double take. "Marie and Desmond?"

Desmond nodded. "So she *does* talk about me. I had begun to wonder."

"Caleb, right?" Marie held out her hand, and Caleb shook it and Desmond's in turn. "I've heard a lot about you."

"Same," Caleb said, his stomach tightening. Why would Delanie's friends have come when Delanie herself hadn't? "You know she's not here, right?"

Marie shrugged. "I already had my plane ticket, and I wanted to see the kids in my costumes. Besides, you never know what that girl has up her sleeve."

Caleb's heart squeezed and his throat thickened. Did Marie know something he didn't? He wanted to ask, but the next people were coming up the stairs. He took another look at the seating chart and cleared his throat. "Looks like we'll be seeing each other again. I think I'm sitting right next to you. Don't let anyone take my seat." He managed a playful smile—at least, he hoped it looked playful. His heart was rattling against his rib cage so loud, he thought it was auditioning to join the tiny live orchestra as the percussion section.

Marie and Desmond laughed and thanked him as they moved past him into the hall.

A short Filipino woman came up behind him and slid into the vacant chair next to him.

"Sorry I am late," Raelene said with a staccato accent. "Grayson could not find his Punchinello hat. I swear, that boy will cause all my gray hairs."

Caleb smiled, taking the next person's tickets and glancing at Raelene's thick, jet-black shoulder-length hair. "Your hair has proven pretty resilient to his devastation so far. Does he have the hat now?"

"Oh, yes." She reached for the tickets of the next person in line. "And I told him he is not to take it home again. He said it was an accident." She rolled her eyes. "What is that saying? He would lose his head, too, if it were not attached to his shoulders?"

Caleb laughed and nodded. "That sounds like Grayson."

A wave of people came through the door—Monica and her parents, followed by Rachel and Oliver and their three oldest children. Rachel had told him she would be leaving the energetic Hannah with a sitter. Dave must be parking the car.

"Finally," Caleb muttered under his breath. There were other things he should be doing besides running the ticket table. Amber was probably having a conniption somewhere. And he wouldn't mind slipping downstairs to get a few photos of Emma with her hair and makeup all done up before the show started.

As the group reached the top of the stairs, Caleb stood to give Oliver his seat, preparing to take a shortcut through the hall and go backstage. But Monica laid a hand on his arm and stopped him.

"Caleb, can we talk for a minute?"

He was about to object, but something about her tone and the look in her red-rimmed eyes said this couldn't wait. He nodded. "As long as it's fast."

She gave a strained smile. "It will be." She glanced at the swiftly filling foyer. "Maybe outside?"

He nodded and followed her back toward the entrance, pressing against the wall to squeeze past people coming up the narrow stairs. His coat was backstage, but he wore a thick large-check flannel shirt, so as long as Monica was right about being fast, he shouldn't need it.

Outside, the sun had set and a thick fog had billowed from the river and covered the downtown area, crystallizing in the frigid air. The fractals amplified and refracted the orange glow of the streetlights so the entire front lawn of the hall—brown and crunchy where it peeked through the remnants of yesterday's snowfall—seemed caught in a glass snow globe. They moved a few steps away from the sidewalk and the people streaming through the doors behind the semi-privacy of a tree, standing right next to where the lawn dropped steeply toward the river side of the hall.

"What's wrong?" Caleb asked. The damp cold was penetrating his shirt faster than he'd expected.

Monica wrung her hands. "Have you given any thought to whether you'll be moving to Brampton?"

Caleb frowned. "Some," he said slowly. "Do we need to talk about it right now?"

She shook her head. "I wanted to tell you that you don't need to worry about it. I'll be staying in Peace Crossing after all."

"You will?" He took a step closer and lowered his voice. "What happened?"

Her voice broke. "I wanted to make it work between Dave and me. I wanted to support him. But my whole life is here, and so is Emma's. My parents. My friends. All of Emma's grandparents and uncles and aunts and cousins. You. I know I told you I wasn't marrying him for the baby, but the more I thought about it, the more I realized I actually was. And it didn't make sense to give up everything we have here to move to Ontario, no matter how much I care about him. It made even less sense to expect that of you."

She wiped her eyes, and Caleb noticed her engagement ring was missing.

"You broke up with Dave, didn't you?"

She nodded. "And I know you're with Delanie now, but I wanted to tell you something I should have said a long time ago—I'm so sorry for how things worked out between us. We had our rough patches, but I know you cared for me in your own way. I think I just had these unrealistic expectations of what love is, and what marriage is. But the people who get a marriage like that are pretty rare." She laid a hand on his chest.

"Dave's a good guy. But he was never you."

She looked up into his eyes, and she looked so vulnerable and sad, he felt pulled toward her and her rosebud lips, just as he had that night so long ago. But her eyes were blue instead of brown, and his heartbreak was too fresh, too raw. No matter how much he missed Delanie, this was one mistake he wouldn't repeat.

When she lifted her chin toward him and leaned even closer, he stepped back, breaking contact.

"I'm so sorry that things didn't work out with Dave. You know I'll always be here to help you and Emma out, but you and me . . . I think that worked out for the best, don't you?"

She drew herself up, but then her face softened and she nodded. "You're probably right. And if anyone is going to have the kind of love they write stories about, it will be you and Delanie." As she moved back toward the door, she paused and laid a hand on his arm. "I wish you both the best."

She walked away, leaving Caleb staring at the swirling crystal-filled mist. *The kind of love they write stories about, maybe. But that doesn't mean the story has a happy ending.*

He looked west toward the river, though all he could see was the fog fading to black. Somewhere far beyond the river was the woman he had hoped to have a happily ever after with. For three days, he'd been trying to resign himself to the fact that it was really over, but every time he thought about it, the hollow ache in his chest threatened to engulf him. At least there was now one less stone weighing him down—he wouldn't have to move to Ontario. But he barely noticed its missing weight compared to the boulder that remained, the one threatening to bring him to his knees on the lawn at this very moment.

"No. Not right now." He had a play to put on. For Emma. For the kids.

For Delanie.

Giving his head a shake to banish that last thought, he turned around to go back to the hall, trying to slow his broken heart.

Once the play was over, he could fall apart. Until then, he had work to do.

Chapter 25

DELANIE SAT IN the dark storage closet in the basement of Mackenzie Playhouse on a stack of molded plastic chairs and stared at the headline on her phone screen, her mouth dry. *Nathan Tait eager to pick up the pieces after being cleared of all charges. Ex-wife Carmelina Gonzales to serve twelve months for battery and assault.*

"I was wrong. We were all wrong," she said to herself. All the anguish of the last two months, the not knowing if her career would survive, of questioning herself, of avoiding hate tweets and emails from her fans, and it had all been based on a lie—judgements made too quickly and a form of mob justice that had been much too harsh. But in the midst of the relief was a twinge of guilt—she could no longer deny that her voice, no matter how seemingly insignificant, had added to a crowd of accusers that had probably been just as hurtful to the superstar actor as the Twitter mob had been to her. Having been on the receiving side of the slings and arrows of public opinion, could she really excuse herself for how she may have contributed to Nathan's problems?

The door of the storage closet rattled, and she sat up, startled. But it was only Amber, who quietly slipped in and then looked cautiously behind her through the door before closing it and turning to Delanie. Her auburn hair was pinned up, and she wore a long, flowing tunic and cropped buttoned cardigan over leggings and flat calf-high boots—casually elegant, but also comfortable. *Huh. Even Amber is finally dressing to Peace Country standards.*

"Are you ready?" Amber whispered. "The show's about to start. I saw Caleb go sit down, so now's the time."

Delanie nodded and hopped off the stack of chairs, straightening her shimmery black tank top and black crepe dress slacks, and tugged on the hem of her silver taffeta blazer—a purchase she had made that afternoon at the local boutique clothing store. She wouldn't usually get so dressed up for a play in Peace Crossing either, but tonight was special, for more reasons than one.

"Thanks for helping me with this," she whispered.

Amber's face lit up. "Are you kidding me? This is the most fun I've had in . . . well, it's been a while." She cracked open the door and peered through it to the wide hallway beyond. "Okay, the coast is clear. Follow me."

Delanie tiptoed behind Amber out the basement walk-out doors, her chandelier earrings tickling her neck with every step, and waved at a few surprised kids standing at the edge of the hallway in full costume. She pressed her fingers to her lips, then crept outside and started scrambling up the snow-dusted hill of lawn that led to the main entrance around the corner, taking extra care in her heels.

Five minutes later, with Amber playing lookout the whole way, she had snuck her way into the narrow canteen off the upper foyer, just outside the main hall doors. On the brown Formica counter behind the closed pass-through window sat a row of sealed sandwich baggies of mixed candy next to a vase of single-stem roses, ready for intermission sales, but the parent volunteers who would be selling them were absent—Amber's doing, no doubt. Delanie was suddenly very grateful for her choice of accomplice. Next to the ancient mustard-yellow fridge, a ladder led through a square hole in the ceiling that opened to the light and sound room above.

Amber closed the door behind her. "I asked Luc, and he said there's no room in the sound booth with him and Darcy during the performance," she whispered as quietly as she could. "But you can sneak up there to hide when they come down during intermission." She raised a brow. "Are you sure you don't want to just watch the show from backstage? I know there's a chance someone will notice you, but—"

"No, I'll be fine," Delanie whispered back, smiling.

She had given up her seat next to Caleb so Desmond and Marie could sit there together, since Caleb was the one she was trying to surprise most. She hoped their presence didn't tip him off—they had both promised to keep their lips sealed until the big reveal. And the last thing she needed was for Emma or one of the other kids to spill the beans during intermission.

"I'll watch one of the other performances. Trust me, this will be worth the wait. And I brought a book." She indicated her phone, on which she actually had dozens of books waiting to be read. If she could calm her nerves enough to focus on reading.

Amber smiled and nodded. "If you need anything, text."

"You bet." Delanie smiled brightly, and Amber stole through the doorway just as the audience in the hall beyond clapped uproariously.

Delanie looked around. The only place to sit was the rather uncomfortable-looking wide wooden step directly below the ladder. The first strains of the opening number filtered down through the open square in the ceiling that led to the booth above.

Luc's face became visible through the opening as he leaned over to look through it. When he saw her there, he grinned and gave her two thumbs up, mouthing, *The soundboard is awesome.* She gave him the A-okay sign, knowing better than to say anything, which would be heard in the hall beyond. He disappeared again.

Bracing her back against the counter, she used her hands to help her hop onto it. The sharp corner at the front edge bit into her thighs through her thin pants.

She grimaced. She never thought she would actually miss the stack of chairs in the storage closet. But in two hours, this would all be so, so worth it.

She hoped. If Caleb was as forgiving as her mother expected him to be.

As THE FINAL soaring strains of the finale filled the hall, Caleb had to admit that, as kids' productions went, this was one of the better ones he had seen. Which was saying a lot, because Molly and her team had worked wonders in previous years. He might be a little biased, what with his daughter being one of the principal cast and with how involved he had been. And because of Delanie.

The thought left him with a sweet-and-sour flavour on his tongue that had nothing to do with the sour peaches he'd been snacking on since intermission. He watched each successive round of bows, which started with the choruses of townsfolk, magical critters, and donkeys, then proceeded to the supporting cast characters, and then the principals.

Finally, Emma emerged from the wings as Lucy and joined Ethan White as Pinocchio at centre stage back. She took his hand before they skipped to the front and made their bows, both of them grinning ear to ear. Caleb stood, redoubling his clapping and shouting bravos, determined that his little girl would be able to hear him above every other voice in the hall.

Lastly came Stella and Geppetto—Ainsley and Joe—bringing everyone still sitting to their feet. Caleb's chest almost burst with pride.

"Your daughter is very good," said Marie's smooth voice in his ear. "She's talented for someone so young."

"Thank you," Caleb said with a smile.

The cast members lining the front of the stage leaned down toward Violet and the musicians with extended arms, and Violet turned to bow on the orchestra's behalf, eliciting another burst of volume from the clapping audience.

On his other side, his mother squeezed his arm. "I can't believe it! She was wonderful!"

"I can," Caleb said, chuckling.

Marcus leaned over Adelaide. "Is it over already?" he asked dryly.

Caleb restrained the urge to shake his head. Theatre wasn't his dad's cup of coffee.

"Not quite, Dad. They have Molly's announcement to make."

"Oh, right, right."

As if on queue, Amber came out onstage holding two wireless microphones and stood beaming as Murray Jones—a tall, angular man with his brown hair combed over his balding spot and a hitch in his step that made him resemble a stork as he walked—made his way from the side section up the stairs at stage left to join her. As he did, the crowd reseated themselves, obviously noticing the festivities were not quite at an end. As Caleb sat, he noticed Desmond glancing furtively sideways at him, then quickly away when he saw Caleb looking. *What an odd guy.* Caleb shook his head and turned his attention to the front.

When the noise in the hall had settled down, Murray squinted into the glare of the spotlight and raised the microphone to his mouth.

"I think that may be one of the best children's productions I've ever seen in this hall. The actors, the musicians, the parent volunteers—all of you outdid yourselves. Molly would have been so proud."

Murray's words were met with another burst of applause. Caleb felt an uncharacteristic lump of emotion in his throat. He wished Delanie could be here to see this. The regret twisted to bitter sadness. She had made her choice . . . and, it turned out, she wasn't the person he had hoped she was. He was just going to have to accept that.

"And, speaking of Molly Davis," Murray continued, "most of you will have heard of her unfortunate passing less than two months ago. This was the final production she had any part in. And, it so happens, today would have been her eightieth birthday, or so I've been told."

More applause, though it was more subdued. Murray smiled and waited for it to subside, then continued.

"So I think it's fitting that we take a moment tonight to recognize her amazing contribution to the arts in this community. She served in many capacities in local theatre and in the performing arts community in Alberta over the past fifty-plus years, but most memorably, she has long directed this annual production with love, patience, and skill. Many of the adult actors who grace this stage throughout the year, myself included, owe much of our passion for theatre to the enthusiasm she instilled in us."

Caleb smiled, remembering Molly's contribution to his own formative years. No, he hadn't ended up pursuing the arts, but he would always look back fondly on his time in the play.

"I could go on and on about Molly's virtues," Murray said, "but somehow, I think that role is better suited to someone who knew her even better than I did. I'd like to invite Ms. Fletcher to the stage to say a few words."

Murray glanced up the aisle toward the back entrance of the hall as a spotlight swung up the aisle. Caleb clapped along with the rest of the audience and rotated in his seat, expecting to see Cheryl making her way toward the stage.

Instead, Delanie was walking carefully down the aisle toward the front.

And Caleb's heart forgot how to beat.

Chapter 26

DELANIE LOOKED LIKE a million—no, a *billion* bucks. As she passed Caleb, she found his gaze and held it. He almost got out of his seat to follow her, to demand to know what she was doing here and why she hadn't called to tell him she was coming—but the fact that he'd received no warning made the reason painfully clear. He sank into his seat, his chest filled with lead, ignoring the glances of his family and Delanie's two friends. If he weren't stuck in the middle of a row, he would have excused himself and rushed outside to get some air, but he didn't want to make a scene.

If I can just get through the next few minutes, I can leave. Maybe I won't even have to talk to her.

He gripped the edge of the plastic cup holders at the front of the armrests and stared straight ahead. He could do this.

When Delanie reached the stage, she spoke for several minutes about Molly and her influence on her own and many others' careers, speaking eloquently about her gratitude that she knew her not only as Molly Davis, but also as her Nan. The words washed over Caleb like waves, barely audible over the blood rushing through his ears. Then something she said broke through the heat and noise that pounded through him.

"As talented as my Nan was, for many years, all I saw when I looked at her was the potential of what she could have been if she hadn't chosen to come to Peace Crossing and have a family. Even though, I must admit, part of me has always been pretty grateful she did." Delanie laughed, and so did the audience.

Caleb drew a deep breath. Why was she talking about this here, now, in front of all the parents and kids?

"While I was helping my family clear out Nan's house," Delanie continued, "I found a scrapbook of Molly's accomplishments on the stage from before she married my Pops. She got to play some pretty impressive roles—Maria from *The Sound of Music*. Anna Leanowens from *The King and I*. Sergeant Sarah Brown in *Guys and Dolls*. She even played Joan of Arc once. Can you picture my sweet little Nan as a fierce warrior woman leading the French to victory?"

Polite laughter rippled through the crowd.

"But that was only one scrapbook of dozens." Delanie glanced around to take in the attentive faces of the kids watching her from the stage. "Nan was proud of the career she'd had before she married my grandfather. But that was nothing compared to how she felt about her work here in this community. She had over a dozen scrapbooks of the productions she'd been a part of in this very theatre, including cast photos and names. I even found a few with a young Murray Jones," she said to the man.

He chuckled and nodded good-naturedly.

Delanie looked back at the audience. "I never understood why that would be important enough to her that she didn't seem to miss the career she could have had. Not until this year. Not until I did it myself."

Caleb swallowed, a flicker of hope lighting in his chest. Had Delanie rethought what she had told him a few days ago in Kamloops?

Now Delanie broke the cardinal rule of actors and turned her back to the audience, speaking directly to the kids. She kept the microphone to her mouth so all could hear.

"Directing the play this year has been the pinnacle of my

career so far. And I hope it will only be the first of many productions I get to direct here. Someday, I hope to have my own collection of cast photos filled with each one of you as you grow. You," she pointed at one of the younger kids, who giggled, "and you, and you, and each one of you, have blessed me more than you'll ever know. You kids are all stars. And I'm so glad I got to see you shine."

Emma burst from her place at the front of the line and raced over to Delanie, throwing her arms around her waist. The mic picked up Emma saying, "I knew you'd come back."

Delanie smiled, wrapping her arm around the girl's shoulders. "How could I miss this?" she whispered, though Caleb somehow heard it loud and clear over his rushing pulse.

The rest of the kids streamed forward and wrapped Delanie in a huge group hug, at least ten kids deep on each side, while the audience whistled and cheered. Caleb watched it all, clapping uncertainly, emotion still clogging his throat. What had Delanie meant? Had she decided to stay in Peace Crossing? Was she giving up on her career on the screen after all?

As much as one part of him selfishly hoped she had done both of those things—that all of this was because she had changed her mind—another part of him balked. How could she make that choice for him?

And how could he let her?

Suddenly, he had a little more compassion for what she must have wrestled with the other night in her hotel room.

Murray wedged his way into the outer edge of the dispersing knot of children and took the mic from Delanie's extended arm, giving a booming laugh as he brought it back to his mouth. "That was even better than I expected."

He waited for the last of the kids to release a rather flushed-looking Delanie, then took a plaque from Amber and held it before him.

"Before I present this, I want to commend Delanie Fletcher

for how she has picked up her grandmother's torch. Thanks to her and her efforts, along with the kids of this year's production and some very generous donors both near and far, not only does Mackenzie Playhouse now have a brand-new sound board, but we will finally be able to replace the wiring that has been such a bother for many years now."

At this, the crowd went wild with applause. Delanie stood there, her face flushing red as a tomato as she beamed around at the crowd, looking embarrassed. Despite his uncertainty about where he and Delanie stood, Caleb joined in whole-heartedly, his heart bursting with pride at what Delanie had done for this community, his daughter, and for him, in only two short months.

When the noise subsided, Murray turned to Delanie. "Now, Ms. Fletcher, it is with great delight that I present you with this plaque, which we will be affixing to the front of the stage. Henceforth, the stage where we stand will be known as the Molly Davis Memorial Stage."

Delanie smiled widely. "On behalf of Molly Davis's family, I accept."

She took the proffered plaque, but whatever she said next was drowned out in uproarious applause.

Murray waved and jogged back down the stairs to his seat. Amber took the mic from Delanie and thanked and dismissed the audience. The house lights came up, and the kids started milling their way offstage to go get changed. Across the heads flowing in opposite directions, though, Delanie met Caleb's eye, her gaze holding the same uncertainty he felt, pulling him toward her with the gravity of a collapsing star. He glanced at the people flowing toward him from the front of the hall in frustration.

Then, he started climbing over the backs of the seats, to a shocked exclamation from his mother and some encouraging hoots from Desmond.

Darn propriety. He needed to talk to that woman.

Right.

Now.

By the time he had moved forward several rows, the left aisle had cleared. Delanie had made her way to the steps at the front of the stage and was hurrying carefully down them in her heels. He pushed his way past the last stragglers in the aisle and ran forward, meeting Delanie at the bottom of the steps and grasping her hands. Some of the musicians, who were putting away their instruments, looked their way and smirked.

"Back here," she said, jerking her chin toward the side doors that led both backstage and to an emergency exit.

He pulled her through them into the dim light and cooler air beyond, then up into the recesses of the wings—now mostly cleared out of kids, though some of the black-clad volunteer stage techs gave them curious glances as they tidied up.

He turned to face her, but he had so many thoughts whirling in his head, the only thing that came out of his mouth was, "What are you doing here?"

She smiled nervously. "Um, surprise?"

"Great job," one of the volunteers called at them on his way by as he gathered up mislaid props.

Delanie smiled back at him. "Thanks."

Caleb glanced at the man impatiently. This wasn't the time for interruptions. "Do you want to go outside for a minute?"

She glanced at the doors below. "It's freezing out there."

He felt in his pocket. "I have my keys. We can sit in my truck."

She gave him a look that made his heart start frolicking like a spring calf. "Okay. Let's go."

DELANIE SHIVERED IN the front seat of Caleb's truck as he

climbed in the driver's side and started the engine. In a few seconds, warm air began blowing into the cab. She angled toward him, her hands in her lap. He looked at her, confusion and uncertainty plain on his face.

"What's going on, Delanie?"

She chewed the inside of her lip. This was what all of this had been leading up to—the finale she had envisioned when she had hatched her grand plan, inspired by Nan's career scrapbook full of larger-than-life musicals. It had gone well so far, but that didn't mean she wouldn't totally bomb at the finish line. For the second time that week, she sent up an actual prayer. *Please give me the right words.*

"I'm sorry, Caleb. I'm so sorry, for so many things. For breaking up with you after high school. For never putting you first. For not believing in us, not even when you proved I should."

She took his hand.

"I've done so many things wrong, and you never stopped believing in me. You never stopped loving me, no matter how unloveable I was. And I don't think I ever stopped loving you either. I don't know what the future holds for me. For us. I just know that if I walk away now, I'll regret it every day for the rest of my life."

He stared at her. In the meagre light offered by the street lamps, his eyes were dark pools beneath bunched brows. "All that stuff you said in there about how you understood why Molly gave up her career to marry your Pops . . . is that what you intend to do? Give up your dream for me?"

Delanie would have bitten her nail, but she didn't want to let go of Caleb's hand. Instead, she swallowed her nerves and dove in.

"I've had a lot of time to think on a couple very long drives this week, and it made me realize that my dreams have changed shape from what they were a few months ago. I want to keep helping kids discover the joy of theatre. I want to have games nights with Emma on a regular basis. And I want to wake up next to you every day for the rest of my life, if you'll still have me." She leaned toward him. "Without you, Caleb, all the rest of my dreams—the fame, the prestige—none of it will matter. *You're* my dream now."

Her next sentence was cut off when he crushed her lips in a kiss that banished any remaining chill, the heat of it rushing through her every vein. She returned the kiss with an abandon she hadn't felt since their prom night—before he had told her he wouldn't be going with her to film school. Before she had stopped believing she was worthy of being first place in someone's heart.

"I take it I'm forgiven?" she asked when they took a breath.

He smiled. "With all my heart, Delanie Fletcher."

He brushed some hair behind her ear, then wrapped her in his arms and pulled her close, tucking her head beneath his chin. She twisted to embrace him as best she could over the centre console, but it was awkward, at best. The sound of a phone clattering between the console and the seats made them break apart.

"I think that was mine," Delanie said, peering down the side of her seat in the dark. She wedged her hand next to the seat and felt the edge. "Yep, there it is. Give me a second."

He looked at the centre console ruefully as she struggled to nudge the phone forward to where she could grasp it. "Usually this thing is so useful."

She laughed. "We can pick up that conversation again later. We should probably go talk to the kids."

He sighed. "I suppose."

She finally got hold of the phone and held it up. "Victory!"

He frowned at it. "What's that about?"

She peered at the screen, just catching an email notification from Tessa Montague before it faded to black. "I'm not sure."

She unlocked the phone and tapped on the notification,

quickly skimming the contents of the email. As she read, her heart swelled with elation.

"Caleb, you're not going to believe this. Tessa wants to collaborate on a reality show designed to spotlight community theatre groups and raise funds for them, and she wants *me* to be the host of the series!" She met his gaze. "It's like the Universe wants us to be together. There would be some travel involved, but I can do this kind of thing from anywhere. Even Brampton."

Caleb grinned. "Or here."

She tilted her head. "Don't you want to move to Brampton so you can be close to Emma?"

"I don't have to. Monica's staying here now, which means I can too." He paused and took her hand again. "*We* can too."

She leaned in for another kiss, this one sweet and lingering. When they pulled apart, he turned off the truck and got out, coming around to open her door. As he helped her down, he said, "I know you think the universe brought us together. But I'm pretty sure there's someone looking out for us who's a lot more interested in the outcome than an impersonal cosmic force."

She met his gaze. She had gone to the same Sunday School as Caleb when they were kids, and had attended the same church until she had stopped going when she left for college. She knew he was talking about God. And for the first time in a long time, she had to admit that it seemed someone up there actually cared about her happiness. Her core warmed further at the thought. Maybe Nan and Pops were back in each others' arms, after all.

"You just might be right, Caleb Toews."

She hooked her arm around his elbow so he could steady her on the icy sidewalk as they made their way back toward the front door, since the emergency exit had locked automatically behind them. Some of the people walking the other way along the sidewalk saw them and smiled. Delanie was sure she was grinning like a lovesick teenager, but she didn't care.

He shook his head, an amused grin on his face. "When are you going to learn? I'm usually right."

She laughed. "I guess we'll find out, won't we?"

"Fortunately, I don't mind sticking around until you do. You'll see what I mean eventually."

She gave him a playful shove on the shoulder. "Alright, Tony Stark. Stop your not-so-humble bragging and let's go find your daughter. I've got a rose to give her."

"And I believe we have some good news to share." He arched a brow at her and clasped her hand in his as they waited for the doorway to clear of exiting people.

She smiled. "I believe we do."

Epilogue

"So, you and Caleb, huh?" Delanie's high school best friend, Stephanie Neufeld, glanced sideways at her with a reserved twinkle in her grey eyes. Her cheeks were rosy from the chill and exertion, and her boots clicked on the pavement with every step. The extra few inches of height they gave her meant Delanie had to look up at her. "I guess it was always kind of inevitable. In fact, I'm surprised it took this long."

Delanie squinted against the bright afternoon sunlight slanting at them from low in the southern sky. She and Stephanie were walking south along the paved path atop the dike toward the downtown centre, sipping drinks they had purchased at Cool Beans before driving to the north end of town for the stroll. It was a warm day for early November, but it was still just below freezing. Their breath billowed around them in frosty clouds. Delanie wished she would have remembered to bring a cozy knitted toque like the cream one topping Stephanie's mahogany curls.

"I suppose." She smiled happily. "There was a lot of water we had to let pass under the bridge, I guess."

"Hmm. Like what?"

Delanie shrugged and glanced at the turquoise angles and arches of the Peace River bridge ahead of them. After everything that had happened between her and Caleb over the last two months, all the years of harbouring hurt and betrayal against him seemed ludicrous. Not only was she ashamed of her behaviour, but it was taking a while to wrap her head around the new reality, and every time she thought of Caleb, it was with a strange mix of emotion—hope that the feelings she had for the man she was getting to know again would last, fear that she would let him down again. But she didn't want to get into that now, not with a friend she had barely seen in the past ten years.

"Just stuff. You know. We were kids. What did we know about relationships?"

Stephanie gave a sardonic chuckle and glanced down at the ground. "Ain't that the truth?" It was a statement more than a question.

Delanie pulled her lips to the side. "How about you? Anybody special in your life?"

Stephanie shook her head. "No. It's hard to have a social life around my schedule at the hospital. Besides that, I sometimes help out at the coffee shop a lot on my days off, and I babysit my nephew, Julien, once in a while, so who has time to date?"

There was a dry note in her voice that made Delanie look twice. "Is it just a time thing? There are plenty of ER nurses with families. Hasn't there been anyone?"

Stephanie looked up. "I did see someone briefly a couple years ago, but . . . it didn't work out."

"Why not?"

Stephanie shrugged. "Just stuff."

Touché.

Delanie peered toward the river, taking in the lovely scenery—the rolling hills on the other side with buildings tucked into their folds like they had sprouted from a landscape that was a study in contrasts. Streaks of dark green where stands of evergreens grew crept up the valley in irregular wedges between hills covered in white. Above them arched blue sky broken only by a few puffy white clouds scudding across it. The sun was already dipping toward the hills on the west side of the river, though it was only around four in the afternoon.

Delanie looked back at her friend, who seemed lost in thought as she stared at her white paper to-go cup. Though they walked next to each other, Stephanie seemed a million miles away. Ten years ago, Stephanie would have been the first person Delanie would have talked to about boy troubles, family troubles—*any* troubles. Now there was a wall of time and distance between them chillier than the autumn air.

And whose fault is that?

"I'm sorry I didn't keep in touch, Stephanie. It's not that I didn't want to. I'm not sure what happened . . . I got busy and distracted, I guess. But that's no real excuse."

Stephanie peered at her, smiling sheepishly. "Yeah, I guess I could have done a little better too. I've heard phones ring both ways."

Delanie returned her smile, understanding passing between them.

"It was Noel Butler," Stephanie said.

"Pardon?"

"The guy I dated. It was Noel."

Delanie nodded. When Stephanie didn't volunteer anything further, she decided that was as much as she was going to share. Maybe it was Delanie's turn.

"I thought Caleb cheated on me with Monica. But I was wrong." She brushed some hair out of her eyes. "Turns out, I've been wrong a lot lately. But I've managed to do a few things right."

She smiled, thinking about the message she had received just that morning from Nathan Tait's publicist. After hearing the news of his innocence, she had taken a page from Amber's book. First, she had removed her video condemning Nathan from her channel and posted an apology video for her part in the mob that had attacked him, empathizing with him after her own recent experience. She had also encouraged her fans and viewers to learn from her mistake and think twice in the future before picking up their phones to cast virtual stones, just as she planned to do.

The message the publicist had sent on Nathan's behalf wasn't mushy by any stretch, but it expressed Nathan's gratitude that she had been big enough to retract her previous stance and to say so publicly. It also expressed well-wishes for her future success. She had sent a note expressing similar well-wishes and gratitude for his forgiveness. Nothing more was likely to ever come of the interaction, but finally, her conscience was clear on the subject.

"Yeah. I heard about what happened to you on social media." Stephanie's expression was sympathetic. "And you lost your job, too. That's awful. No one deserves to be treated like that."

"Thank you. But it could have been worse. And the job thing was kind of a blessing in disguise."

"How's that?"

Delanie looked skyward and smiled. "Because now I get to be here with Caleb and Emma. Besides, it showed me I'm not as powerless as I thought I was."

Her agent had sent Crystal McLean a scathing indictment of Josh Rosenburg's behaviour, along with the recording Delanie had taken, copying the email to every executive at the studio and threatening a wrongful termination suit. So far, the studio had been dragging their feet on their response, but Sandra said to give it time—at the least, the recording would ensure Delanie got a decent payout to smooth things over. And that the executives wouldn't believe the lies Josh was probably telling about her behind her back.

And *somehow*, that recording and the story of Josh's behaviour—and what Delanie was doing about it—had leaked to everyone on set. Delanie had her suspicions, but Desmond had never admitted to anything. He *had* relayed Xander's news that one other girl had already come forward with accusations of sexual harassment against Josh. Delanie had a solid hunch that it wouldn't be long before there would be more. And she had another solid hunch that the studio wouldn't want to associate themselves with *that* kind of controversy either. One way or another, Josh wouldn't get out of this scot-free.

She smirked. Des might only have a yellow stripe belt in Taekwondo, but he made a pretty fabulous guard anyway.

"You know what?" she added. "In a weird way, I'm glad it happened."

Stephanie glanced at her in surprise. "You are? Why?"

Delanie smiled and turned to her friend. "Because if I hadn't crashed and burned that way, I never would have learned what I really wanted. *Who* I really wanted. Or, you know, who I am."

Stephanie nodded. They walked several paces before she spoke again, a pensive look on her face. "Sometimes, I think I need to do that."

"What? Crash and burn?" Delanie laughed.

Stephanie cracked a rare smile. "No. Figure out what I want. I have a hard time getting to know people. I'm always afraid they'll let me down, so it's easier to keep them at a distance." She glanced away so Delanie couldn't see her face. "I think it's what came between me and Noel. He probably thought I was too much work." She squinted into the distance. "Sometimes I think I'm better off alone."

Delanie stopped and laid a hand on her friend's arm. "Hey, no. You don't mean that. No one is better off alone."

And if something turned Noel off of Stephanie, it wasn't a fear of hard work. Maybe she'd hear his side of the story someday.

Stephanie turned and looked at the pavement beside her. "But being with people is so risky."

"Not every person, right?" Delanie ducked her head to catch

her friend's eye. "You've still got me. I'm sorry I let you down before. But I'm not going anywhere anytime soon. I promise."

Stephanie nodded and dabbed at her wet cheeks with her knit gloves.

"Say," Delanie continued, "do you still like playing board games?"

"Sometimes," Stephanie said. "I don't have much time for it these days. Nor opportunity, with how busy Autumn and my folks are."

She glanced away again, and Delanie filled in the rest. It was hard to play board games when you didn't have people to play them with.

Delanie put on a cheery smile. "Caleb and Emma and I are having a games night this Sunday. You should come. Emma's a little whiz at, well, everything, as far as I can tell. She whipped me pretty soundly when we played *Settlers of Catan*."

Stephanie laughed. "That's not intimidating at all. Being beat by a nine-year-old?"

"Tell me about it. Good thing she's such a good sport about it." She tilted her head. "So, will you come?"

Stephanie studied her. "Will there be anyone else there?"

"There wasn't going to be, but maybe Caleb would like to invite some people over too. I'll have to ask him." She frowned. "If there are, would you still come?"

Stephanie hesitated. "As long as Noel isn't one of them."

"Deal." Delanie grinned and resumed walking. "I'm glad we reconnected, Steph. All my best memories of growing up in this town are with you."

Stephanie arched a brow. "*All* of them?"

Delanie blushed, thinking of her many memories with Caleb—memories that they intended to keep adding to for years to come. "Okay. A *lot* of them." She gave a shy smile. "And we can make a few more, if you'd like."

"I'd like that."

They shared a long look, and Delanie's heart warmed. Marie had been thrilled to meet Caleb, of course, but she had secretly expressed worry to Delanie that she didn't seem to have many other close friends here. *I know you don't need a lot, girl, but you do need at least one. Tell me you have one.*

It was Marie's nudge that had prompted Delanie to call Stephanie at last. And now Delanie could tell Marie what she wanted to hear—she had a friend in Peace Crossing.

She smiled to herself, thinking of the photos Marie had sent her of her and Desmond at the Starlight Gala. When Delanie had suggested Marie use her ticket to take someone else to the gala, she hadn't expected her friend to ask Desmond out. Neither had he, but the two of them had been inseparable since. Delanie couldn't be more thrilled. It seemed she wasn't the only one whose dreams had started coming true lately.

"What's so funny?" Stephanie asked.

"I was just thinking how funny life can be. Like, you can make all the plans you want, but sometimes happiness lies in the place you least expect and weren't even looking."

"Like back in the place you started?" Stephanie asked, arching a brow.

Delanie swept the river with her gaze, then glanced to her left and realized she could see Caleb's house on the street they were passing.

"Yeah. Exactly like that."

Want to hear what happens when Delanie and Emma bake up a birthday surprise for Caleb?
(Hint: Delanie gets the biggest surprise of all!)

Download the bonus epilogue at
https://www.talenawinters.com/ests-bonus.

Dear Reader,

I HOPE CALEB and Delanie's story gave you some joy. (If you loved it, I would really appreciate a review. And be sure to read on to learn more about the next book in the series, *Every Bell that Rings*, featuring Noel and Stephanie.)

For me, this book was a chance to return to one of my favourite fall activities—the local kids' community theatre production.

I got the idea to write a sweet small-town romance series set in an analog of my current hometown of Peace River near the end of 2021. I had just finished publishing a massive two-year project, an epic fantasy that was dramatic and intense and which was definitely not supposed to take two years. Between that project, the pandemic (speaking of dramatic and intense), and several family crises, I needed a little lightness and hope in my life.

And the Peace Country Romance series was born.

When I moved to Peace River in 2005, one of my favourite things about the town was the thriving arts community. The reputation of Peace Players preceded my move, as one of my college music professors had once lived here and told me about the organization.

But I had no idea what a treasure the local community theatre would become for me and my family. My children have all been involved in the local fall kids' production, which has been led for years by an amazing and talented team of volunteers. To Teresa Bell, Donna Brunham, Chantelle Bentley, Joanne Kyle, and the many, many other volunteers who have made Peace River theatre productions what they are over the decades, this work is my grateful tribute to you.

Peace Crossing is similar but not identical to Peace River. (It's fiction, what can I say?) However, the Mackenzie Playhouse is as close as I could make it to the real-life Athabasca Hall, one of the oldest buildings in the community. The stage of Athabasca Hall is named after Don Weaver, one of the founders of Peace Players. However, other than their passion for community theatre that resulted in the stage being named for them, I did not draw any of Molly's history from Don Weaver's.

My own background is in music, but theatre, especially musical theatre, has always been close to my heart. (Fun fact: I actually outlined an entire kids' musical adaptation of Pinocchio, song titles included, for that one chapter of rehearsal I showed you. Maybe I'll even turn that into its own thing someday too.)

Even if theatre isn't quite the passion for you that it is for me, I pray that the hope, sweetness, and love in this book made your day a little bit brighter. Because sharing hope is why I do this.

Talena Winters
May 30, 2022

Acknowledgements

As EVER, I would like to thank my lord and saviour, Jesus Christ, for blessing me with the words to tell this story and with a story worth telling.

Thank you to my support team, who cheered me on when I presented this idea: Brenna Bailey-Davies, Jennifer E. Lindsay (whose insightful comments also helped develop this story), and Jessica Renwick. You three are such a blessing to me. I'm so glad you're in my life.

Thank you to my mom, Laurel Easton, whose unwavering support and belief in me has often kept me going in this career. (And thanks for being both beta and proofreader, Mom!)

Thank you to my other beta readers, Donna Brunham and Chantelle Bentley, for helping me get the theatre production details right. (Any remaining mistakes are definitely mine.)

While I was wrapping up the revisions on this book, I had yet another family crisis to deal with. Fortunately, I didn't have to do it alone. I want to thank my family, especially my husband and sons, for holding down the fort at home while I handled the situation elsewhere. And to my extended family members and friends who provided ongoing support throughout the crisis—thank you so much. (You know who you are.) They didn't contribute directly to the writing of this book, but I would never have made my deadline without them.

And thank you, dear reader, for supporting my work. I appreciate you beyond words.

Every Bell that Rings

CAN HIS CHRISTMAS SPIRIT BANISH HER GHOSTS OF CHRISTMAS PAST?

STEPHANIE NEUFELD DREADS Christmas. Where others see a season of joy and connection, she sees only the anniversary of her sister's passing. But when she agrees to cover a coworker's shift in the ER during the Peace Crossing Santa Claus Parade, she doesn't expect her old crush to show up—the guy who ghosted her after a single date.

Carpenter Noel Butler doesn't have time for relationships, nor to be laid up for weeks right before his favourite holiday. But since he can't work with a broken leg, he thinks up a new challenge: make the attending nurse he almost dated once fall in love with Christmas. Easier said than done when she literally won't give him the time of day.

After Stephanie and Noel reconnect on a sleigh ride, another accident reopens old emotional wounds. Will misunderstandings keep Noel and Stephanie frozen in the past, or will they discover a warm new reason to celebrate the season?

Every Bell that Rings is the second standalone title in the sweet small-town Peace Country Romance series. If you like enemies-to-lovers interracial romance, heartwarming stories of healing, and joy-filled white Christmases, you'll love this clean and wholesome love story. **Coming Christmas 2022!**

Reserve your copy at www.talenawinters.com/every-bell.

SOMETIMES TO FIND HEAVEN, YOU HAVE TO GO THROUGH HELL...

SARAH APPEARS TO have the perfect life—she's made sure of it. But behind the façade, her respected lawyer husband abuses her, she hates writing the books that have made her a success, and she is tortured by demons from her childhood. When she receives a cancer diagnosis, her carefully constructed lies begin to crumble.

Then she has a chance encounter with Steve, a compassionate humanitarian who is everything she's never known. But the undemanding, honourable love he offers must have a catch—she just hasn't found it yet. Can Sarah be saved, or is it too late for her to find heaven?

Finding Heaven is a standalone gripping emotional page-turner about second chances and redemptive love.

"One of the most beautifully written books I have read."
- Kristin Dyck, editor of *Mile Zero News*

Learn more at www.talenawinters.com/finding-heaven.

Also by Talena Winters:

CONTEMPORARY ROMANTIC FICTION:

Finding Heaven
The Friday Night Date Dress

Peace Country Romance series:
Every Star That Shines (Book 1)
Every Bell That Rings (Book 2)

In the same world, heartwarming family fiction:
All I Want for Christmas (novelette)

YOUNG ADULT EPIC FANTASY:

Rise of the Grigori series:
The Waterboy (prequel novella)
The Undine's Tear (Book 1)
The Sphinx's Heart (Book 2)

SCIENCE FICTION THRILLER:

Jack Reynolds:
Up in Smoke (novelette)

TALENA WINTERS is addicted to stories, tea, chocolate, yarn, and silver linings. She writes page-turning fiction for teens and adults in multiple genres, coaches other writers, has written several award-winning songs, and designs knitting patterns under her label My Secret Wish. Master of the ironic GIF response. She currently resides on an acreage in the Peace Country of northern Alberta, Canada, with her husband, three surviving boys, two dogs, and an assortment of farm cats. She would love to be a mermaid when she grows up.

You can connect with her at www.talenawinters.com.